Cherry

CAROLYN DENNIS-WILLINGHAM

NO HILL FOR A STEPPER

A NOVEL
BASED ON A TRUE STORY

EMERALD
BOOK CO.

PAMPA
AMARILLO
LUBBOCK
NEW MEXICO
ROTAN
HAMLIN
ROBY
SWEETWATER
FT. BLISS
EL PASO
CRANE
MEXICO

OKLAHOMA

FORT
WORTH   DALLAS

UTH
END   LOUISIANA

NGER

S

TEMPLE

AUSTIN

HOUSTON

SAN ANTONIO

GULF OF
MEXICO

CORPUS
CHRISTI

McALLEN

HARLINGEN

Published by Emerald Book Company
Austin, TX
www.emeraldbookcompany.com

Distributed by Emerald Book Company

For ordering information or special discounts for bulk purchases, please contact Emerald Book Company at PO Box 91869, Austin, TX 78709, 512.891.6100.

Design and composition by Greenleaf Book Group LLC
Cover design by Greenleaf Book Group LLC

Publisher's Cataloging-In-Publication Data
(Prepared by The Donohue Group, Inc.)
Dennis-Willingham, Carolyn.
  No hill for a stepper / Carolyn Dennis-Willingham. — 1st ed.
    p. ; cm.
  "A novel based on a true story."
  ISBN: 978-1-937110-00-0
    1. Adult child abuse victims—Fiction. 2. Boxers (Sports)Fiction. 3. United States. Air ForceNon-commissioned officersFiction. 4. Fathers and sons—Fiction. 5. Texas, West—20th century—Fiction. 6. Biographical fiction. I. Title.
PS3604.E656 N65 2011
813.6   2011927559

To my father, the cream in the pitcher,
who beyond all odds, rose to the top.

PS: I know you're listening
"Per Aspera Ad Astra"

To all the folks who have heard Cono's stories
straight from the horse's mouth, especially
Rusty, Jonica, John, Pat, John Mc, Andy, Nikkie, Terry,
Jenniffer, Uncle Andy, David S., and Stella
who heard them more than once,
but pretended it was the first time.

MY GRANDFATHER DIED when I was five years old. My parents told my sister and me to get dressed up. "We're driving to Temple to visit Grandpa Dennis before he goes to Heaven."

I pictured him sick, lying in a hospital bed, a white sheet covering him up to his chin. I pictured hugging him good-bye. Instead, we drove to a funeral home where I saw him lying in state. I was confused and thought to myself, *How can I say good-bye to him when he's already dead?* As Dad would say, I remember that moment as clear as a bell.

One afternoon years later, when I was around fourteen, I was sitting with my mother and Grandma Dennis at the kitchen table, and we were talking about my grandfather. As Grandma Dennis spoke of "Wayne," she said, "I wouldn't go through that agin if ye paid me a million bucks." I thought, then, it was a strange thing to say about her deceased husband. Later, I would understand more clearly.

Still later, in March 2008, when my mother was at home under the care of hospice, my father, "Cono" Ray Dennis, shared stories with me of growing up in West Texas during the Depression. Even as a child, I had heard bits and pieces of the events that had shaped my father's life, the fragments of endurance, the pieces of a childhood that should not have imposed themselves on a man as decent as my father. Those years of hardship and abuse developed the pattern for his life—what to change and what never to forget in order to develop a soul and character more like his grandfather's and less like his dad's.

The history of abuse in his family died along with his father. It never showed up to rear its ugly head in the direction of my sister or me.

When my mother died in June 2008, my father resumed the telling of his story, and I believe that in a small way our conversations helped him release the intense grief he felt from my mother's passing. My mother, as well as her parents, had showed Dad what a loving family could be—and changed his life.

In November 2008, Dad and I took a road trip back to Ranger and Rotan, the places of his memories. On December 18, for his birthday, I gave him an unfinished but accurate version of all those stories he had recounted to me. The book, *Cono's Texas: The Truth Bein' Told*, created a deep sense of pride in my father. It stayed on the end table next to his favorite recliner in his family room, making it easily accessible for any and all visitors, neighbors, and, later, the hospice workers to see. My father knew that even though he would not live long enough to see it published, the expanded version of his story would unfold and live long after his death.

Cono Ray Dennis died from a broken heart at the age of eighty-one. He was buried on what would have been his and Amelia's sixty-first wedding anniversary.

This is his story.

⊰ ★ ⊱

Author's Note: The events in this story are true. Some names, dialogue, and details have been added for the novel's purposes. The terms *ye* and *ya* (ye sounds like the "i" in yick, ya sounds like the "u" in duh) in some of the dialogue are used as Texas dialect in place of the word "you." "Ye" is not meant in the Old English or biblical sense. The italicized term *tar* in the story is the Texans' colorful pronunciation of the word *tire.*

CHAPTER 1

San Antone, Texas,
Lackland Army Air Force Base

1946

I CAN'T HELP the way my dad is. Hell, I didn't make him—he made me. You'd think that when a fella created something he'd take care of it, admire it, and pay it a little attention: kinda like a landscape painter who protects his canvas by bringing it in from the rain, or an author waiting for the ink to dry before gently stacking the pages he's just written in a pile. I'm the "book" Dad started to write, but he handled my pages carelessly, and then threw the whole thing into a dusty corner.

The truth of it is he didn't even spend much time creating me. His part of the making probably took all of fifteen minutes or— bless my mother's heart—thirty if he was Cooter Browned from Pearl beer. As a kid, I kept thinking that someday he'd pick up his

"Cono book," dust off the front cover, open me back up, and start writing again.

⊰ ★ ⊱

"Son, don't you never ever let yer mother run outta wood!" At seven, I was swinging that axe over my head and down hard onto that chopping block. My axe became my best friend. I held on to it so tight that the fingers on my right hand gradually made indentations in the wooden handle. When I had to grab ahold of my must-do, learned-to-respect weapon, my fingers sunk into the familiar worn grooves of the handle just as they would later learn how to comfort themselves around the grip of my .22. I kept my axe sharpened and shiny, covered it when it rained, and always knew where it was and how to get to it real quick if I needed to. I took care of it, giving it the attention it deserved.

I often thought of other uses for it, like how I could use it to "take care of Dad" when his temper flared, but my axe never landed where I'd pictured it. So far, my axe has only split open big pieces of wood.

Yeah, growing up I did want to kill my father, cut his head plumb off with my axe or blast him with my .22. I held on to those ideas as tightly as a cowboy holds on to the reins of a wild stallion. But Dad was always faster, stronger. He knew how I felt about him, and because of that, he was good at anticipating my moves. He was like a polecat ready to spray anything that crossed his path, anything that didn't sit right with him. That's one thing I learned from my dad—how to defend myself, to cover up if need be, like a boxer in the ring who has to protect himself at all times.

I tried to keep away when I could, but sometimes I couldn't move an inch out of the way before one of his big paws found me.

Dad never hurt my sister Delma, and I'm sure glad about that. But I knew she was scared of him anyway. She learned fear by watching the way Dad treated Mother and me.

You don't really know much when you're born, but that's where it starts alright, whether you like it or not. When you're just a little suckling pig on your mamma's teat, all you really want to know is that the teat will keep filling up so you can start suckling all over again. Once you reckon the food's always gonna be there when you're hungry, you move on to wondering whether you're gonna be kept safe from harm and warm when it's cold. As you get a little older, you find out that maybe there isn't always going to be enough to eat after all, and you won't always be warm either. This is especially true if you were growing up during the Great Depression in Texas, in the western part, where any stranger is sized up from boot to hat—if, that is, they're lucky enough to own both.

Texans trust themselves first and foremost, and then maybe one or two of their kinfolk, as long as they've found that trust to be right as rain, if the sun can set on their words. I grew up trying to figure out who to put in which category: those I could trust and those never to turn my back on. I learned what I know from watching those who crossed over and the others who stayed on their own side.

I did both.

Ike, my grandfather, is not mean like his son. Unless he's breaking a horse or doing something else with purpose, he's got a smile perched on his leathered face. He stays cool as a cucumber even when times are tough. I hardly ever see that worry bubble dancing over his head like the cloud of Texas dust most of us stand under. Ike got rid of his worry when, at the age of two, Great Grandpa Jim put him on top of a horse, teaching him how it felt to rise above the smallness. If trouble comes knocking on his door, he just wrestles it down until all that's left is the *T*.

Lathering up my face for a close shave, I look at myself in the mirror. I'm wearing a master sergeant's standard-issue uniform with patches from Lackland Army Air Force Base in San Antone, Texas. Five-foot-ten, one hundred and fifty pounds, complexion listed as "ruddy," and not an ounce of fat on my eighteen-year-old body. If my reflection showed anything but, I wouldn't be the physical training instructor responsible for over ten thousand men. I can jump a rope like Joe Louis, crossing it under my feet until the nylon disappears.

I stepped up my game a few years back. I left behind the body of a small, skinny kid everyone picked on for a new, stronger body like I had squeezed into a pair of tight overalls bought from the "Don't Ever Touch Me Again" department.

I look at my cheekbones, the prominent ones I got from Ike, who's part Cherokee. I rub my hand over my chin and cheeks checking for straggling whiskers. There are none. But give me a couple of hours, and I'll need to put my brush back into the shaving cup and lather up all over again.

Now that my duffle bag is packed with a few days' worth of clothes, I'll take the train from San Antone to Temple, visit Mother and Sis, and find out whether or not Dad's really gonna spar with me. It was his idea in the first place, and it threw me off for sure. A sparring session with Dad and a chance to hit him back! Don't that beat all?

This is what happened. A couple of months ago I had gone home for a short leave and showed Dad my red boxing trunks, with "Kid Dennis" stitched on the bottom left leg. He eagle-eyed my trunks up one side and down the other, but when I showed him my eight-ounce gloves, he held them in his hands, carefully feeling the fine leather and laces as though they were newborn pups. Then, for whatever reason, I said, "Here Dad, you can have them. I'm not fighting for the army anymore, no how." He looked up at me from the couch he was sitting on, rubbed his index finger back and forth around his thumb, and said, "Then next time ya come, bring another pair and I'll spar with ya." *Well I'll be damned*, I thought. *This son of a bitch still isn't done hitting me.* As soon as I got back to San Antone, I didn't waste any time. I went and bought myself another pair of gloves.

Ha! Wayne "Denny" Dennis, the one-time carnival boxer, doesn't stand a chance. I'll look him straight in his eyes, like I used to when he hit me for no good reason. But this time when he rears back with that big fist of his, I'll be ready with my own.

Up 'til I was about twelve, we had lived in a lot of different places—with my mother's folks, Ma and Pa, in Ranger; at Tourist Courts in Rotan, Crane, South Bend; and several times with Mother's sister, Aunt Nolie, and her husband number one or number two—until we finally ended up in Temple. But when I turned fourteen, Dad didn't just step over the line into the territory of no forgiveness, he leapt over it like a cougar pouncing on his prey. That's when I knew it was time for me to leave. I boarded the train to Anything's-Better-'n-This.

After the train dropped me off in Ranger, I went straight to Ma and Pa's. I stayed there long enough to put a little flicker of light and comfort back on my pillow. I found out that Fire Chief Murphy let the football players sleep in the firehouse if—as was my case—their homes were so far away they couldn't easily attend regular practice. As much as I loved Ma and Pa, I didn't like walking the two and a half miles back and forth from their farm. So

I stayed in the firehouse, sweeping floors to earn my keep, and began playing a little football.

Before long, I traded in the pigskin for the comforts and companionship of real cowboys: my Uncle Thurmond and Coots Rutherford at the Martin ranch outside of Hamlin. That's where they found me. Ike was still living in Temple back then, and he told me I could live with him instead of at home with Dad. And anyone who lives with Ike learns a whole lifetime in less than a year. But when Ike moved, I soon discovered there was nothing left for me in Temple, nothing left except for the agitation of having a lighter checkbook in my pocket.

But now it's time to go back to Temple. I stuff these sparring gloves into my duffle bag and I have to laugh out loud as I recollect why I had to borrow them. We can pull things over on folks sometimes, especially when it's not expected. But when we feel so sure of our own skins that we forget to be sure of our own surroundings, we're ripe for the picking and there's nobody to blame but our own selves. "Always pay attention te what's around ye," says Pa. "'Cause if ye don't, something'll come up and bite ye on the butt."

That's what happened all right. I was bitten on the butt by ol' Vargo, the snake. But his venom wasn't of the poisonous variety. It only made me laugh, both at him and at myself. Shoot, if I was in his shoes I might have done the same thing.

Now I look down at my own shoes, my standard-issued army boots I'd traded my cowboy boots in for. When I was just a kid, H. Govan told me, "Little Dennis, sometimes you jes' hafta change yo' shoes 'n do sumthin' different." He said this to me after I'd asked him why he'd changed jobs from shining shoes at the barbershop, where I got to see him all the time, to working at the bank, where he cleaned up the money dust and footprints of rich people. Needless to say, I never got to see him at the bank. My poor feet never had the right shoes for walking into a place with money. My feet were busy doing things like walking down to Rotan's railroad switching station and picking lamb's-quarter for Mother to boil for supper.

When I was in grade school, I had heard how H. watched some of the high school football players go off and fight the Germans. H. Govan, a colored man, was the only one who wrote to those boys—not the coach and not the teachers.

H. is now the water boy at Rotan's high school, working for the Yellowhammers football team. That man loves football; he's found shoes I don't think he'll *ever* take off. Next time I get back to Rotan I'll have to show him my army boots. He'll stare down at them and say something like, "Well look at you, Little Dennis, those are alright. Yes siree, those are alright." Mostly he'd like them because I do, at least for now.

I'm not real sure how long I'll wear these army boots, but I can tell you one thing. When my feet start to smart, I'll trade them in for something better, just like H. did. Ike told me once, "If ya don't like what yer doin', what's the point? A rich man that hates his job ain't rich a'tall." Settling for something can kill a man just as easy as being shot on Main Street in Rotan or being beaten to death with knucks and a tire tool in Ranger.

I've been around these army boys for two years now, and come to think on it, most of them aren't real "standard issue" either. They've walked their shoes in places I've never heard of and brought along with them some of the strangest notions. For now, my shoes fit me just fine. But their comfort didn't happen overnight.

I had just turned sixteen when I heard that OilCo Construction

Company of Tulsa, Oklahoma, was building a pipeline to the border outside of Pampa, Texas, a small town in the panhandle. Woody Guthrie grew up in Pampa and even wrote a song about how bad the dust storms were. It was wintertime and the Great Depression was just dust from the past. So when I heard about the job openings, and before anyone could stop me or spend any more of my money, I lit out like a penned bull when the gate opens. It was January 1944, and working on that pipeline was the chance to earn my own money and get to keep it for a change.

The Santa Fe Railway carried me from the Martin ranch to Pampa. From there, I hitched a ride to the outskirts of town where the pipeline was being built. My new straw boss met me; he looked around forty-five years old but was said to be in his mid-thirties.

He sized me up one side and down the other and said, "Stay with me, and I'll teach you what you need to know."

A couple of fellas handed out picks and shovels. It didn't take me but a split second to size them up and figure out that they were fixin' to have me dig a goddamn ditch.

Now, I'm not exactly sure what I was expecting, but ditch digging wasn't at all the picture I'd put in my mind. I guess I figured I would go home each night with that liquid Texas Gold staining my clothes and the smell of *rich* penetrating my nose holes, just like my Great Uncle Will McClesky had done in 1917 in Ranger, when the oil spewed like black lava from a wooden volcano.

The straw boss took me and the rest of the rookie crew to a section already lined off with binder twine. My eyes followed that string for a lot longer than I cared to see. Next, the straw boss told us how deep to dig. Problem was, that ol' ground was frozen solid and harder than a full tick on a cow's hide. I had on every bit of clothing I owned, but it didn't make no difference. If it wasn't for that welder who started the fire in the tin barrel, I'd have been as dead as the goats that died at my feet during that awful winter sixteen years ago.

I was only two years old when Grandpa Ike and his friend J. B. Aimes went into the goat business together. A freeze came to town that winter, and the goats bleated their agony until their throats froze up. Frozen dead goats were everywhere, even in the house, since we had brought many of them inside trying to save them. It was like living in a barn. But the goats all died anyway, lying right there on our kitchen floor like unskinned rugs. Since the goats were about my size, and being that I was so young, I kept thinking I was going to die from the cold too.

I remember moving closer to the warm fireplace, close enough to get the feeling back in my hands. Then I got a harebrained idea. I reached into the fireplace, grabbed a hot chunk of red coal, and sizzled a layer of skin off my right hand. The pain and my stupidity were bad enough. But that wasn't all.

Ike ended up losing all his money, and him and J. B. liked to have had a shootout. To this day, I hate the cold—and I hate goats even more.

It did help me to understand something, though. When Ike would be close to winning a hand at poker, he'd tell the other players, "Well, boys and girls, it's time we separate the sheep from the goats." I suppose that meant one was better than the other, and there in Pampa, I sure knew which one I didn't want to be.

But there I was again, in the freezing weather outside of Pampa, Texas, feeling like a damn goat. We'd been out digging since early morning, and I was cold. God, I was cold. I swung my pickaxe, but it wasn't anything like chopping wood. When my pickaxe hit that frozen ground, my entire body buzzed, and the ground looked just as it had before I swung at it. With every hit, my teeth clenched and my eyeballs twitched like they were rolling back in my head; probably like how a cow feels when blue lightning hits its horns. To make matters worse, it looked like there was nothing between me and my pickaxe and the North Pole except for a barbed wire fence—no barns, no trees, nothing. Only cold winds whistling and laughing at us, telling us how stupid we were.

After a couple hours of that misery, I told Mr. Straw Boss, "Ye sure were right. Ye taught me all I needed to know. I'm leavin'! I'm goin' to town, and I'm gonna join the damn military 'cause this ain't for me. I'd rather get bullets than this. I'd rather jump in a foxhole than stay here and freeze to death like a stupid goat."

Whitney, another young fella who'd started on the same day as me, threw down his pickaxe and said, "Ye wanna ride?"

As I was getting into Whitney's truck I hollered back to Straw Boss, "Ye know the difference between a sheep and a goat?"

He stared at me like his eyeballs where frozen, which I have to say they had a good chance of being.

I answered my own question: "The sheep's still alive."

After I'd said it, I felt kinda sorry for the poor fella—first because he probably didn't know what the hell I was talking about, and second, as he watched us get into Whitney's truck, I knew it wouldn't have taken much for him to jump right on in and come with us.

I went to Pampa with the idea of becoming a marine paratrooper. I figured that if I could learn to use a toothbrush on my own after having my face slapped, and to tie my shoes before I could be slapped again, becoming a soldier would be a walk in the park. At least the marines wouldn't let me freeze.

I got to the Pampa post office where the recruiters were and remembered I was only sixteen. Then I realized that if I signed up for the draft they'd have to take me. I walked over to the draft board.

"I gotta register fer the draft 'cause I'm eighteen today," I said, lying through my frozen teeth. They signed me up.

When I went back to the marine recruiter's office, they were all out to lunch. *OK, then I'll be an army paratrooper*, I thought. They were out to lunch too. The navy? Out to lunch. There was only one recruiter anywhere around, and he was from the army air force. I walked straight up to the recruiter and said, "They're fixin' to draft me. Do ye want me?"

"I'll take ya," he said.

Right away, they put me on a bus heading for the Amarillo Air Force Base. They gave me a hotel room, swore me in, and before I knew it, I was on another bus heading to Fort Bliss, where German prisoners were being held.

We stayed on the side of Franklin Mountain in five-man huts made out of tarpaper. And wouldn't you know it? It was cold, cold, cold. There was one little gas heater sitting in the middle of the hut, and the only way to get warm was to practically sit on top of it. The only thing better about being at Fort Bliss than digging that pipeline outside of Pampa was that I wasn't holding a goddamn pickaxe.

I tossed and turned the cold from my back to my front, from my head to my feet, until I finally fell asleep around three o'clock in the morning. An hour later, some little corporal came in blowing his whistle and yelled, "Come on and get up." He marched us down to the chow hall, where I ate a biscuit, a piece of bacon, and two watered-down scrambled eggs. Then he tried to put a couple of us on KP duty. In the kitchen next to the mess hall, the pots and pans were stacked up to the ceiling. "Ya'll clean all these pots and pans and don't come back 'til it's done." I figured he'd picked at least one wrong man for the job.

Looking out the window, I eyeballed those German prisoners walking in squads, their sergeant drilling them. I shifted my eyes back to those grimy pots and pans and thought to myself, *Well this sure ain't gonna cut it.*

I went outside and hollered at the pudgy sergeant. "Come here and bring that squad with ye." He marched them over to me like I was a general. I focused in on those German prisoners and said, "Ye see all those pots and pans? Don't ya'll come out of here 'til you've finished cleanin' 'em all up." They might not have spoken much English, but they sure knew what a finger point was.

So, while they started in on their new job, I went down to the PX and drank me some nice hot coffee. That's when I had my first good thought in over a week: *This army business might not be so bad after all.*

A few days later, they bused us to the town of El Paso, in the very western corner of Texas, just so they could ship us out to Harlingen Army Air Force Base, further south than a bird can fly for winter. We were on a troop train wearing full gear, our knees touching, and I couldn't sleep a wink. I was used to sharing a bed with kinfolk, but these were strangers from around all parts of Texas, places I'd never even heard of before. Besides, I might have been poor growing up, but I never had to sleep sitting up.

Something occurred to me as I looked around at the sleeping strangers. I realized we were all related in some way, all wanting something different, something a whole lot better than what was behind us.

The train pulled in, and before I knew it, we were standing in parade dress waiting in single file for the chow line. I was standing in my flight section of fifty-four men. All the ranking men had gone except for the second lieutenant, who was greener than a gourd. He was the squadron commander over everything, and he walked straight over to me and asked, "Soldier, you've done previous service, haven't you?"

"No sir," I said, standing in rigid attention and trying to figure out why he asked me that question.

"But you've had previous training, haven't you?"

I thought real quick. Hell, I'd had previous training alright—previous training in ranching and sandwich making, not to mention in bank robbing conversations, fighting, and escaping. So I said, "Yes sir, I've had previous trainin'."

"Where at?"

I knew what he was thinking, so again I lied through my teeth and said, "ROTC, sir." Every officer likes to hear that.

"Can you drill men?" Shoot, I'd seen enough picture shows to know how to drill men. Any idiot can drill men. I'd been drilled all my life—told what to do, what not to do, when to do it to boot.

"Yes sir!" I said.

He called over the little corporal, pointed to me, and said, "This is your new assistant."

I had no inkling of an idea of what it meant to be an assistant to a corporal, but I learned quickly enough. An "assistant" meant wearing a piss pot, a little blue helmet that identified you as an assistant just like a piece of tape with your name on it identified you as the newcomer at a Baptist revival.

Little Corporal put that piss pot on my head, and I marched those soldiers straight to the classroom. Then I went to the PX to drink some more coffee.

After breakfast, they put me in pre-mark, where they're sup-posed to teach you how to break down weapons. That was funny to me. How could anyone be sixteen—or worse, have passed that age—and not already have known how to break down a rifle? I broke down and put back together everything they threw at me.

I'd barely had a chance to size up everybody when the decision was made to shut down Harlingen's Army Air Force Base.

Before I knew it, I was on my way to San Antone, Texas, home of the Alamo. Finally, I would get to see the real Alamo, not the little plastic model that we sold at Weber's Café in Temple. The real Alamo!

I remember wishing I could take my piss pot along with me to San Antone. Not that I liked wearing it, but I sure liked the name. It reminded me of Ike's favorite horse, P. A. "P. A." stood for "Pissant" unless the women were around. Then we'd call him "Prince Albert."

It was here in San Antone that I met West Point Colonel James T. Posey, a real thoroughbred. I love that old man, and not just because he shares the same name as my childhood friend, Harold "Hoover" Posey. Colonel Posey sees something in me that nobody else has, kinda like he can look right through me and know where I've been, and he knows better than I do where I'm heading.

A few months ago Colonel Posey sent a lieutenant colonel over to me and asked, "You're an athlete, aren't you, Dennis?"

"Yes sir."

"Boxing and football?" They'd been watching me alright.

"Yes sir, that's right."

"I'm sending you over to the physical training department."

"Yes sir."

When I got there I reported to the lieutenant, who said,

"Dennis, you are now a physical training instructor." I taught class the next day. I was just fixin' to turn seventeen.

Next thing I knew they gave me one stripe, and then two stripes. I got my third stripe this past December right after I turned eighteen years old. I'm a buck sergeant. I have twenty instructors, and I'm responsible for all those men.

I look in my duffle bag and see the sparring gloves Colonel Posey lent me yesterday. He had looked tired to me, like a man defeated by grief but still trying to stand up straight. His hair was graying, and his eyes had lines at the corners like a map of a busy town. But his kindness sat on my chest like Pa's and Ike's kindness, stayed there perched like a redbird.

I thought about when Colonel Posey's little daughter had died six months back from some disease the doctors didn't know how to cure. I thought about Ervin Clay Carter and Gene Davis being dead and how hard it was on their parents and, maybe, how hard it was on me. They were just kids, and life had sucked the air out of them easier than sucking a chocolate malt through a wide straw. Then I thought about Private Henderson.

After I'd told Colonel Posey about sparring with my father, he said, "You know, whatever picture you've formed in your head about sparring with your father might not be what really happens."

I knew what he was talking about. I thought of other pictures I'd made up in my head that didn't match the truth, like working on that pipeline. That picture wasn't anything like what happened. I thought of more pictures from long ago, like me owning my own guitar, or having a real conversation with my dad, or not being able to reach my .22.

I swing my duffle bag over my shoulder and check my old watch, the one Pa gave me. Walking towards the mess hall I see a bunch of new recruits doing a few push-ups, sounding like their insides are about to pop out. One or two of those boys struggle like they're drowning in the quicksand of a Tarzan movie. I laugh out loud so they can hear me, and then I say, "Hell, that ain't no hill for a stepper."

The time those words were said to me I had stepped up as good as any boxer can be in his last round of the fight, tired, with only a little air still left in my lungs but still not ready to quit. Those words gave me the push that set me back upright, moving forward again. After my unsolicited comment to them, I knew some of those grunting new recruits on the ground were gonna glare at me and wish that I'd fall under the hooves of wild horses. Others would remind themselves that no matter what, they considered themselves "steppers" and could pop out fifty more if they had to. Those are the men who will make it, both in this army and out.

A light sprinkle mixes in with the beginning of a fresh spring air. I catch the bus to the train station, knowing each minute that passes gets me closer to showing my dad a thing or two about how a real boxer fights.

Dad never had a problem with hitting hard. He was so strong, and his hands so big, he could slap someone with an open palm and knock 'em down as flat as if they'd been swatted by a big-pawed bear. But now I have strength, technique, and accuracy. When I get to Temple, he doesn't stand a chance. I keep thinking that I should pop him one for that poor ol' truck driver who made the mistake of coming to the wrong house; maybe one for the man at the domino hall who never got to get out of his chair; maybe a bunch for my mother. The other punches will be for me.

I get inside the train station just as the sun makes a quick appearance over Alamo city. In the waiting area, I try to get my butt comfortable on the hard metal seat. I watch the comings and the goings of the passengers, normal-looking folks for the most part, on their way to do something different.

While I wait for the train to arrive, I think on the last couple of months and what they've been like. I think about my promotion, about Vargo, about the cooks' barracks. The only thing that doesn't put a smile on my face is thinking again about Private Henderson. His life was over just when he was about to start something new, to make something of himself. But it wasn't my fault.

"What's takin' so long?" I ask the man behind the ticket counter. I'm ready to get going and think about something else.

"Railway strike makes everything late." I'd forgotten about the strike, thought it only affected the folks up north.

Of all the places I've lived, only a few are worth going back to. Ranger is one of them, a small town where a fella can't turn around and take a shit without the entire town knowing what he's had for supper. At least, for the most part, they are good folks who make sure you have something to eat. Still, the best thing about Ranger? That's where Ma and Pa live, the nicest people on earth.

We left Ranger when I was five and moved further west to Rotan. Rotan was just a tad bigger, so there were only a few more people to size up before we could feel comfortable. What's the best thing about Rotan? That's where I met some of the best friends I've ever had. Gene Davis, who didn't get a chance to learn to shave, and Hoover Posey, who spoke like molasses was stuck to the roof of his mouth. Hoover spoke so slow a fella could fall sound asleep before he'd even finish a sentence. And, of course, Rotan had H. Govan and Mr. Sam Green.

The best thing about going back to Temple? Not a damn

thing except for Mother and Sis being there. Ike's no longer there. Even though his sandwich business was going well, Ike needed to change back into his cowboy boots before the smell of cattle and horses left him forever. He works on a ranch in Walburg now, not too far away from Temple. I've made up my mind to go see him on this trip, put lead in my pencil and an ease on my mind. I miss his smirk-like grin when I do something stupid and he says, "Well aren't you smart!" It's something about the way he tilts his head under his hat and looks at you sideways that makes you laugh and feel comfortable at the same time.

The man behind the counter is yelling, "The three o'clock train to Austin, Temple, Waco, and Dallas is ready for boarding." Finally!

Getting on the train, I'm thankful it's not crowded. Too many people too close to me is something I'll never get used to. I find a seat towards the back like I always do. A back up against the wall is a back protected. I need to see what's going on around me at all times. And, like always, when I hop on a train, I hope that my head is still attached when I get to where I'm going; not like our friend, Wort Reynolds, who hopped on that train to Clyde, Texas, the train that grabbed his head and kept right on going.

"Ticket, please."

I turn my eyes from the curved tracks outside my window to the ticket taker. Handing it over, I watch him punch the hole without even looking into my eyes. How many years has he done this, I wonder. Does he like the shoes he's wearing?

My ears focus on the sound of the train's idling, eager-to-go engines. Where the hell would I be today if I didn't have those railroad memories chugging along with me, some good and some anything but?

Just as I'm feeling comfortable, that I won't be crowded, I feel something getting comfortable in the worn seat next to me, making me anything but. It nudges me. I ignore it and then tell it to go away. It doesn't listen. The memories want me to pay them a little attention. I know the train is about to pull out. I know the train is taking me to Temple. But my mind and my uninvited seat companion start to take me somewhere else, somewhere I've already been before, somewhere I don't care to go back to. It starts speeding me down the track a lot faster than this train will ever go—and a whole lot faster than I can put a stop to.

The first memory is safe. It makes me wish, "If only it could have all been this easy." But past wishes were reserved for the other folks with good seats.

Not for me.

Cono, Lackland Army Air Force Base, Age 18

CHAPTER 2

Stirring Up a Baby Sister with a Tiger Stick

1930

"CONO, I'M LEAVIN' fer a bit te pick up yer Uncle Joe," Aunt Nolie called to me. "I'll be back 'for long. Ain't nothin' gonna happen fer a while anyhow."

"OK," I tell Aunt Nolie. She's all gussied up like she's going to a dance; red lips to match her red dress. I sit on the bottom step of our front porch, my bare feet touching the dry Texas dirt, and I watch her drive away from the house. Dad's standing on the front porch next to me and is lighting another cigarette. Except for his matches and the flickering lightbulb on the front porch, it's dark out. Dark and noisy. The sound of my mother screaming inside her bedroom is louder than the sounds of the June bugs chirping. I can't for the life of me figure out why Dad's not doing anything to help her. But there's someone else in there with her, some lady from town named "Midwife," who said for us to "Skedaddle 'n go do somethin' else, fer cryin' out loud."

I make circles in the dirt with the stick I'd picked up under the resting tree earlier in the day, when I could still see all the way to the end of the world. I twirl it round and round in the dirt between my bare, dirty feet. The ground's real dry; I think this could be my chance to see a real doodlebug. "Doodlebug, doodlebug, please come out. Yer children 'r asleep, and yer house is on fire."

Sure wish something would happen. All this waiting makes a fella real tired, and every time I hear my skinny mother yell, I feel crawly all over, like a bunch of daddy longlegs are throbbing on my head. Even though there's a baby in her belly that she's trying to force out like a stubborn mule from the safety of its barn, you'd never be able to tell she had a big belly by watching her walk away from you. But when she turned around? The front of her looked like she swallered a watermelon and tried to hide it under the blue-checkered dress Ma made for her when all her clothes got too small.

My bony elbows rest on my bony knees so my hands can hold up my head, the part causing me to be a bit restless and tuckered out at the same time. I close my eyes and pretend Ranger's late train is making its sounds; that my head's on my pillow, where it's supposed to be at this time of night.

I worry that Mother's not in the hospital. A few days ago I heard Aunt Nolie tell Mother, "Elnora, it'd be a whole helluva lot safer if ye had that baby in the hospital like ye did Cono." They talked about the Great Depression that sat on our shoulders and wouldn't get off. They said it makes us hungrier than usual and poorer than we've ever been.

"Hospitals cost money, Nolie. We don't have no money fer a hospital."

Ma and Pa say it's because of President Hoover that we don't have no money. Others say it's because we ain't had rain in a coon's age, that all the crops—cotton, corn, and maize—have turned into a dust that you could just as easy blow away like a fly acrost the lonely couple of peas sitting on your plate. A farmer and his family, like Ma and Pa, can't live on dust, and since there's no money around to gamble with, a man like my father can't collect none.

I hear another scream from the bedroom. Dad shifts his weight from one foot to the other. It's hot out, so he keeps rolling up his sleeves, but they keep creeping back down again. He won't take his shirt off, though. Even though we're not in town, he says that taking your shirt off in public is uncouth, no matter how hot it is. Whatever "uncouth" means. He lights another Camel. With my special stick, I stir a little faster and dig a little deeper. It might be just a piece of wood to some folks, but to me it's a magic tiger stick and will make doodlebugs come out and help Mother stop hurting. And, it will grow me a baby brother or sister.

I start thinking that unless it figures out how to catch up with me I'll always be older than the baby coming out of my mother. I like that. I like the idea of being older. It makes me feel bigger and important. Also, I don't need nobody else telling me what to do.

Just before I start feeling too big for my britches, I hear the huff and whirr of an engine pulling up to the house. I look up and squint into the headlamps of the familiar flatbed grain truck. The engine stops. The headlamps turn off. Aunt Nolie jumps out of the driver's side and walks over to us. She's still wearing the red dress she left in an hour ago. I look for Uncle Joe. I hear him before I see him. He's stretched out in the back of the truck sucking in hard air and trying to force it back out again.

"Any word yet, Wayne?" Aunt Nolie asks Dad, tussling my towhead at the same time.

"Nah."

"I'll jes' go on in and check," she calls over her shoulder as she wiggles and waggles her rear end off to Mother's bedroom.

Aunt Nolie is a tough booger, and it's good to have her on my side. She can kick anybody's ass from now into tomorrow. She said one time that she'd rather fight than talk, but she does plenty of both. She's not quite as skinny as Mother, her hair's not as black, and she's not nearly as pretty. But she speaks her mind so you don't have to guess what's on it.

I make myself scrape the dirt some more even though all I want to do is fall asleep. Dad's still staring at something in the dark, something far away that I can't see. I'm only two and a half years old, so I'd much rather be stirring at something I can see than staring at something I can't. "Doodlebug, doodlebug, please come out . . ."

Before I have time to get comfortable again, Aunt Nolie comes outside and kneels down beside me. Her watery eyes stare into my tired ones, and she's saying real quiet-like, "Cono, ye got yerself a baby sister."

I feel my eyes pop out and my chin drop down. I'm not real sure what to do next, seeing as how I've never had a baby sister before. Stuff is stuck in my throat, way in the back, where I can't get to without choking.

I make myself spit out, "Kin I see?"

"Go right on in," she says.

I guess Dad thinks it's OK for him to come in too since he follows me into the house and into the room, which smells like hard work and soft babies. It's the room where I meet my baby sister for the first time.

I tiptoe up to Mother's bed. Since her ankles are no bigger

round than her thumb and middle finger put together, I can't figure how she got that baby out of her tiny body. But I'm sure glad she did. There lying in my mother's skinny arms is the cutest little thing I've ever laid eyes on. Her little nose is no bigger than a kernel of corn.

My mother's eyes are closed, like she's said good-bye to us for a while and hello to something else.

"What're we gonna call her?" I ask.

"Delma Jean's her name," she whispers.

I start to lean towards my new sister. "Careful now," says Aunt Nolie.

"I know," I say.

I get real close to one of her tiny baby ears and whisper so only she can hear, "Since I'm older, Delma Jean, I'm gonna have te take care of ye."

I mean it too.

Dad looks down at my sister and strokes her little hand and lets out a little smile. I think he likes her. I look at my hand and decide that I'll never touch another goat ever again, alive or dead. I won't touch another piece of fire either, and I'll teach my new baby sister not to. I don't want her to get hurt like I did.

"She's a cute li'l thing, Elnora," he says.

"She shorly is," says Mother.

Aunt Nolie shoos us out of the room, telling us that Midwife needs to finish up.

And as I walk away from Mother and my baby sister, I hear Aunt Nolie say to her, "Yer only eighteen and ye did it again. Now ye got yerself two babies and yer still alive. It's all gonna work out jes' fine, Elnora. You jes' wait and see."

A few days later, my Grandpa Ike leaves Rotan and comes to

Ranger to meet Delma. He brings her a little baby rattle shaped like a horse. He gives me a cigar box. I lift the lid, but there's nothing inside except the smell of old cigars.

"What's it?" I ask.

"Well, that there's a box for you ta put your specials in."

"Like what?"

"I s'pose anything that's important to ya that can fit inside."

I keep staring inside the empty box, thinking about what special I could put inside.

Just as I'm thinking that Delma's too big for a cigar box and wouldn't like it anyhow, Ike says, "Maybe you can start with this here," and he hands me a real pocketknife.

I feel the heavy in it, turn it over and over in my hands, and look up at Mother, who's caught Ike's eye and is holding it. The side of Ike's cheek goes back towards his ear as he makes a little clicking sound inside his mouth.

"But you'd better not open it so ya don't cut yerself," he says.

"When kin I?"

"I reckon you'll know when it's time. But it won't be t'day or tomorrow. Leave it in thar fer a while. Let it get used to its new home."

"Thanks!" I say and run off to the other room before Mother can take the knife away from me.

Aunt Nolie and Uncle Joe like my Grandpa Ike. They talk and laugh when they get together with him and act like they're kin to Ike and not Dad. Dad doesn't seem to get on well with Aunt Nolie, and she doesn't seem to get on much with Dad neither. Being so much alike in the rough department, you'd think that Aunt Nolie and Dad would get along good, but they don't. Sometimes when they're in the same room, Aunt Nolie looks like she's just waiting for Dad to smart off to her so she can hit him upside the head with a crowbar full of bad words. Once I saw her lock her eyeballs on his and not let go even for a split second. It was like she was holding him down and waiting for him to fess up at the same time. But Dad just sat there quiet, cleared his throat, stood up, and walked away. The truth is, Aunt Nolie looks at Dad like Ma and Pa do—with a raised eyebrow and a squinted eye. I don't think they like the way Dad takes care of Mother.

Just like Aunt Nolie and Uncle Joe, Ma and Pa help us out a lot too since they live just outside of Ranger on their farm. Without Ma and Pa and Aunt Nolie's help, I think we'd just blow away like tumbleweed.

We settle in, the five of us, and now we're together with my baby sister, of course. Delma cries sometimes, but Mother says it's OK and for me not to worry none. She says, "It's normal, babies doin' that." I can't see how crying is normal. If I cry, which I try not to, Dad tells me to cut it out 'cause, "There ain't no room fer it in the house." Aunt Nolie's house is small, so I guess he means you gotta fill a house with furniture and food and sounds of crying babies, not the sounds of crying from a big, strong brother like me.

Wayne and Elnora Dennis

CHAPTER 3

148 Miles to Temple

SURE WILL BE good to see Delma Jean when I step off this train. She's sixteen years old now, the same age I was when I signed up for the army.

Some say it's peculiar that I remember so much from my first few years of life. But some things, like the burning of a hand or the birth of a little sister, stay with you forever. I also remember things like putting a pot on my head to make her laugh, helping to pin her cloth diapers around her butt, and, later, pulling her toes to make them pop. I'd smile and say, "They ain't long enough yet, Sis. I'm gonna hep 'em grow." She'd always run away laughing.

I also remember using that pocketknife Ike gave me. It came in real handy in first grade.

I got another knife when I first came to San Antone. I had a cowboy hat I really loved, but I found something I liked even better. With the trade of my hat, I became the new owner of a

Mexican bowie knife that came with an engraved scabbard. It was a real beaut. Sometimes you have to trade in something good to get something better. I'd learned that long ago.

This train has its rhythm going now. The passengers have settled in. Most are trying to sleep just to make the time pass. I lay my head up against the hard window and watch as the city starts to slowly slip by. I close my eyes to see if I can nod off like everybody else, but it's only an idea. Sleep is knocked out by that presence in the seat next to me. More memories keep nudging me, crowding me up against the ropes, where none of my boxing defense skills seem to work. No, these are stronger opponents. They jab my chin, then power punch me in the gut. It's more painful than a broken nose. They make me remember.

Delma, Age 14

CHAPTER 4

Busted Toothbrushes and Beaten Backsides

1931

I STACK UP all the devil's claws I find so I can see how high they'll go up before they all fall back down again. Here at Ma and Pa's farm just outside of Ranger, where we're living now, devil's claws are everywhere. They start out as pink wild flowers, but they always end up looking like a dry piece of horned wood. I've tried to find a family of devil's claws, the small baby ones, the middle-size ones, and the biggest king of all devil's claws. So far, they all seem about the same, so I just keep stacking them up. Sometimes if you ain't paying any attention, one will snag you around your ankle and make you think you've been bitten by a ratt'ler. I can't bring them into the house, though, 'cause Dad says, "There ain't no room in the house for more weeds."

"Cono? Cono? Where the hell are ya?" Like Ma says, speak of the Devil.

"Over here," I say, getting up and dusting off my britches.

"I got ya somethin' today."

Dad never brings me nothing. Ever. Not even a stick of chewing gum. But now he's standing in front of me, dressed as always in his khakis and clean short-sleeve button-down shirt. His big hand reaches into the sack from Adams Grocers and pulls out a brand-new toothbrush. I've seen Mother and Dad use one before, so I guess that I must be big enough now to use one too since I'm a big brother and all. I want to show Dad how grown up I am.

I look at that shiny white toothbrush like it's a precious jewel and think I should be saving it for a Sunday.

"Well now, go ahead on. Give it a shot." I stick it in my mouth and chomp on it like it's one of Ma's old biscuits. I hear a crack. The handle comes out but the brush part stays in.

Dad can catch a housefly in one hand without blinking, so it shouldn't have surprised me none that his open palm slams fast across my face.

As I put my hand to my face, he says, "Oh fer cryin' out loud, Cono! I'll swannin', ya bit it in two! Can't ya do—"

I don't hear the rest of what he's saying since he's walking away from me shaking his head back and forth. Now half of my face is stinging like it's been resting on a yeller jacket's nest. How can you build up something so high just to watch it fall down so hard? With the brush part still inside my mouth and its handle still in my hand, I think I've found the baby devil's claw after all. It's me. I'm the baby.

I think about what I'm supposed to do with these two pieces. Maybe I can just swaller the brush part that's not doing anything but napping on my tongue. At least then half of my dumbness will be covered up. Then again, Ma is always saying to me, "Cono, ye need to 'member that anythin' ye swaller is gonna have te come out the other end." She reminds me about this all the time, ever since she saw me swaller that penny a few months ago. No sir, she won't let me forget about that penny. I'd picked it up off Pa's night table, looked at it, sniffed it, and after licking that penny, it just slid down my throat as easy as ice cream.

When Ma saw that penny go into my mouth and not come back out, she said, "Times bein' hard, ye gotta look at yer ba'll movement ev'ry time ye do one. Don't use the outhouse. Go in the fields. When ye find it, clean it off real good and hand it over to yer Mother. She needs it a whole lot more 'n yer belly does." I knew she was right. No one has much money. Most folks around here are six pennies shy of a nickel.

I watched each poop that turned up. I waited, hoping it had melted and I'd already peed it out, but that didn't happen. A few days later, when I saw that penny come out, I stared at it for a while. I just didn't have it in me to pick it out of my poop and clean it off.

Every few days Ma would ask, "Find that penny yet, Cono?"

"No ma'am," I'd say. "Must be makin' its way back up."

Now if I would have swallered that penny in front of Ike, he would have grinned and tilted his head to the side and said, "Well aren't you smart!" Then we both would have laughed and that would have been the end of it. Except that ain't the way it happened. It was Ma who saw me swaller that penny.

A few days after that penny had come out and I'd stared it into staying put, Pa took me to Adams Grocers to get us some cheese and crackers like we always do on a Saturday. After walking back home, we sat on our favorite side of the house, the breezy side, and watched the nighttime roll over to our part of town. It was so quiet that our crunching sounded like a two-man band. And when the music of summer bugs joined in, we sounded better than a revival choir.

"See this tooth right here?" Pa said jabbing his finger on a back tooth.

"Yeah?"

He put that finger up to his nose, sniffed it, and said, "It shor do stink!" Pa sure is funny sometimes.

Spitting out a cracker crumb with his tongue and a puff of air, Pa reached into his pocket, pulled something out, and said, "Here ye go, Cono. I think this is yer'n." I looked down and smiled at his open palm. There, sitting smack dab in the middle of his calloused farm hand was a shiny penny.

"Thanks, Pa," I said, staring at its purpose.

"Mm, hmm," said Pa. "Ever'thin's copacetic, ain't it Cono?"

"It sure is, Pa," I said. Pa loves that word, "copacetic." He told me copacetic means that things are tasting good on your tongue and everything's going to be alright.

I put the penny in my pocket and kept it safe while I ate my crackers. When we'd finished eating and as the sun was getting farther and farther away from the day, I ran into the house and said real loud to my mother so Ma could hear, "Mother, I think this is yer'n."

I decide not to swaller the top part of my toothbrush. I spit it out of my mouth and carry it and the bottom part into the house. I pull my "specials" box out from under my bed, lift up the lid, and spit the top half of the toothbrush inside next to Ike's pocketknife. I reach in my pants pocket and pull out a devil's claw. There might not be room for a devil's claw in the house, but it fits just fine in my box. I close the lid. The other half of my toothbrush I lay under my pillow.

Several days go by. Dad's ignoring me as usual, but I guess that's better than a slap on my face. Mother dries off the breakfast skillet, picks up a fussy Delma, and says, "Cono, yer goin' te town this weekend te sleep over at Mamaw's."

"How come?" I ask.

"Aunt Marguerite and Aunt Eva are there. They wanna see ye."

Well, I can see all the way down to the truth, and it feels like I've swallered a ratt'ler. Dad's still mad that I bit that toothbrush in two and doesn't want me around. I don't want to be around him either. Still, I don't want to go. I like Dad's sisters well enough, but I want to stay here with baby Delma, pull that little kernel of corn in the middle of her face with my pointer and middle finger and say, "I got yer nose!" just so I can watch her laugh.

Mamaw, Dad's mother, is the toughest grandma I know. It would be a whole lot easier if I just ran away and caught a train to somewhere else. As I sit on that idea like a chicken warming her eggs, I decide against it. Everybody says that the trains are filled with starving hobos on their way to California. They say they like to eat children under the age of twelve. I'm afraid they'd eat me too even though I'm little and skinny.

Mamaw's real name is Lizzie. But since Ike is divorced from her, he calls her "a pain in the butt." She's probably the one who passed off the meanness bug to Dad, since Ike's bug is more of a calm, cool caterpillar instead of a mean-ass scorpion like Lizzie's bug. Besides a tricycle being there, the only good part about going to Lizzie's is being across the street from the firehouse where

Chief Murphy lives. I hope there'll be a fire so I can chase the fire truck on my trike to watch the fire being squirted out. After that, maybe I'll just pedal myself around the world.

I pack up a few things and put them in my drawstring knapsack. My Great Uncle Clyde and Great Aunt Maddie, Ma's sister, pick me up in their wagon and take me into the town of Ranger for a weekend where I hope I won't be eaten—just chewed up a bit and spit back out. Like a toothbrush.

I don't get to see no fire. I only get to see poor ole Bill Preston get the crap beat outta him. Bill's about eight years older than me. He was about ten when his parents decided they didn't want him anymore. They just packed up their belongings, including their oldest son, and headed off to California, leaving Bill standing next to Lizzie looking dumbified. His folks probably just said, "Here ye go" and handed Bill over like he was a piece of gum that was supposed to stick around for a while. Or "Here, feed this 'til we git back," like he was a dog or something.

I don't guess Mamaw Lizzie cares much for Bill. That belt came down on his backside, "Whack, whack." To hell with this! I walk out the front door, get on my tricycle, and take off towards the Bankhead Highway, back towards Ma and Pa's. I know Mamaw didn't see me leave. She was too busy paying attention to Bill's backside to notice. But before I can make it to the end of the street, I hear my aunts yelling, "Hey, Cono! Where ye goin' off to?"

"I'm runnin' away," I tell both of them since they've already caught up to me.

"How come?" says Aunt Eva.

"Don't like it here," I say, still pedaling away from Mamaw's house.

"Come on back now, Cono," says Aunt Marguerite. "It's gonna get dark soon and ye won't be able to see the snakes."

Snakes?

After thinking about which snake I'd rather be bitten by, I slowly turn the handlebars around and start pedaling my way back to Mamaw's. Aunt Eva and Aunt Marguerite both stroll along beside me while my feet keep going in circles, a lot slower now that I'm heading away from Ma and Pa's and back to Mamaw's.

Then, out of nowhere, Aunt Eva says, "Cono, who do you love most?"

"Mother, Delma, Ma, Pa, and Polo," I say without having to think twice. I think they're trying to trick me, like if I say, "Mamaw and ya'll," then they'll want me to stay. I see the look my two aunts give each other before they turn their backs to me and walk inside the house.

Before I go in, I sit on the front step and listen for more whacking, but I can't hear none. I can't help but think the same's gonna happen to me. I'll be left here forever and ever with belt marks on my back. I mull over running away again. But what if Mamaw's the one who comes to find me instead of Aunt Marguerite or Aunt Eva? I'd be a real goner then. I decide it's better if I just go on in the house.

I stick it out. I stay there for the longest weekend of my life, trying to have the look of a three-year-old cute kid instead of an eleven-year-old stupid one who gets beat up all the time. When I see my Great Aunt Maddie and Great Uncle Clyde pull up in their wagon, I'm filled with happy all the way down to my toes. I'm going home. Before I leave, I hide a little present under my pillow just for Mamaw, the bottom half of my toothbrush.

I finally get home to see that Mother has bought me another one. Ain't no way I'm biting this one in half. Never again will I bite down so hard, unless it's on one of Ma's old biscuits. I say goodnight to Ma, Pa, Delma, and Mother. Dad's not home, which suits me just fine. Usually he finds some bootlegged Pearl beer and hustles dominoes at this time of night. And since he knows Ma and Pa don't like him much, he'll wait 'til they're sound asleep, so he can stumble in peacefully without any pesky stares.

The windows are open, and the summer breeze floats across my bed like a puff of air that puckers and ends up whistling out a happy tune. Anything bad that might have happened during the day has been blown on through and out the window. I hear the sound of the train chugging by every so often. When the steady kaplunk, kaplunk of the oil wells helps push the blood through my veins, I start to get sleepy.

But when I hear that nicker that Polo makes? I know I'm almost out like Lottie's eye. Tomorrow, I'll ride him like a wild Indian.

☆

The morning shows up and knocks on my window like the red-birds do when they peck on the glass at their own reflection. I know that Pa has already put in a half day of work. Pa's a real good man and a real good farmer. "Gallasses," what Pa calls his suspenders, have helped to hold up his pants ever since he got ruptured on a bucking horse early on. Pa said, "That horse swallered his head is all. I must 'a had the reins too tight." Pa keeps going like nothing ever happened. He doesn't believe in "bellyaching." He says, "Thar ain't no room fer it." The sound of no bellyaching is music to my ears. That's one thing I'm glad there ain't no room for.

Pa gets up at four every morning, and you know it's four in the morning 'cause that's when Pa gets up. He starts the kindling in the big white cookstove and pours the water and coffee grounds into a pot for boiling. He has a big round cup that sits on a saucer, like a bird in a nest waiting for a worm. Off he goes to check on his team and give them a little breakfast before he's even had his own.

Ma has his breakfast ready by the time he gets back. She gives him the same thing every morning. Not because that's all she can cook but because that's all he wants. There, sitting on the table along with his coffee, are two eggs (three if we have enough), some piece of fried pig, and fresh-baked biscuits. Ma likes it when he eats a big breakfast. I know because she's always saying, "Some a ya'll don't eat enough to keep a cat alive."

She's one to talk. Ma's skinnier 'n a post. I think she's mostly talking about Mother.

After breakfast, Pa reaches over and gets the milk bucket and heads for the cow lot. By the time he's back with the milk, Ma has the dishes washed and put up. Next, Pa goes and harnesses up his team of mules with the double britching harnesses and starts gee and hawing them left and right up and down the fields, plowing or harvesting his corn, wheat, or oats. I love getting up in the morning and seeing somebody I love do something important.

I eat some leftover breakfast and then holler for Polo, the best Shetland pony that is and ever was. He moseys over to me and I jump right on top of him even though he's not wearing a saddle. I don't need to use a saddle when I'm on Polo. My hind end fits just right on his white-and-brown speckled back. None of my cousins can ride him like I do. It's like his backside was made just for me.

I look into Polo's big brown eyes and he stares back at mine of the same color. He knows what I'm thinking most of the time—sometimes it's good just to get away. I hear Pa yell from the barn, "Where in the Sam Hill are ye goin'?"

"I ain't sure yet," I yell back. When Polo and me are riding fast like this, it doesn't matter where we're going.

We find ourselves already through the farm and over to Connelly Creek, our swimming hole with the rope swing. I tell Polo, "Someday I'm gonna teach myself how to swim." I tell Polo things I know he wants to hear, things about toothbrushes and beaten backsides. He nickers at me, so I know he's paying close attention to what I have to say. I listen back when he tells me that the nights when I'm asleep are short, but the days can be long. Right now it's the noon hour, and Polo knows this time of day makes my belly stir.

"Time to go back, Polo. Almost time fer dinner."

I ride him up to the front of the house but start slowing down when I see a car pull up in front of Ma and Pa's. Not just any car, but a brand-new four-door 1931 Cadillac that I know Great Uncle Will paid through the nose for.

"Cono!" I hear Aunt Nolie yell. "Come say hello to yer Uncle Will." I ride Polo over to Great Uncle Will as he's getting out of his fancy car wearing his fancy suit, his five-dollar Mallory hat, and carrying his fancy walking stick. Since he's married to Ma's sister, my Great Aunt Oler, I know I need to be polite, but it's hard to be since he's always such a horse's butt. His money never helps us out none. I'm not sure it helps him either 'cause it sure doesn't make him a nice feller. Last time he came over he looked at me and said, "Why Cono, ye haven't grown an inch. You better watch out or yer little sister's gonna catch up with ye." Then he laughed. I didn't like what he said one little bit.

Polo and I ride up close to him and he says, "Well hello there, Cono."

I'm just waiting for another report about how I'm not growing, and I'm about to say, "Hello, sir," but I don't get the chance. He walks over to me and pulls me right off Polo with the crook of his fancy walking stick. *Well I'll be damned* is what I'm thinking; the shock of it all doesn't let me think of anything else. Great Uncle Will laughs. I can't believe it, but he reaches in his pocket and thumb-flicks me a shiny penny.

"Save it up fer a rainy day there, young fella."

I pick it up off the ground and mumble, "Thank ye, sir."

Great Aunt Oler and Aunt Nolie don't pay me no mind; they just go on talking. I get up, grab Polo by the reins, and walk slowly back towards the house. I don't want Great Uncle Will to know that underneath my hat my dander is up. So what if he's got an oil rig named after him? So what if he just gave me a shiny new penny? It ain't like I've never seen one before! As far as I'm concerned, Great Uncle Will's just a short, fat, king of a fancy man, and I wish I had his Cadillac and he had a wart on his butt. I'm just gonna go put that penny in my cigar box until I think of something to do with it.

Probably buy some paper to wipe my butt with.

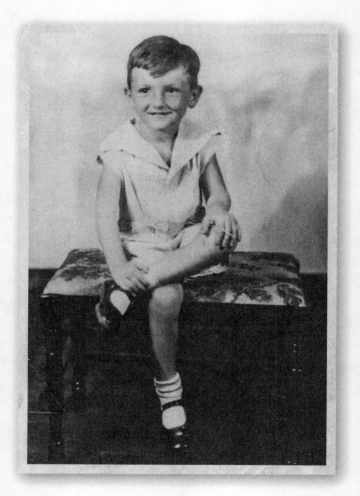

Cono, Age 4

CHAPTER 5

New Shoes and a Hammered Head

1932

WE'RE BACK IN town now, living with Aunt Nolie and Joe. I know Ma and Pa are glad to get rid of Dad. I don't blame them. I'd get him outta my house too if I had the chance. I'd brush my teeth any way I'd want to.

I'm watching Mother herd flies out the door when Dad walks in and hands me another present. "Cono, I got somethin' for ya."

I want to say that whatever it is no thank you very much. But I wait and watch as he walks over to my bed carrying a box under his arm. I take it from him, slowly opening the cardboard box and hoping a snake won't pop out and bite me between the eyes. Inside the box is a brand-new pair of brown shoes, the kind with laces that I have no inkling as to how to tie.

"Thank you," I say. I'm not about to ask him what to do with those strings. Instead, I sit there on my bed almost the whole morning, even missing breakfast, while I try to figure out how to tie these damn shoes. I shove one lace under the other, cross and circle them a few times, flip and curve them in different directions, and pull them enough so that finally they look close enough like shoes that have been tied. At dinnertime I come out of my room and start towards the kitchen with my new tied shoes on my feet, walking slowly so they won't come apart.

"Ain't it time te eat?" I ask loudly, puffing my chest out like a rooster and looking down at my shoes.

"Almost, Cono," says Mother, not looking up from the cook-stove to pay me any mind.

"Remember, we need ta go to town today," says Dad, staring at Mother, who nods her head.

I stand straight and tall waiting for Dad to say something about my tied shoes, how I'd done it all by myself without breaking a string. I probably could stand here all day waiting, but he doesn't say nary a word. He's got a newspaper to read. I don't care. They're my shoes, on my feet, tied my way.

We eat some beans and cornbread and Aunt Nolie stops chewing long enough to say, "Cono, yer Mom and Dad have business to attend to this afternoon and you need to stay here. Punk Squares is comin' over and he's bringin' his son, Freezer. Yer gonna have somebody to play with."

"What about Delma?"

"I cain't watch her, so she's gotta go with yer folks."

I don't ask Aunt Nolie why she can't take care of Delma. I don't complain about that good-for-nothin' kid coming over. He's younger than me and acts like a baby, always booger fishing and eating his catch. No, it's best to stay on Aunt Nolie's good side.

I walk some comfort into my shoes for about an hour until my folks leave. I go to the back of the house where my sandbox is, the one Aunt Nolie and Uncle Joe built for me. They'd taken an old worn-out tractor tire and filled it with sand. Except for the gritty pieces that usually end up in my teeth and hair, I like digging holes, building up sand piles that I turn into buildings.

After taking off my new shoes so they won't get dirty, I get a head start on my buildings.

Just when I start to like my new creation, Aunt Nolie yells, "Cono! Freezer's here." He walks over to me and sits on the tire like he owns it.

"What a' ya makin'?" he asks, his finger up his nose as usual.

"Nothin', just building."

"Buildin' what?"

"Adams Grocers," I say just to satisfy his nosiness.

"It don't look like that," he says, shooting his mouth off like he was the King 'a Builders.

"So?"

"Looks like a pile 'a sand."

"You make it, then." He shrugs his shoulders and starts piling up sand on his side of the sandbox.

"What's that?" I ask.

"Adams Grocers."

"Well, it sure the hell don't look like that," I say.

He throws sand at my chest, and before I know it I throw some back.

"Cono! Ye got sand in m' eyes!" Then he leans over across my own Adams Grocers and slugs me a good one right on my nose.

I feel the sting from my nose holes all the way up to my

eyebrows and back down to my toes. It hurts so bad that I run back inside the house and over to Aunt Nolie. Her and Punk are having their own sand fight, fighting over words I don't understand.

She stops talking and says, "Cono, what is it?"

"He, he, he, hit me," I say, slobbering boogers and holding my nose.

"Well, don't jes' stand there pitchin' a conniption fit! Git back out there and clobber him back, or I'll be the one hittin' ye next."

I stare at her seriousness for a second and realize it's as true as daylight.

On my way back outside, I grab an old hammer sitting on the kitchen counter, walk straight over to Freezer, and hit him on the top of the head with it.

When he starts crying, I stop. He has a goofy look on him. His eyes are wiggling like when you take a penny and spin it on its end. Punk hears him and stomps outside like he's being interrupted from a meeting with the president. He scoops him up and throws him into his Ford pickup. Then, when Punk takes off down the road, he stirs up more than just a little dirt.

I know Aunt Nolie, and she's true to her word too. But still, I didn't mean to make his eyes cross like that. I'm gonna try not to think about it.

CHAPTER 6

125 Miles to Temple

I SHAKE MY head a few times; try to clear it since I can't sleep anyway. In the seat in front of me, there's an old man snoring like I want to be doing. His clothes—old too—are clean and pressed. Earlier he was reading the *San Antonio Express*, so I know he can at least read. *Why would anyone with any sense want to go to Temple, for crying out loud?* Maybe to see relatives who had sunk their teeth and bodies into the quicksand of Temple, like mine had?

Even though my mind is set on Temple, I start to think about Ranger, how it was there long before my own story. Ranger made its own history when my head wasn't even the size of a grape. Before my pulse started to throb or even know where it was going to end up, the pulse of Ranger was beating strong. I like thinking about that. I like thinking that Ranger had other things to offer, things other than lost pennies, beaten backsides, and broken toothbrushes.

Ranger, the town of my birth, was named after the Texas Rangers, the ones who killed all those Comanche across Texas. The Rangers had a camp nearby, but when the Texas and Pacific Railway Company was built, they moved on over to those tracks and the town of Ranger sprung up like a bubbling spring.

In 1917 the drought came and the ground turned into a dust that just blew around the heads of the town's people, a continual reminder that life was tolerable at best. Later in that same year, the McClesky No. 1 oil well hit its target and spewed out black, sticky dollar bills to the lucky oilmen, my Great Uncle Will McClesky being "number one" among them. This made for more railroad tracks, more people to set down roots in Ranger, and lots more money for my Great Uncle Will.

The bad news was, even though the oil was spewing, the drought ended. You'd think that was a good thing, except it rained so hard in both the fall and the winter that Main Street became a river. Some folks even saw a mule drown in that river. As it turned out, all that water made many a folk get plumb eat up with typhoid and the flu. Then, as if that wasn't enough, the oil that came in with a gush went right on out with a drizzle.

Ranger had to settle in and be grateful for what it was, a West Texas town with a railroad station on top but empty of oil underneath. I'm just grateful that Ranger, Texas, is where Luffy and Jim Brewer live, my Ma and Pa. When I was a kid, we used to go there almost every summer. That place became my safe haven, my calm in stormy weather. Even nowadays, just like back then, I go over the little hill right before their farm, knowing it will only be moments before I'm reunited with Ma and Pa. And never failing, my throat gets thick with a mixture of homesickness and relief. Next leave, I plan to visit them. This time, my mind is set on something else.

My great-grandfather, Ma's daddy, Matt Henson, was a real Texas Ranger. We crossed each other in between life and death since he died the same year I was born. I didn't get to know him. What I do know is that after he died, his wife got fifty dollars a month because her husband had been a Texas Ranger. She took that money too; not like Great Granny Dennis, who couldn't take Cherokee Indian money because if she did, her frowned-upon heritage would be out in the open.

As a youngster, I'd pretend Great Grandfather Texas Ranger Matt Henson died in a famous shootout. Instead, he died just because it was the thing he was supposed to do at the time. All that being said, I used to tell my school friends that I was part Cherokee, part cowboy, and part Texas Ranger.

Ranger is also where my folks met. According to Ma and Pa, Dad stole Mother out from under them when they weren't looking. She was fifteen. Mother and Dad took off somewhere and Pa sent the sheriff out looking for them. So Dad said, "Elnora, we should get married so I don't have to go to jail." For the life of me, I don't know what was going through her head when she said OK.

For a while, Pa and Dad hated each other with rabid-dog fury. For the first couple of years, after what Pa called the "kidnappin'," Pa carried a gun just in case Dad came within eyeball distance. And Dad packed a gun too just in case he had to defend himself against Pa. Ma didn't like Dad much neither, a fact she kept mostly to herself. But after Dad got stove up with spinal rheumatoid arthritis that made him limp, she called him "Slewfoot" when he wasn't around. Ma would never cross him, though. Shoot, Ma had so many children of her own she didn't have time to fuss over a son-in-law. Ma and Pa's other kids were Loodie, Nolie, Carmen, Johnny, Mark, and Dalgo, who died from a disease when he was a boy. My mother was the last born, and so was known by her family simply as "Baby."

After all those kinfolk had been born, it was my turn. I was born in the Ranger hospital in 1928, the same year Mr. Hoover got elected president. On that cold day in December, I was given the name Connell Ray Dennis, at least on my official birth certificate. My "real" name, the one that seems to be stamped onto my forehead like a tattoo, is Cono, pronounced like "Don-O." I hated it when folks got confused and called me "Cone-O."

Ike gave me that name. He's good about giving people names that stick like a fly killed on a swatter. For instance, Harold Posey, my old school buddy from my second, fourth-grade year, didn't go by "Harold" after Ike got a hold of him. Ike thought he looked like President Hoover, so "Hoover" it was. Ike never calls Pa by "Jim," his real name. He calls him "Logchain," the name of his cattle brand. In my mind, parents around Rotan should have waited until Ike had a good look at their young 'uns before coming up with a name. It would have saved a lot of time and confusion all around. Ike's real name is Isaac Newton Dennis. I'm not real sure where he got Ike from. Maybe he named himself.

In February 1934, right after we moved to Rotan, Bonnie and Clyde robbed the National Guard Armory in Ranger. The armory was where Clyde got his favorite weapon, an automatic rifle. He cut off part of the barrel, got three ammo clips, and welded them together so it would shoot fifty-six times without reloading. That's why Clyde called it his scattergun.

I don't know why, but it makes me kinda proud that Clyde's best weapon came from the town where I was born. Bonnie and Clyde would enter my life one way or the other several times before the Texas Rangers finally gunned them down.

Amelia Earhart was another celebrity who came through Ranger. She landed her Autogyro at the Ranger airfield in 1931. It's a shame that she went missing just six years later.

But for me, the real celebrities from Ranger are Ma and Pa.

I close my eyes again, but it's no use. My seat companion says, "You ain't done yet, Cono." Again, I give in to the nudge and open up that old cigar box of "specials," the things I don't care to see. I picture that tiny little girl sock, the one that belonged to my kidnapped little sister.

Ma and Pa Brewer

CHAPTER 7

A Baby Girl Sock Without the Baby Girl

1932

I HEAR JOE moaning and groaning in his bed. Mother and Aunt Nolie are in the kitchen so I sneak over to Joe's bedroom door and open it slowly, hoping it won't creak too loudly. It wouldn't matter. The condition he's in, I don't think any noise would wake up Uncle Joe.

The man lying in the bed doesn't look anything like my Uncle Joe. His head is all swelled up, and a long, bloody cut runs from his forehead, over his eye, and down to his chin. There's another cut over his nose, a deep gash across his forehead, and a couple more roost on his chin. Mother comes up behind me with a fresh washcloth and scares the tar outta me.

"What happened to him?"

"Punk Squares and Hammit Bashem beat 'em with knucks and a *tar* tool," she says.

"What fer?"

"Don't rightly know fer sure."

"When's he gonna get better?" I whisper.

"Ain't sure he is, Cono." I don't really want to know why Punk and Hammit beat up my Uncle Joe. I'm afraid to.

Three days later, after plenty of moaning, my Uncle Joe dies. Earlier that morning, when he took his last breath, Aunt Nolie covered him with a blanket and cried, "He didn't deserve this." She wipes her nose and eyes with the back of her hand. Except for his cuts and bruises, Uncle Joe's whiter than a bed sheet.

Now some men in a big black car come to take away my stiff-as-a-board uncle.

We ride to the cemetery in Ma and Pa's Model T Ford. I lie in the back under the window having to listen to Aunt Nolie cry and blow her nose. Ma pats Nolie's hand, but it doesn't seem to help much. Aunt Nolie keeps on crying.

Dressed-up men lower my Uncle Joe into a deep hole in the ground. The preacher's talking about ashes and dust, which seems like a strange thing to be discussing at a time like this.

The women sniffle and wipe their noses and men take their hats off. I wonder if Hammit Bashem or Punk Squares would take his hat off if one or both were here. But they're not.

I hear people whispering around me, so I know those killers are still in town and not locked up in the county jailhouse. That makes no sense to me whatsoever, considering everybody in town knows that those two men used their weapons all over Uncle Joe's head.

For the next few weeks, I wait for Aunt Nolie to rub my head as she usually does when she walks past me. I wait for her to say, "Cono, where ye been?" But she doesn't. Aunt Nolie, usually filled to the gills with talk, hardly says anything to me. I guess I can't really blame her. I was the one who'd riled up Punk Squares by making Freezer's eyeballs twitch. I stayed to myself, not wanting to talk to anybody no how.

Dad's been gone for a few days, but today he comes home. Me, Aunt Nolie, Mother, and Delma are sitting on the front porch when he drives up. Sis is just a baby, only fourteen months old. She toddles where she wants to go, then plants her cute little nose right in the ground. Mother's holding Delma in her skinny arms, and Dad walks towards them. He's clenching his jaw, which makes his brown eyes look black. He looks different, like something bad is about to happen.

"What're ye doin', Wayne?" asks Mother. Dad doesn't answer. He just keeps walking up to the porch.

"Wayne?" says Mother again. Dad snatches Delma right outta her arms, turns back around, and starts walking back to the car he had borrowed. Then all hell breaks loose.

"Wayne, what the hell do ye think you're doin'?" says Aunt Nolie.

"It ain't none of yer concern, Nola," says Dad just as calmly as if he was taking a sack of groceries to his car instead of my whimpering baby sister.

Mother cries and pleads with him to bring Delma back. She follows on his heels, pulling on his sleeve, but he shakes her off like a horsefly. When Dad puts Delma into the car, Sis starts crying too. I know she must be as confused as we are. She never goes anywhere without Mother, and now she's watching Mother cry and try to get to her. She's watching me too. I'm helpless. I can't move. I can't do nothin'.

Dad leaves, and I can hear my baby sister crying for me to

come rescue her, but I can't. I just stand there, holding on to Mother's skirt. Mother's holding on to Aunt Nolie's arm.

"That crazy son of a bitch," says Aunt Nolie.

"I hate his guts," sobs Mother.

Right then and there, so do I. I hate him. He has taken my little sister and left my mother's arms raw from the friction of loneliness.

First Uncle Joe, and now this.

"Let's go back in, Baby. We need to sit down an' think on it."

So that's what we do. Aunt Nolie puts on a pot of coffee. This time it's Mother who holds another tissue up to her nose. I put on my best "everything's gonna be all fine" face. It doesn't feel real comfortable on there, like it doesn't fit right, but I put it on to help me keep from crying. My insides feel shaky. I know all this nose blowing is my fault. I run to my room and get Tiger Stick and run back outside to sit in the dirt. Tiger and me dig around and around in the dry soil, hoping we'll dig deep enough to make Delma appear like we did on the day she was born. Then I start crying, and I think I can fill the hole with the water from my own eyes.

I go back in and see Aunt Nolie loading up her coffee with more sugar. She clinks her spoon round and round the coffee cup just like I did with Tiger in the front yard. Her eyes stare inside the cup like they're waiting for an answer to jump out and into the saucer.

"Let's call up Cleave Barnes," says Aunt Nolie. "If anybody can help, it'll be Cleave."

"Why Cleave?" asks Mother, lighting another cigarette with shaky hands.

"Cleave's earned his money robbin' banks." She turns to me

and says, "Cono, he doesn't do it all the time, and never around Ranger." I'm glad Aunt Nolie's back to talking to me again.

Then back to Mother she says, "Remember, he's the one who taught Wayne how to use a gun."

Aunt Nolie turns to me again and says, "He hardly ever took it with him on a robbery 'cause he never wanted to hurt nobody. He jes' needed the money's all." She keeps on. "But he learned how to be real smart in his scoutin' and escapin' from the law. So, if someone's gonna commit a crime, all Cleave has te do is think like a criminal."

Mother goes straight to the phone and calls Cleave. A few more cups of coffee later there's a knock on the door, a sound more like a present than the banging of knuckles on a wooden door.

Mother opens the door fast, like she's trying to shoo out a family of rats before they run back into the walls. Cleave walks in and gives her a little pat on the back. He doesn't look at all how I had expected him to. I thought he'd have scary, wild-animal eyes and angry red scars crisscrossing his face. He's shorter than Dad's five feet eleven inches. Cleave's arms are skinny of muscle too. I can't see how he's gonna help at all. Dad could whup him faster than a heart beats at the first sign of trouble.

Cleave gives a hat's-off greeting and sits at the table, taking the cup of coffee that Aunt Nolie gives him. He offers Mother another cigarette before lighting his own.

After listening to the kidnapping story, he makes one short click on the left side of his cheek like Ike does when he's pondering something. I like that. I like that a lot. He might be good at finding my baby sister after all.

Finally, he says, "Don't you worry none, Elnora. If he's anywhere nearby, we'll find him, and we'll get yer baby back."

We pile in Cleave's good, robbery-paid-for car and take off searching, asking, scouting, poking, prodding, scoping, and snooping. But it's like chasing a chicken that knows her head's about to come off. I know Dad and Sis aren't anywhere nearby.

The whole world seems quiet without my baby sister.

Nobody knows a thing about my sister's whereabouts. Nobody but my dad.

I lie awake and wonder what he's done with her. I know he's never hurt her—he's never hit her like he's done me—and so I'm not too worried about that part. I'm more worried that I'll have to keep on living without her, that Mother won't have her "little girl baby," and the good things that could have been are now shoved in a box we can't open.

I flip from one side to the other. Mother and Aunt Nolie probably think I'm fast asleep, but I'm not. I hear every word they say.

"What was the fight about, Elnora? Yer fight with Wayne before he left?" asks Aunt Nolie.

"It don't make no difference now. My baby's gone."

"I figure it does make a difference. I can understand him up and leavin' like that 'cause he's done it before. But takin' Delma? That's a meanness he's never had."

Mother doesn't answer.

"Go on, tell me now."

"You ain't gonna like it."

"I don't like Wayne much either, so what diff'ernce does it make?"

Mother's quiet. I look through the crack in my door and see her fingering the buttons on the front of her dress. She lights a cigarette, smoking more today than I've ever seen her smoke before.

"First, I gotta ask ye somethin'," says Mother.

"OK."

"Punk was here not long before he and Hammit killed Joe." Mother pauses for a second and then keeps on.

"Remember? It was when Freezer came over to play with Cono."

Now Aunt Nolie sits on the quiet.

"Why'd Punk come over here? I know it wadn't because those boys wanted to play together."

"No, he didn't come over for that. He came over to ask me . . ." She paused for a bit, making me wait.

"Go on."

"Punk came over to ask me if I thought there was anythin' goin' on 'tween my Joe and his wife."

"Thelma?"

Aunt Nolie nods and twirls her hair.

"What'd ye tell him?"

"That he was crazy as a jailbird."

"Why'd he think somethin' like that?"

"He said he'd seen Joe and Thelma talking real serious-like at the store."

"So?"

"Like I said, Punk's crazier than a jailbird. Joe didn't do nothin' wrong but get beat up," says Aunt Nolie.

"Punk ain't the only crazy one around here," says Mother.

"What d'ya mean, Elnora?"

That's when Mother tells Aunt Nolie what had happened the night Joe got beat up.

There was a party at the Draygers'. Everybody brought in their bootlegged liquor and were pretty much three sheets to the wind, especially Punk, Hammit, and Joe. When Punk saw Joe and Thelma talking to each other, Punk shoved Joe, Joe hit back, and Punk's sidekick, Hammit, joined in. They took Joe outside and used the knucks and an old tire tool all over his head. Thelma screamed, but nobody listened. And the whole time Joe was getting the tar beat out of him, Dad just sat there, watching, not doing a thing to stop it. He didn't defend Joe, didn't move a muscle. He just watched.

"How do you know all this, Elnora?"

"From Thelma. Saw her at Adams when she asked how ye was doin'."

Aunt Nolie tilts her head to the side like she's trying to picture what happened.

"Thelma and Joe weren't doin' nothin' wrong, Nolie. He'd been askin' her what to get ye fer yer birthday. At least that's what she told me."

I hear Aunt Nolie sucking up snot. She wipes her eyes until she finally says, "I don't know who I hate more, Punk Squares or Wayne."

"I know. Me too. That's why we had that fight. I couldn't believe m' ears. Even Thelma was shocked Wayne didn't help him none."

Mother hangs her head down low like she's trying to pray and says, "If ye want us outta yer house, I'd understand. I'm real sorry."

Aunt Nolie dabs her wet eyes with a napkin, shakes her head, and says, "Well it sure came in handy, the sheriff bein' Thelma's cousin 'n all."

Mother nodded and kept on. "I told Wayne that he'd done ya'll wrong, 'specially after all you've done fer us. Then he got mad at me, accused me of tyin' in with you and not him, said it wadn't none of his business te get involved. He jes' said, 'Elnora, I'm gonna ask you this one time and one time only. Am I yer family or's Nolie?'"

"What d'ya say?"

"I jes' said, 'Ye killed Nolie's husband jes' as if ye swung that *tar* tool. God Almighty, ye even tried to get him te drink water when he was laid up in bed. What kind 'a man are ye anyhow?' He says, 'A man who wants to know if yer with me or not.' But I didn't answer him, I jes' went to bed. Now, he's taken my baby girl." Mother looks down and rubs her palms together like she's squishing a June bug.

"Why d'ya marry him, Baby? Was there a time ye ever really liked him?"

"Sure there was, a little over three years ago, right 'for and a bit after we got married. He looked like a movie star. I guess I liked that part of him, 'least fer a while. Then the meanness took over."

"Ye think Wayne was too drunk te hep Joe?" Mother stared into Aunt Nolie's eyes.

"That would explain a lot, wouldn't it?"

"Sure would. He wouldn't admit to bein' too drunk."

"Still," said Mother.

I'm tired. I think I've heard enough anyway. A time when my dad was nice? I wonder where that man had gone off to. But I can picture my dad being too drunk to help. A little drunk wouldn't matter, but a lot drunk would. He wouldn't risk getting a beating and not winning the fight. Come to think on it, I wonder if Dad even came home that night.

I wake up the next morning. Nothing's the same. At least now I know that it wasn't my fault, none of it. Joe dying and Delma being kidnapped weren't because of me.

Mother has made my breakfast without even a "Here ye go, Cono," like I'm used to. All she says is, "Clean up yer room, OK, Cono?"

I walk off to Delma's and my room. Except for the screaming of mad in my head, Ranger is still quiet. All I can hear is Delma crying as Dad drove away from us. I hate him. God I hate him.

Cleaning up, I find one of Delma's tiny socks under the bed, and I hold it up to my cheek. Then I put it into my cigar box so I won't have a chance of ever forgetting her. I miss my baby sister something awful.

Cono and Delma

CHAPTER 8

115 Miles to Temple

THE NEXT DAY in Ranger was just as quiet, not like this train with that mother hollering for her baby to settle down a few rows up. Aunt Nolie kept telling Mother, "It's all gonna turn out fine, jes' ye wait and see. He's mean and onary, but he knows he cain't take care of a baby by hisself." Aunt Nolie was mad with worry for her sister and for Delma.

On the third day, I heard a car pull up. I thought it was probably Ma and Pa coming to check in on Mother and my kidnapped sister. But it wasn't. It was Dad.

Mother flung open the front door and yelled, "Where's my baby, Wayne?" I think this was the first time I ever heard her voice so strong and clear.

"She's in the car."

Mother ran out to the car, picked up my sleeping sister, and held her tight like they'd both break into tiny pieces if she let go.

Delma smiled and flapped her little arms like a baby bird trying to fly home. I wanted so bad to run out there too; hug my sister and tell her how sorry I was that I didn't take care of her like I'd promised. But I didn't. I could see that Mother needed to tell her that first.

With Delma still in her arms, Mother walked past Dad back into the house. She sat in the chair rocking her baby as if Delma was just a day old. The tears she poured out were mixed with relief, love, and anger.

Aunt Nolie touched Delma's little foot and said, "Yer back where ye belong now, ain't ye baby girl?" That made me remember something. I ran to my bed and pulled out my box of specials from underneath. When I got back to Delma, she was sitting on the floor playing with her horse rattle.

"I got something for ye, Sis," I said. And, even though the other one was someplace else, I put that baby girl sock on her foot where it belonged.

Dad had followed us back in. Mother stared up at him from the chair and said in a calm, determined voice, "Where were ya'll?"

He told her the truth, but he said it like he was telling us about a vacation he'd been on. "We took the train from Ranger to Sweet-water and on to Rotan to stay at Granny Dennis's house. When I told her what I'd done, she said, 'Wayne, you take that baby right back to her mother right now.' So I'm back," he said, like he should win an award for minding his grandma.

Then we all watched as Dad walked into the kitchen and looked in the icebox for something cold to drink.

I still think it's a crying shame that I had to spend so much time thinking it was my fault. I guess that's what we do sometimes, take the blame for things that just aren't our fault, especially when we don't know any better. But back then I didn't have a Colonel Posey to tell me any different.

Last week on the base, that responsibility was especially tough, and I don't feel much like I lived up to it. I was right in the middle of running a training exercise when a young private missed the rope leading down from the climbing wall. He fell fifteen feet to the ground, landing wrong. We all ran over and circled him like a bunch of buzzards.

"Sergeant Dennis," he says, "my neck. I don't feel so good."

"Aw, you'll be all right, son," I told him. "They're coming to take ye to the hospital. You'll be all right."

But he wasn't. Private Henderson died later that day.

So far, almost every night since then, I imagine him lying there on that hard ground, his eyes staring into mine with confusion and fear. I'd lied to him.

Colonel Posey told me I had done nothing wrong, that it wasn't my fault Private Henderson had died. He told me I was the best sergeant he'd had so far, told me how he appreciated me. I looked at him for a few seconds, until most of the guilt flew off my shoulder like specks of dirt in a windstorm. Most, but not all.

I'll always be grateful to Granny Dennis. I picture her setting Dad straight while she was spitting her snuff clear to Oklahoma to make her point. She did right. The problem is, Mother's never been the same. Since then she answers to everything Dad asks, never argues, and never says boo about something that might put her in such a position again. I think she should have sewed him up in a sheet when he was asleep and then beat the crap out of him with a baseball bat. But she stayed, tolerated him, and gave up. I'll never do that. I'll never give up. Boys from Rotan and Ranger, we never give up.

It seems like ever since that day he's been snuffing her out like a dirty old cigarette butt. I'll be damned if I'm gonna be part of his ashtray ever again. Ashes to ashes, dust to dust . . .

I watch the woman a few rows up who's holding her squirmy baby. He's fussing and wants down off her lap. She's smacking him on his backside and that just makes him cry and squirm even more. I keep thinking, *If you just let him down for a bit, he can run around a couple of times and then he'll want to run right back to you and settle in.* Some people don't know a damn thing. One thing I know. I'll never treat my kids like that—if, that is, I ever find a woman who makes me look twice.

After the kidnapping, things at home were quiet, at least for a little while. I like to think it's because Dad settled in, that he felt bad about what he'd done. But maybe it was because Dad kept his mind occupied on something he was good at, something that made him feel strong outside the house, so he didn't have to use his muscle under the same roof the rest of us shared with him. I liked being at home then. But it wouldn't take him too long before he let the meanness back in.

Up the aisle, the baby and his mother have settled down. He's sleeping on her lap rocking back and forth to the rhythm of the train. I can't help but wonder if she knows how lucky she is to have her baby with her, safe and warm.

Elnora

CHAPTER 9

A Tiger by the Tail

1932–33

MOTHER AND AUNT Nolie pool their money and come up with the quarter to get my haircut. I've never had one before, and I don't see why I need one now. We're going anyhow, walking to the barbershop. Mother carries Delma on her hip and walks next to her sister, both of them walking faster than me. I drag my Tiger Stick along with me. A tiger, 'specially mine, can be quite ornery at times, even if he did make me a sister. He's hungry too. He hadn't had anything to eat since that cold biscuit at breakfast time. "Well, ye should 'a gotten up earlier," I tell him.

"OK, Cono, here we are." Aunt Nolie gives me a little shove towards the door, but I'm happy just to peek inside and call it a day.

"Well, go on in," says Mother. "I'll git ye settled, then Nolie and me 'er gonna fetch a few things at Adams Grocers. We'll come back directly te get ye."

I look up at her and nod.

"An' leave that stick outside!"

Huh? I'm goin' in unprotected? Tiger's not gonna like that one iota. He's still young and doesn't like to be left alone without me.

I do as Mother tells me. I lean him up against the window so I can make sure he doesn't get kidnapped. At least he can look in the window to see if I'm alright.

"Cono, say hello te Mr. Grady Healer."

"Proud to know ye," says Grady. I shake his hand, and he hoists me up into the barber's chair like I'm a sack of taters even though I could have gotten up there all by myself. I don't get to sit on the padded part of the chair. I have to sit on a hard board that he'd put over the arms of the chair. Board or chair, it wouldn't have made no mind. I don't like being hoisted.

He throws a big barber apron around my shoulders and starts wetting down my hair. I turn towards the window to make sure Tiger is still on lookout when Grady says, "You best be still, Cono, or I might accidentally snip off a bit 'a yer ear, ha-ha."

I don't like him, and I don't like this haircutting business. Still, I stare straight ahead like I'm told, straight into the mirror and at my own self. My eyes move through the mirror and onto the back wall. I can't read yet, but I see a poster of a mean-looking man holding up boxing gloves. I stare at it for a bit, wondering what it means, when Grady says, "Ye gonna go see the fight?"

"What fight?"

"Carnival's comin' to town. That there's a picture of Tony "the Tombstone" Tucker. They're gonna put up a big tent jes' outside 'a town, and any fella who wants to kin fight him fer money."

I'm thinking about how fun it would be to go to that fight when he says, "I hear yer dad's signed up."

My ears perk up, and I'm ready to jump outta that chair, go straight to my mother, and get down on praying knees. "I think I'm goin'," I say, hoping it's the God's honest truth.

"There, at'll do'er," he says, dusting off my shoulders and taking the silly apron off of me. This time I get down outta the chair by myself before he tries to lift me off like a baby. I might be small and skinny, but I ain't helpless.

"It was good to meet you, Cono. You come back again real soon."

"Yes sir," I say and start to walk out the door.

"Hey, ye better wait fer yer mother."

"Yes sir, gonna sit on the curb."

"Alrighty then," he says and starts sweeping up my gone-forever hairs.

Tiger's still waiting for me when I get outside. He stares at my head like I'm a stranger. "Oh fer cryin' out loud," I say. "It's still me." Then I tap him up and down on the checker table that Grady sits at when he's not cutting hair.

I look at those red and black squares and wonder about the game. I want to touch those checkers but I don't. I know Mother would be proud of me for not messing them up. "Someday," I tell Tiger, "we're gonna learn to play this game." I sit on the curb making little dust bowls in the dirt waiting for Mother and Aunt Nolie and trying to be patient. I have a very important question to ask. "Be patient." Aunt Nolie and Mother tell me that a lot. "Be patient, Cono, yer dinner's almost ready" or "Be patient, Cono. Delma will be up soon, and then ye can play with her."

The Model Ts are stirring up a little dust as they drive past. The little gusts make hairs on the back of my neck feel itchy. I watch the people across the street, the ones who are going in and out of the Gholson Hotel. Most of them look like they have real money in their pockets, not like us who pull our pockets inside out to show our Hoover flags.

Mother, Delma, and Aunt Nolie show up, and I don't waste any time. I tell them what I'd learned from Grady.

"Oh, fer cryin' out loud. Is he plumb outta his mind?"

"We already know that, Baby." Aunt Nolie snorts.

"So, kin we go?" I ask, and then I quickly add a "please" to go along with it. "We can stand in the back, and we don't hafta stay the whole time."

Mother is walking faster now, either from anger or because Aunt Nolie is having her turn at carrying Delma.

Mother isn't paying me any mind. She walks like a soldier about to go to a battle, and I wonder if I'd said something that should have been kept just between Tiger and me. But I'm only four and three-quarters years old, and I haven't learned yet how to keep things to myself like my mother has.

Aunt Nolie slows down a bit and walks next to Tiger and me.

"Why're ye holdin' on to that stick?"

"It ain't a stick," I say, 'cause now I'm the one getting ornery. Can't they tell the difference between an ordinary stick and a magic Tiger stick?

"Then what in tarnation is it if it ain't a stick?" She snickers.

"Never you mind," I say. She laughs again.

After passing a few more blocks, Aunt Nolie leans towards me and whispers, "Cono? Maybe there's a way I can take ye to that fight tomorr'a night."

"OK" I say. Then, of course, Tiger wags his tail all the way home.

⊨ ★ ⊭

Mother doesn't say nary a word to Dad while he's tying up his boxing shoes. They're not what Dad calls "official" boxing shoes but, he says, "They're close enough to git the job done."

He walks towards the door, turns around wearing a piece of grin, and says, "See ya when I come back with money in my pocket." He's out the door heading for the fight, a real one this time.

Aunt Nolie holds on to my hand real tight as we walk towards the carnival tent. The place is crowded with Ranger folk and others I've never seen before.

Dad isn't the first contender to step up to the challenge. There's a couple of other fights, but they don't last long. Tony the Tombstone has flattened them out like old rugs.

"Denny Dennis," the announcer says.

Denny? He might not have official shoes, but he's got himself an official name.

Dad looks like he's got an itch and the only way to scratch it is for him to put on his six-ounce gloves and step into that boxing ring. Aunt Nolie stands on her tiptoes trying to see over some tall man made taller by wearing a cowboy hat. It doesn't take long before she taps him on the shoulder and says, "If ye take that fine hat off, maybe the rest of us could see the show."

The man looks behind him to see Aunt Nolie with her hands on her hips and a wink coming from her left eye. "Yes ma'am!" he says, ogling her up one side and down the other like he's buying cattle. Me, I creep up towards the ring, turning sideways between the sweaty bodies until I'm almost within reaching distance.

I see Dad eyeballing the Tombstone, staring at him like he's already pinned him in a corner. They dance around each other like feral cats waiting to pounce on a rat. Even though I can see better now, I don't get what they're doing. They look like they're play-fighting.

"What's happenin'?" I ask Aunt Nolie, who's followed me up closer to the ring.

"The Tombstone is throwin' a few jabs."

"What 'er 'jabs'?"

"Well, see, a jab ain't usually a hard punch, but it lets the other fella know yer in the game. Jabs kinda make the other fella pay attention. They're holdin' their gloves up by their heads 'cause in boxin', ye gotta protect yerself at all times."

The Tombstone jabs, trying to get Dad's attention. Dad's smiling like he's watching a funny picture show. Aunt Nolie tells me more. The Tombstone throws another jab, then a straight right, but Dad easily ducks under it and comes up with a left hook to the jaw.

"Well lookie there, he's done it," says Aunt Nolie.

The Tombstone went down fast, laid out flat on his back, out like a light. The fight is over before the first bell had a chance to ding. Dad had been paying attention alright.

The Ranger folks—some who like Dad, and some who don't—hoot and holler that one of their own just beat a stranger, a foreigner, on Ranger soil. My dad is a hero.

Dad doesn't brag, though. He smiles without his teeth showing while he stares down at the bloodied man. The referee counts to ten. The Tombstone twitches his eyeballs. Knowing he's not dead, the referee raises Dad's right hand up in the air and declares him the winner.

Walking home, I think about how good it was to see Dad do something good like that, something better than drinking Pearl beer and ignoring me.

The next morning I ask, "Were ye scared, Dad?"

"Naw, I ain't afraid 'a nothin'. Besides, that pissant couldn't fight the gnats off his butt." I laugh at the picture of the Tombstone trying to swat gnats off his hind end wearing bandages on both hands.

That part about Dad not being scared of nothing ain't true. He's scared to death of cyclones. He came home from a trapping trip a few months ago and told Mother he'd seen a piece of straw that had gone right through a wooden post from the same cyclone that took out the town of Peacock. I guess he'd learned right then and there that a cyclone is something you can't tangle with, something you can't beat with an open palm or a closed fist. Ever since, when he sees a few storm clouds brewing, he stares at them all night until they pass on through. I guess Dad's found something a whole lot tougher than his own self.

A few weeks after the first fight I get to go to another one of his fights. I can barely see the punches being thrown, since the taller folks are all crowded around the ropes. But I sure do have a good view of Dad's feet. Shorty Haughton is beating the tar outta Dad, but Dad keeps right on going. He won't stop punching.

Aunt Nolie says, "Yer Dad's getting his shoes shined."

"Huh?"

"Shorty's hittin' him with fast left an' right body shots."

Dad stumbles then straightens back up. I see my Dad's blood crawling all the way down into his shoes. Dad doesn't stop, though; he doesn't give up. He goes ten rounds with Shorty and ends up losing anyway. My dad takes as good as he lays out.

The next morning I sneak into his room. Dad's lying in his bed, black circles around eyes he can't see out of. They remind me of the coons he traps. All my mother can say is, "He's crazy, plumb crazy." I sure wish I had a nickel for every time she's said that.

She brings him another wet towel. I think about how Uncle

Joe looked after his beating. This is different. Dad is grinning like he'd won. Uncle Joe had nothing to grin about.

Dad doesn't mind the swelling or the bruises that show up. He says, "It's all part of the territory." But not being able to get cleaned up and shaved is a splinter in his craw. He always shaves and puts on clean clothes before starting his day.

"Denny Dennis" toured around West Texas with the carnival making five dollars every time he laid somebody out. If the guy was two hundred and fifty pounds, it wouldn't matter. Dad would say, "Bring 'em on." I don't think it was that gold dust he was yearning for, 'cause a body can only take so much even for five dollars a bout. I think he did it for other reasons.

Denny Dennis's boxing bouts don't bring us much money, but then again, neither does Wayne Dennis's gambling money. Even so, at almost five years old, I'm starting to have a little bit of a craving for the boxing sport, 'specially if I can be the one still standing when the rounds are over.

⊰ ★ ⊱

The summer's almost here and Dad has stopped boxing. He's antsy again. He says we're moving to Rotan, that he'd bought a domino hall with his friend Blackie Patterson and now we're gonna have "an established business." I think we're moving because we've worn out our welcome at Aunt Nolie's.

I don't know much about Rotan other than it has dominoes. But it doesn't really matter. As long as I can still take care of Sis and still be able to see Ma, Pa, and Aunt Nolie before too long. Besides, I reckon I'll find out all I need to know about that town soon enough.

Dad's yelling, "Hurry it up now. Blackie's in the car waitin'."

I get most of my things, put them in the car, and say, "I jes' gotta get one more thing."

I turn back and run into the house as Dad's yelling, "Hell, c'mon, Cono. Get in the car!" Dad's not too patient when it comes time to be going someplace, and he hates waiting on folks even more.

First, I have to do something important. If I'm not gonna have Polo to talk to, at least I'll have Tiger and my cigar box of specials. I know as sure as rain that Dad's not about to let what he calls a "stick" inside Blackie's car. He'd say something stupid like, "Throw that damn stick out. If ya need a stick so bad then find one in Rotan." I'm not about to give him that chance.

I hurry into my bedroom, pick up Tiger, and say, "I wanna take ye with me, but I gotta make ye shorter so ye can fit in this here box." I hold him carefully, feel his length from my fingers to my elbow, and know what I have to do.

"I'm gonna break ye in half now, so you can come with me." Tiger tells me he doesn't want to be broken in half, but I say, "Think of it as a nice haircut, jes' like I got from Grady 'cept I'm makin' yer tail shorter's all."

I think he's OK with that, so I put him over my knee and push on both ends. It takes me a few minutes of twisting since Tiger's being stubborn, but I keep at it until he's the right size to put in my box. I take the upper part, the part holding his head, and put it in my cigar box next to my pocketknife, toothbrush top, devil's claw, and penny.

"There, at'll do 'er. It ain't so bad to be short. Hell, I've been short all my life, and I can still go on a trip."

I leave his leftover tail in the room. You never know who might find it next and need a good tiger's tail. I close the cigar box, carry it to the car, and sit down in the backseat next to Sis.

"Wha's dat?" asks a nosy Delma.

"My box 'a specials," I say.

"Wha's in it?" she asks while having the nerve to try to get a peek inside.

Dad surprises me by saying, "Now ya never mind about that, Delma Jean. A boy has a right to keep some things to his own self."

"Ain't that right," says Blackie. Then he looks over at Dad and they both laugh. Mother rolls her eyes.

I feel a little unsettled in the back seat of Blackie's car. Not because I'm crowded by Mother and Sis sitting next to me, but because we're leaving Aunt Nolie, who takes me places and protects me by holding down Dad with her eyeballs.

CHAPTER 10

108 Miles to Temple

I LAUGH WHEN I think about Tiger's "haircut." Shoot, that haircut wasn't anything like the one I got for the army. I laugh harder when I think about a story barber Grady had told me when I went back for a visit.

Early on, when my head was still the size of a grape, Ike got to know Pa real well. Ike had left cowboying for a bit and moved to Ranger during the oil boom so he could become a butcher. Pa called Ike "Is'ral." Maybe because to Pa it sounded close enough to "Isaac." So "Is'ral " and "Logchain" had a plan.

According to Grady, Logchain and Is'ral got real liquored up one time, the two of them drunker than Cooter Brown. They hopped on top of Nellie, Ike's old gray mare with the bell around her neck, and rode straight into the lobby of the Gholson Hotel. As if that wasn't bad enough, Nellie's bell started swaying back and forth and ringing, like it was announcing that the two Cooter

Browns were itching to wreak havoc. Fire Chief Murphy chased after them, hollering for them to stop their nonsense. Instead of stopping, they roped ol' Fire Chief Murphy and pulled him around a little bit. They didn't hurt him none, but the madder the chief got, the more they laughed their fool heads off.

When Fire Chief Murphy finally freed himself from the rope, he just brushed off his clothes and mumbled, "Damn fools." Then he walked off shaking his head like he still had dirt in his ears from being dragged in the road.

That wasn't the end of it. Ike told Pa he needed to go to the barbershop for a shave.

Pa says, "Aye, God, Is'ral, ain't no need te pay Grady for a shave. I'll do'er fer free."

"Well," says Ike, pondering the idea and probably clicking his cheek, "alrighty then."

They stumbled into the barbershop, and Ike walked over to Grady's barber chair, where he plopped down his dusty butt. Pa threw the shaving towel over him and lathered him up real good with the shaving brush. Grady said he just stepped aside and leaned up against the wall with his arms folded. He told me it was better than watching a picture show.

After the first nick, Pa slapped a little piece of paper over the cut and kept on shaving. After the second cut and the second little piece of paper, Ike says, "Don't ya be drainin' m—" but Pa slapped a piece of paper over his mouth so he'd shut the hell up, saying, "Quit yer bellyachin', Is'ral."

By the time they walked out of the barbershop, Ike's face was covered with those tiny pieces of paper. From cheek to cheek and nose to chin, he looked like he'd walked out of a mummy's tomb.

Grady said he was laughing so hard he barely heard it when

Ike mumbled, "Logchain, it's a miracle ya didn't cut my head plumb off."

Then those two crazy cowboys got back on that old gray mare, her bell still just a ringing, and rode off to who knows where to do who knows what else.

I take my mind off the picture of those two crazy cowboys and settle it back on the hard window of the train, trying to get comfortable leaning up against it. I open and close the fist of my right hand and try to compare it to the size of my father's. There's no comparison. Mine are still nothing compared to his.

I love boxing. I've had my nose broken twice from the sport. I like to tell folks that the first time, my nose shifted to the left, and the second time, it shifted to the right, which straightened it back out. Truth is, I have a bump on the top of my nose, but it's probably from my Cherokee side and not from my nose being broken. Either way is OK by me.

I love making contact when my opponent's not looking. I love fading to the left quicker than a right cross can touch my chin. I love fighting taller men, when I can throw an overhand right and end up lifting them off the ground with a left body shot. I realize that maybe I come by it naturally, that my bones, speed, and fists can find their target. I loved boxing for the army, wearing my red "Kid Dennis" trunks, marking my black boxing bag with the name of each person I beat. I'm done with boxing now, at least officially. I still spar and do my boxing workouts, but I don't take part in amateur fights anymore.

I wanted to keep going, keep boxing for the army to see how far I could go. I had an opportunity to take a fight in Mexico. I was gearing up to fight in the lightweight class, but Colonel Posey didn't want me go. My respect for him was stronger than wanting to be in that fight, so I dropped it out of my mind. I didn't go. He said that I had other things to accomplish in this life, and he was worried about that fight. Come to find out, Colonel Posey was right. It was a real setup, a fraud of a fight that would have matched me up with a middleweight just so I could be the fall guy.

⊣ ★ ⊢

Specials. I wish I could have put Aunt Nolie's brown radio in my cigar box. That radio taught me that a whole world lived outside of Ranger and Rotan, Texas. Through that brown box, I met Joe Louis, my boxing hero. It was 1939.

We'd known about the Joe Louis–Max Schmelling rematch for a while, and we were eat up with excitement. The Brown Bomber lost to Schmelling in 1936. Joe made the mistake of dropping his left-hand jabbing, and when the German figured out Joe's mistake, he ended up beating him with it.

Later, Joe made a comeback by beating Jack Sharkey, which put him back on top. Schmelling was fit to be tied, and the rematch, even though over the radio, was about to soak our poverty-stricken souls with hope. I remember thinking that if Joe could win, there might just be something for the rest of us to look forward to.

I listened to those summer bugs, the cicadas; the ones that sound like sandpaper being rubbed together. Aunt Nolie's radio started to crackle. We knew we were getting close.

Finally, we heard the announcer, Clem McCarthy, saying that the fight was about to start right there in New York's Yankee Stadium. I tried to picture Yankee Stadium, but I had no reference for it. Instead, I pictured a crowd a whole lot bigger than the carnival tent in Ranger.

"*In the red corner, Max Schmelling, weighing in at one hundred and ninety-three pounds. In the black corner, Joe, the Brown Bomber, Louis, weighing in at one hundred ninety-eight and three-quarter pounds.*"

The crowd on the radio roared. We sat real quiet, listening to every sound that came through Aunt Nolie's brown box. Even Dad sat there with us, leaning forward with his hands folded under his chin like he was really there.

Joe had Max up against the ropes and then knocked him down three times. In two minutes and four seconds, Schmelling got in only two punches. The fight was over.

Joe Louis, the man who says, "He can run but he can't hide" and "Everyone has a plan until they've been hit," had marched right into that ring in front of thousands of people—heard by a million more—and showed us a thing or two about how to get things done.

Boxing's not my career; it's more like a survival skill that keeps me alive. I'll use those skills when I need to, like when I arrive in Temple in a couple of hours, stare into my dad's eyes, and say, "Ding, ding, round one."

Ike Dennis, Age 21

CHAPTER 11

You Can't Beat That with an Ugly Stick

1933

IT'S MY BIRTHDAY. We make a stop at Mamaw's before driving to Rotan, leaving Blackie in the car to wait for us.

"Don't need to come in," he says, leaning back in the driver's seat. "A little peace 'n quiet suits me jes' fine right about now."

Lizzie might be a real pain in the butt, but she can make a cake better than Mother, Ma, and Aunt Nolie all put together. I'm five years old today. Mamaw wishes me a happy birthday by not beating Bill, who sits there quiet-like, stuffing cake into his mouth one bite after the other.

"Ya know anything about Rotan, Elnora?" Mamaw asks.

"No, jes' that Wayne has a new business there, a new domino hall."

"Ya set it up with Blackie?" asks his mother. He nods and takes another sip of his coffee.

"It's gonna be a long drive, Wayne, a hundred and forty miles. Kids might get a little restless."

Dad shrugs, not paying her any mind.

"Well," she keeps yapping, "I happen ta know a little bit about Rotan other 'n Ike lives there. I know because he's told me a few things." She says it like she's got a badge pinned to her chest that Ike still speaks to her sometimes.

Nobody says anything but she keeps going anyway.

"Well, Rotan was named after Mr. Ed Rotan, who gave money so they could have a railroad. Can ya'll imagine havin' a whole town named after ya?"

I don't say anything, but she sure is right. "Cono, Texas" has a real good ring to it.

"Some folks there have a job at the National Gypsum Company."

"What's gypsum?" my mother asks sipping on her black coffee.

"It's white sandy stuff that lives just under the ground. They use it for all kinds of things. Ike said they use it to make chalk for the schools' chalkboards. He also told me they put gypsum in those little wrapped-up cakes called Twinkies you see at the grocers. I'm not the least bit interested in eating chalk, but smearing a little cake on a blackboard might be alright."

Finally, we say our good-byes. Mamaw has that look in her eyes, mad that we're gonna get to live in Ike's town and she's not. We get into Blackie's car and wave bye. Then Mother says to Dad, "Mamaw Lizzie still thinks Ike's gonna take care of her, don't she?"

"When hell freezes over," says Dad.

I haven't been around my Grandpa Ike much, not nearly as much as Pa, but I sure look forward to it. As I see it, anyone who can give me a pocketknife and divorce a woman who beats the backsides of orphans is fine in my book.

Dad and Blackie sit in the front seat, and me, Delma, and Mother sit in the back. We take off on that red brick Bank Head highway, the one that runs from Ranger to Abilene to Sweetwater and north to Rotan. Blackie is a good driver, which is a good thing since Dad can't drive a lick. Shoot, I could drive better than Dad if only my feet could reach the pedals on the floorboard.

I don't quite know what to expect, but I sure do like this red brick highway leading to someplace new. I'm thinking that everything's going to be "copacetic," like bright colorful times might be ahead, like we're following a pot of gold at the end of a rainbow. "Copacetic" makes me think of Pa and his stinky teeth, and I get a little throat-lumpy.

Mother's not saying much and doesn't stare out the window as often as Delma and me. Delma's eyes are as big as a Walking Liberty half-dollar coin. I saw one once. Some fella came through Ranger and got his hair cut at Grady's. He flicked that coin at Grady and didn't even want change back. Grady showed it to me, and told me he'd never let it go.

Delma stares out the car window and watches the land move while Mother keeps looking down at the passing red bricks. I don't know what she's thinking, but I have an inkling of an idea that every brick that goes by is just one more that's taking her farther and farther away from Ma and Pa and Aunt Nolie. Maybe she's just tired.

I don't want to look down. I want to look between Dad and Blackie and see what's ahead.

Delma mashes her little nose up against the window of the car. I stay quiet, thinking about what Rotan will be like. I try to picture it, a town with gypsum snow under the ground, a town where Dad is happy, a town where—

"Where we goin', Cono?" Delma whispers.

"I ain't so sure, Sis, but it'll be someplace good 'cause looky here, we're ridin' in a four-door automobile!"

She turns away from me then and keeps pressing her little nose up against the window until she finally gives in to sleeping on Mother's lap. At least we are together, Delma and me. I want to keep her close by so nobody can snatch her away again. As long as I can do that, it doesn't make no difference where we are.

The car keeps humming slowly down the highway. I try to sleep but I can't. Instead, I think about Mr. Ed Rotan and decide right then and there that Cono, Texas, won't just have snow gypsum under the ground and a railroad on top of it. It'll have oil underground and derricks on the top, pumping night and day. I call them jacks "grasshoppers" because that's just what they look like when they're pumping up and down. They're grasshoppers trying to hop away, but they're stuck and have to settle for hopping up and down in the same place.

My town will have at least two good cafés that serve T-bone steaks and tea iced in clean tin jars. It'll all be free to me since it'll be my town. I don't know much about T-bone steaks since one's never been in my mouth, but I do know about cold iced tea. A while back, Pa and I went from farmhouse to farmhouse following the thrasher, and it was the first time I ever got a swaller of iced tea out of a fruit jar. A couple of them farm ladies knew how to make it real good. But the best was when one of them ladies had cleaned up an oilcan good and shiny. She poured the tea into the can with a bunch of ice and sugar, and when I tasted it, it was the coldest and best drink I had ever had. Ice is few and far between around here, sometimes as scarce as food. So when Pa took a sip he said, "Aye God, ye can't beat that with an ugly stick."

Cono, Texas, will have at least two different picture shows that run every day in two different theaters. And a boxing ring. Oh, and a rodeo every night.

When I was in Ranger, Aunt Nolie took me to my first rodeo, the Stanford Stampede, and then later to the Fourth of July rodeo. She taught me to fall in love with bulldogging, roping, steer wrestling, bareback riding, and saddle-riding broncs. I even fell in love with a pretty palomino named Real Rita. That horse could do every trick you could imagine and even some that you couldn't. Seems like every time I'm with Aunt Nolie I learn something new. I'm gonna miss her, but I heard Mother talking to Dad about how some fella is courting her. Maybe she needs a little time to settle in to something new, just like we're doing.

My mind leaves Cono, Texas, and I think again about Ranger, the town where I learned how to brush my teeth, where Ma and Pa have a farm and a house that you'll always want to go back to, where Polo takes me anywhere I want to go. Ranger is about haircuts that teach you about boxing and about boxing that teaches you to keep standing up. It's a town where a Tiger can stir the ground and make you a little sister. Oh yeah, Ranger also teaches you that goats freeze, but hands burn.

I go back to the comfort of Cono, Texas, finally off the poor list and high on the hog. I fall asleep there.

Delma wiggling next to me wakes me up. I play with her, tickle her under her armpits, and pull on her corn kernel saying "Got your nose" until Dad yells, "Ya'll hush up!" Then what seems like a hundred years later, he says, "We're here."

We drive right up Rotan's Main Street, take a few lefts and

rights, and end up at our new house. It's a real house too. I barely have the chance to get out of the car to have a look inside before a scrawny kid across the street pokes his head out of his front door and yells, "Hey, there. That gonna be yer house?" He throws a real football up in the air and catches it on its way back down. Rotan just might be copacetic.

CHAPTER 12

105 Miles to Temple

LITTLE GENE DAVIS, the scrawny kid with the football, became my best friend. He had a way of making things better than they were. I'll never forget him—ever. He didn't even wait to size me up. He just came on over and started talking to me like we were old friends. I often wonder what would have happened if he'd stayed alive and kept growing up like I did. I wonder what he'd be doing now and if we'd still be friends. At least I got to have him around for a while. But he died way too young, just like the daughter of Colonel Posey.

As my feet kept growing out of Rotan and later into Temple, they were finally able to reach the pedals on a car. Now I can say, unlike my father, I'm a good driver. One of the good things about living in Temple was learning how to drive. I got hired out at the Texas Power and Light Company to be a meter reader. When I interviewed for the job, the boss, Mr. McDonald, asked, "Can you drive?"

"Yes sir," I lied.

"Well, OK then. You're hired."

It was a good thing that my coworker, O'Connell, knew how to drive. Because when we went out to the country areas, he was nice enough to start teaching me. When the time came to get my license, I risked losing my job, but this time I knew that truth telling was necessary.

"Mr. McDonald?" I said, after entering his office.

"Yeah, Cono."

"I need to tell you the truth about something."

"OK."

"Ya see, when ye first asked me if I could drive, I lied to you. I'd never driven before in my life."

"I figured that," he said.

"Well, I can drive now."

"And I guess you need to borrow my car so you can take the driving test?"

"Yes sir."

"Well, go on then."

That's how I got my license.

Lying got me to where I needed to be and telling the truth pulled me along a little further. I guess they both serve their purpose when it comes right down to it, but then again, I guess I've known that all my life.

Dad always preferred to be driven, or he'd walk if he was feeling up to it. Until we moved to Temple, he never owned a car long enough to learn how to drive it without scaring the rest of us or, for that matter, long enough for me to learn to drive. He was the odd man out, never having an interest in cowboying or even getting on top of a horse like the rest of the Dennises. Still, he's just as bad of a driver as he is a bull rider.

He tried to ride a bull once. Maybe it was a low point for him, but for me it was anything but. We were living at the Dennis ranch when one evening Dad came home drunk and decided it was time to act like a real rodeo star. I was standing outside the corral, where we kept one of our two-year-old bulls. Dad sauntered over to me and slurred, "Cono, grab that bull o'r yonder. Hold 'em still 'til I get on. I'm gonna ride this son of a bitch."

"Sure I will, Dad."

It was better than watching a real rodeo with a hundred palominos. While I was putting the rope around the bull's neck, Dad went over and fixed Ike's spurs to his shoes. Not to his boots, because he didn't even own a pair of boots, but to his shoes! Then he slapped on Ike's chaps. I helped him get on top of the bull and stood there holding his rope.

"Whenever you're ready," I said.

"I'z ready," he slurred.

I let go.

Dad put one hand up in the air and said, "High, ho, Silv—"

That bull didn't even buck. He just turned around real slow, like he was trying to see what kind of idiot wanted to sit on his back. That slow turn around was all it took. Dad fell right off that lazy bull and straight into the dirt, Ike's spurs dangling from his shoes.

I turned around and looked in the other direction so Dad wouldn't see the smile on my face. If he was paying attention, he would have seen my shoulders quivering from laughter.

He got up and staggered back to the house, mumbling

something about killing steak for dinner. Some things sure were funny back then, but other times? You couldn't find "funny" anywhere you looked.

CHAPTER 13

No Hill for a Stepper

1934

WHILE THE REST of us feel settled in, Dad's restless all the time and complains about his back. It seems like ever since we took that walk up Double Mountain he's been limping and complaining more and more.

The Dennis ranch sits at the bottom of Double Mountain, a real important place in West Texas and even more so around Rotan. Ike runs the place, but times being hard with the Depression and all, he only makes fifteen dollars a month instead of thirty. It's bone-hard work too. There's branding to do, mending fences, feeding cattle, breaking and shoeing horses, and kicking salt blocks out of truck beds, just to name a few of the things Ike does.

A few days after we got to Rotan, we went to visit Ike and Dad said, "Let's all take a walk to the top 'a the world." So, the four of us started the climb up that mountain. We'd gone only halfway when my feet started hurting from the smallness of my shoes, so I started slowing down. Delma kept saying she wanted to be carried.

"Ah hell, what's the matter with ya'll?" Dad asked, looking straight at me. "Why, this ain't no hill fer a stepper!"

As soon as he'd said it, I knew he was saying something good, like he knew I was tough and could make it to the top. Sure enough, even though Dad was limping more and more, the four of us made it up to the top of the world.

"Look out there now, boys and girls," Dad said. "You can count seven towns from here."

That's when Dad started humming The Light Crust Dough-boys' song "I'm Sittin' on Top of the World."

It sure was a nice change to look down for a while. It made me feel like we had plenty of money and plenty to eat and that if your feet could make it all the way up to the top of Double Mountain, shoot, they could make it anywhere. No hill for a stepper.

Dad's the one who had a hard time getting over that walk. Now he does even more yelling, more cussing, knocks things off the table if they don't suit him, throws aspirin at the wall if it doesn't help.

I heard Dad say, "I just don't feel like myself."

"Go ahead on to the doctor then, Wayne, see what's wrong."

"Fer cryin' out loud, Elnora, I jus' started a business. I can't go spending money on no doctor."

"Ye wanna feel better don't ye?"

So the next day, Dad goes to the doctor and when he comes home, he's hardened even more than usual.

"Well, what'd he say?"

"He says I got real problems and I ain't gonna be worth a grain of salt."

"What ye mean, Wayne?" Mother asks with worry written all over her face.

"He says I got stove up with spinal rheumatoid arthritis."

"What's that?"

"Well, it ain't a fuckin' cold is what!" and he storms out the door.

All of a sudden, things don't seem so copacetic anymore.

⇥ ☆ ⇤

Ever since Dad went to the doctor, he threatens to kill every doctor that crosses his path. "They don't know a damn thing about makin' people well," he says, and "All they want is my money." I don't know what it feels like on the inside to have spinal rheumatoid arthritis, but I know on the outside it makes you limp and cuss and drink. Dad says that Pearl beer and whiskey help him, but it doesn't help us one iota. A meanness swirls around him like a moldy leaf in a whirlwind. The good thing is, at least he doesn't treat Delma in a mean way like he does us. Delma doesn't talk much to him, and when she does, he's usually nice to her.

Me, on the other hand, I'm just one good whuppin' post for him. He yells and swats at me for the most oddball reasons. Just the other day I brought a horny toad in the house to show Mother and Sis and you would have thought by the sting on my face that I'd invited a rattler to sit with us at the supper table.

Gene and I have gotten to be real good friends. Turns out, Gene is a grade ahead of me in school. He sure doesn't look like it, though. Gene's shorter than I am and skinnier too. I like that about him. I like that a lot. I get tired of being the small one. I want to grow up big so next time I see Great Uncle Will he'll say something like, "Well, now look at you, Cono, you've shot up like a weed." And, even though I still have that penny, I'll say, "Maybe it's the toilet paper I bought with that penny ye give me."

Gene's dad told him that Dad was running a poker game and had a falling out with one of the players. Dad hit that man four times. Whoever that man was he bled in those four places and never even had the chance to get out of his chair. Sometimes I don't want to hear what Gene has learned from his dad. Other times I think it's better to know, just so I can be paying attention, kinda like watching out for a jab. But I sure wasn't paying attention the other day. Mother and I were sitting at the kitchen table snapping beans. I said, "I hate him. I don't like him one little bit." When I looked out the open window, there was Dad standing right there on the other side.

"Cono," he said, "let's you and me take a walk."

"Where ye takin' him, Wayne?"

"Ain't none 'a your concern, Elnora. It's between me and the boy."

CHAPTER 14

Another "Special" in a Cigar Box

1934–35

I WAS THINKING how I'd really done it, how I was about to be deader than a doornail. I walked out the front door, looking back to see Mother watching us out the kitchen window. I followed Dad down the road, preparing myself for his big paw across my face. My lips were glued down real tight and my jaw was clenched tighter than a coon trap.

"Why don't ya like me, son?"

I told him the God's honest truth. "'Cause you're mean," I said.

He was walking slowly, limping more and more, and finally he said without even a glance in my direction, "Well that ain't no reason to hate me."

"OK," I said.

A few steps later he said, "You can go back now."

Dumbfounded, I turned around and walked back home. But

Dad, he kept walking away from the house, away to someplace else.

"Where's yer Dad?" Mother asked when I reached the door.

"Don't know. He kept on walkin'."

I told her about our quick conversation, and all she could say was, "Well I'll be damned."

A few weeks later Mother tells me that Dad is in the hospital. She says he got real weak and thinks he's going to die. Mother, Sis, and I get a ride to Roby, where the big hospital is. We walk in to find Dad laid up in a bed wearing a white gown, covered up halfway with a white sheet. He looks almost dead-white himself. I knew from the moment I saw him that he didn't feel good, since his hair was all messed up. He opens his eyes and gives us all a piece of a smile. Then he says, "How ya'll doing?"

"Fine," I say.

"Fine," says Delma.

"How're ye feelin', Wayne?" asks Mother.

"Not worth a pot to piss in," he says.

"Well, these here doctors'll take care of ye. Ye'll be better 'for ye know it."

"Maybe so."

Dad looks over at me and says, "Cono, come over here to me. I wanna tell ya somethin'."

I walk over to the side of his bed and wait. He looks me straight in the eye and says, "If I get outta here I promise I'm gonna be better to ya."

"OK," I say.

Maybe this spinal rheumatoid arthritis isn't so bad for the rest of us.

⊣ ★ ⊢

Most of the summer clopped along real good. Gene has a skinny old Shetland mare. We ride on her together all over Rotan, Gene in front and me in back. Sometimes we pretend we're Texas Rangers looking for outlaws. Other times Gene sits on top of his old mare while I sit in his red wagon and he pulls me along with a rope.

Dad's home now, but he doesn't say much. He just stays to his own self and leaves us alone, like he's only got the energy to be trapped inside his body and not let anything else come in or go out. No surprise to me, then, when the days pass and the antsyness crawls back under his skin.

"I'm goin' trappin'," he says. He leaves again.

Mother has been seeing to it that my clothes are sewed up and my shoes are looking good for my first day of grammar school. I'm not real sure what to expect other than what Gene has told me, but I want to be prepared. It sure makes me feel good that Gene will be there too.

"Did I ever tell ye what yer cousin Dickey Dennis did one time 'for his school was te start?" asks Mother.

"No, what?" I say, trying to clean off my shoes with a wet cloth.

"He was a little older 'n you when his mother sent him off to town te git his school supplies."

"What 'er school supplies?"

"Ye know, paper, pencils, a ruler, things like 'at. The stuff we already got fer ye. Anyhow, Dickey goes off te town and when he gits back, he ain't carryin' no school supplies, not one bag."

"How come?"

"Instead 'a carryin' school supplies, he was leadin' a donkey by a rope." Mother laughs and keeps sewing the patch onto my britches.

"Did he get whupped by his dad?"

"Nah, Lawrence, ye know, he's like his brother, yer Grandpa Ike. He jes' laughed when Dickey told him he'd gotten such a good deal on that donkey that he couldn't pass up such an offer. Anyhow, Dickey rode his donkey te school without neither a piece 'a paper or a pencil te write with."

I don't know Dickey very well since he's a second cousin and not a first, but I sure like the picture in my mind of him leading a donkey back home, probably whistling a happy tune all the way.

Mother also told me that not only did Dickey have a donkey, he also had himself a musical instrument. I'm not sure how he earned his, but he had a fiddle and could play it almost as good as his daddy, my Uncle Lawrence. Maybe Uncle Lawrence bought it for him 'cause he's got a good job at the gin as a bookkeeper. Anyway, Dickey would invite hobo street musicians to his house for a free meal as long as they stayed long enough to play a few songs with him. When those hobos walked away from Dickey's house, they always had full bellies and new tunes in their pockets.

Dad came back from his trapping last night, and I slept fairly good even though today I have to find out what all this learning stuff is about. I'm wearing the clothes Mother got ready for me and Dad looks me up and down and says, "Ye'll do jes' fine." I think I've just puffed out like a rooster.

Mother and Dad walk me outside the house, give me a finger point in the direction of the school, and I start walking. But I have to stop and turn back around. Delma is holding on to Mother's dress looking a little unsettled. I don't want her to be scared. I want her to know that everything's gonna be copacetic. I give her a little wave and a smile. "No hill for a stepper," I mumble, turning towards the school and looking straight ahead.

I get to my class in time to see the kids wiggling around at their desks, waiting for our new teacher. She's talking to some other grown-ups in the back of the room, which means nobody's late except maybe herself.

She's as pretty as a fresh-baked apple pie. Her hair's all done up in a soft bun, not like an old lady's bun that's too tight and makes her eyes squint. This teacher has curls around her powdered face and red on her cheeks.

A kid they call "Spur" walks up to the front of the room and lays an ear of corn on her desk. I stare at that corn a minute and look over at Spur, making my eyes say, "Why in tarnation would anyone put an ear 'a corn on a teacher's desk without shuckin' it?" For crying out loud, it was like handing someone an apple pie without the crust. So, I stroll on up there, shuck it real nice, and lay the husk and silk in a neat little pile on the corner of her desk, proud of myself, thinking, *At'll do 'er*. I go and sit back down.

The teacher finally decides school should start. She walks up to the front of the room, and I can see her shiny blonde hair and her dress that looks fresh out of a Sears and Roebuck's catalogue.

She looks down at her desk and stops. "Who made this mess on my desk?" she says, pointing her finger down at the husk and silk pile. I fess up to what I do—most of the time anyway.

"I did, ma'am."

"Well then, come on and clean it up." I've only been in school five minutes and I've already made my first mistake.

I pick up the husks and throw them into the wastepaper basket beside her desk. When I sit back down, she smiles at me and says, "Good morning class. My name is Mrs. Alexander. Welcome to first grade." Her smile's still sitting there on her face, making me think that everything is going to be alright after all.

At recess I find Gene, and we walk straight over next to the sandbox to claim our territory just like we'd planned. Gene pulls out a little drawstring sack filled with marbles and my eyes widen from all that shininess. We start to flick a couple until I feel something draping over me, kinda like a dark cloud does when you don't want it to rain. I look back to see who's making a shadow over me. The kid looks familiar, like someone I'd seen earlier, who'd given me the once-over when I wasn't paying attention. Well, I'm sure paying attention now. He's got that smirk on his face, the kind that wants to start something; the kind that wants to pick on someone younger, a smaller kid like me.

Ike always says, "Ye can tell a lot about a fella by the shape of his head." Well, Big Kid's head is shaped like a squash, so I know he's no good. He smiles down at us and says, "I'm gonna take them marbles."

"No you're not," I say, but I don't smile back.

"I'm gonna bump yer heads t'gether."

"No you're not," I say again and flick another marble, red this time. He leans down towards Gene and me about the same time a pocketknife shows up. I grab it, flip it open, and shove it right in the middle of his fat bully thigh.

"Aaaahhhh!" he squeals.

The teachers see the blood and start squealing too just like a pack of pigs. One of them teachers yells, "Tommy Burns, what in tarnation happened to you?"

Gene and I collect our marbles and put them back inside the little drawstring tobacco sack and stroll away like we're taking a Sunday walk. Nobody follows us. Nobody says boo. Mr. Big Kid Tommy Burns is a goat. He should be lying frozen somewhere, maybe skinned and used as a rug.

I worry someone's gonna come get me and throw me out of school my first day.

After recess, we go back to the learning part of the day, and nobody says diddly-squat about the blood by the sandbox. I start to relax a bit, but I'm getting tired like I usually do when I sit too long. I'm ready to go home to check on Sis.

It's OK, though, if I have to wait just a little longer. I like looking at Mrs. Alexander, at her nice smile and her fancy dress. I just keep picturing my mother getting to wear a dress like that someday.

Right before it's time to go home, Mrs. Alexander starts to teach us a new song called "Home on the Range." I like the words. They make me feel almost as good as when I'm riding on ol' Polo, free and easy like deer and antelope playing together without any bickering. I like it that she tells us what the words mean. She says that "discouraging" means that you don't like something much, like something makes you feel uncomfortable, something spoils your spirit. So now I can say that "Home on the Range" is my new favorite song. I can also say that recess today sure was discouraging.

I sure am glad I thought to look in my cigar box of specials this morning and even gladder I had a pocket in my britches. Ike sure was right; I knew when it was time to use the present he'd given to me when Delma was born. I just hope nobody finds out.

⛭ ★ ⛭

Dad's been trying his niceness out, I guess, to see how it fits. So far it's fitting him like a good hat.

"Cono, you wanna come with me into town? I'm gonna get my hair cut."

"Sure," I say.

Dad has his hair neatly combed as always. We might not have any money, but somehow Dad has to go to the barber at least once a month, and he always seems to have enough for beer and cigarettes.

"There's someone there I want you to meet. His name is H. Govan, and he shines shoes."

"Like a boxer shines shoes?" I ask.

"Nah," Dad says and smiles, "like a real shoe shiner shines shoes."

"OK," I say.

"Now, he's a colored man, but don't ye pay that any mind."

"OK," I say.

I'm a little scared of colored folk. We didn't get many of them around Ranger, but even so, folks around there told me things about coloreds that are a bit discouraging. They said things like "They'll steal from ye when yer not looking" and "White women need to look the other way if one talks to them." They said, "Not only are they stupid, but they'll pretend to be nice, then they'll stab ye in the back when yer head's turned." Now that I'm going to meet one, I figure that since Dad's with me, this colored man won't hurt me none.

We walk into the barber's shop, and Dad shakes hands with Mr. Kindle, Rotan's Grady Healer. It looks pretty much the same as Grady's in Ranger, but instead of a boxing poster, there's a framed picture of President Roosevelt. And there's something else different too. There's a colored man standing in the corner holding a rag. Dad walks up to him, shakes his hand, and says, "How ya doin', H.?"

"I'm jus' fine, Mr. Wayne. How 'bout yerself?"

"Any better 'n I'd be dead."

"Well that's fine then, jus' fine," he says and laughs.

"H., this is my boy, Cono." H. bends down, looks me square in my eyes, and says, "Well, it's a real pleasure Little Dennis, a real pleasure."

I like how he's squatting like that so he can see my eyes, like we were playing on the same team. I don't have to look up to him, and he doesn't have to look down on me. I stare back into his eyes, where I can see right into the middle of him. What I see is safe and comfortable. So I say, "I ain't never met a real colored man before." I hear Dad laugh.

"'S 'at right?"

"Yeah."

"Yes sir," corrects Dad.

"Yes sir," I say.

"Well, Little Dennis, I've never met a young man so strong and smart lookin' as you." Dad gets into the barber's chair, and H. pulls up a stool to start shining Dad's old black shoes.

I stare at H.'s face for a while, wondering how it got to be so brown and mine so white at the same time.

As Dad's face is getting brushed up with lathered soap, I finally ask, "Why're ye in Rotan?"

"Well, I came here to Rotan before you was born. I picked a lot of bolls. I got married and decided I wanted to do somethin' diff'rent, so I got myself a job in this fine establishment shinin' shoes. Where'd you come from, Little Dennis?" he asks while shining Dad's shoes.

"Ranger."

"Ranger, huh? Went through there once. Wadn't there long, but it seemed like a nice little place."

I like the way H. looks at me, like I'm worth a jar full of quarters. "Where were you born, Mr. H.?"

"I was born in Crockett, Texas, yes sir, in 1897."

"Crockett, Texas, like Davy Crockett?"

"Yes sir, one and the same." Now I was thinking about how another fellow got a whole town named after him.

"How you know about Davy Crockett, Little Dennis?"

"My Pa told me he fought at the Alamo in San Antone."

"Pa's his grandpa on his mother's side," Dad says, talking out of the side of his mouth that's already been scraped of hair and soap.

"Well, yer Pa's right. Before Mr. Crockett fought at the Alamo, he stopped off in Arkansas, Texas. Later on, that town was renamed 'Crockett.' Davy Crockett fought real hard at the Alamo. He died there too."

"Did he know Dan'el Boone?"

"Can't say if he did."

"Some people call my dad 'Dan'el Boone' since he can trap and all."

"Well, do they now?"

"Yes sir. An' he can throw a knife right into a tree too!"

"'Cept I didn't fight at the Alamo," says Dad, and everybody laughs. "But then again, neither did Dan'el Boone."

"Are all colored folks born in Crockett, Texas, same as you?"

Everybody laughs again, so I must have said something wrong. Mr. H. doesn't laugh, though. He says, "Some 'a us were born there, but not all. Coloreds're born everywhere, same as white folk."

"Oh," I say. I have to think on that a while.

As always, Dad and me don't say much on our walk home. His hair is shorter, and his face is, as he says, "Smooth as a baby's butt."

My mind is full of questions about the colored man I've just met. Finally I get the courage to ask, "Dad, would you let Mother and Delma talk to Mr. H.?"

"Why a' course," he says, looking at me like I'm a complete idiot. I decide not to ask any more questions.

⊣ ☆ ⊢

A few months more of learning go by. Tommy Burns leaves me alone, but I have a new best enemy. Her name is Mrs. Berry, and she's not even my teacher. She's a short, skinny woman not much bigger than me.

One morning I was heading back to class from recess when I took a peek into one of the other rooms, just to see if I was missing out on anything. I wasn't bothering nobody. But Mrs. Berry must have thought I was cheating a preacher out of a Bible, 'cause she slapped me on the back of the head, hard like, with not even a warning. I don't tolerate getting slapped, and besides, Mrs. Berry isn't even kin to me. I turned around and stared into her wrinkled face, and then I knocked her old skinny ass down on the floor before she could kill me. She just picked herself up and stared a fire into my eyes. She didn't say one word, but her eyes told me all I needed to know.

After school, Gene and me sit on the school curb. I tell him all about Mrs. Berry and the slap on my head.

"Cono," he says, "that scratch she's got on her arm? The one she says comes from her rose bushes? I bet it's from one 'a her twenty-seven cats."

"Huh?" I say, still rubbing the back of my head.

"Yeah. I bettcha at night she throws all them cats in the cellar with only a scrap 'a food just to see which ones 'er still alive in the mornin'.'" I know what he's trying to do. He's trying to make me feel better.

"'For she goes to bed?" he whispers like it's a secret he can't tell anyone but me. "She packs mud-colored cream on her face hopin' that the wrinkles'll go away. Then, when she wakes up in the mornin', she peals the mud crust off her face like it was a crusty scab, but leaves just enough still on so we gotta stare at it all day." He's got me laughing now.

"Ya know what else, Cono? Before she comes to school in the mornin', she let's her twenty-seven cats outta the cellar, goes up to her four-foot-tall husband, Mr. Mrs. Berry, and tells him good-bye by slappin' him on the back 'a the head." Gene and me laugh so hard we slap our knees and then fall back on the ground holding our bellies.

There's a lotta people I can say I love in my life; Gene is now one of them. There's also a few I can say that I hate. Pa always tells me, "Cono, if ye don't like somebody it's jes' 'cause you hadn't got to know him well enough's all." That sounds like something H. would say.

"Hey, Gene. Ye want to meet a real colored man?" I ask.

"Sure I do. Who is he?"

So I tell him what I know. I tell him about the man with dark skin and kind eyes. I tell him how he looked at me like I was a real person and not just a stupid little kid.

The next day after school, I take Gene to the barbershop.

"Hi, Mr. H.," I say.

"Hey there, Little Dennis, what you know good?"

"This here's my friend, Gene."

"Well, it's a real pleasure to know ya, Gene," and he sticks out his hand for Gene to shake. Gene waits a second, stares at H.'s big brown hand, then pumps it up and down like the handle on a water well.

"Well now, that's a mighty fine handshake ye got there, young fella. Ya play any football?"

"No sir, not really. I jes' throw the ball around a bit's all."

"Gene's real good at throwing the football, H."

"I can tell that, I shorly can. Besides my wife, Teresa, that's one thing I love. I love that game 'a football."

"Why don't ye play, then?" I ask.

"Well, I s'pose that window has closed down on me already, but I been going over to the Yellowhammers to watch them practice. They've started to let me be their water boy. I sure like it, too."

"Maybe we kin watch a game with ya sometime," says Gene.

"Anytime, boys. I'd like that. Uh-huh, shorly would."

"Ya like shinin' shoes?" asks Gene.

"Shor I do. I get to talk ta all the folks. Real nice folks here in Rotan."

The barber's door jingles as a man walks in. He's got enough fat on him he could be two people instead of one. After he takes off his cowboy hat and hangs it on a hook, he props up his booted feet on the footrest of the barber's chair and says, "Shoe shine, boy."

"Yes sir, it'd be my pleasure. Ya better look out now, yer shoes're gonna be shinin' to the next county in jus' a few minutes."

The fat man doesn't say anything. He just opens his newspaper and starts to read while H. starts to buff his shoes.

☆ ☆ ☆

A month passes and I hear that H. isn't at the barbershop anymore. He's got a new job as the janitor at the bank sweeping up the footprints of the rich folks. I miss seeing him at the barbershop because I hardly ever go to the bank. If we do go in there, Mother and Dad walk out cussing and arguing with each other. Except for H. being there, I have no business in a place that holds other folks' money.

Gene and I are on our way to school one day when we see H. walking to work. We run up to him and I say, "Hey, Mr. H., why ain't you shining shoes no more?"

"Because Little Dennis, I'm all done with that."

"How come?"

"Well, if you get stuck in the same shoes for too long, they'll jus' take ye to the same ol' place over 'n, over again, and ya won't never get to go someplace new. Old shoes get to be like two pieces 'a stale bread. You can settle for 'em if need be, but ya knows there's some fresh slices out there that'll taste a whole lot better. Maybe even a whole loaf."

"White bread or brown bread?" asks Gene, laughing at his joke.

H. laughs too and says, "Any kind 'a bread as long as it's fresh."

"'S 'at what the bank is to ye now, Mr. H.? Fresh bread?"

"Fer now, Little Dennis, I s'pose that's exactly what it is."

"Until ye get to play football?"

"Not play football, no sir. But maybe help out a bit more. I love watchin' them Yellerhammers, I shorly do." He pats my shoulder and walks on towards the bank, whistling a song I've never heard before.

I whistle myself back to the house. I'm still not real good at whistling, but I like practicing. Pa whistles a lot, especially when he's calling his horse. I manage to blow out "Home on the Range."

When I get home, I find out that the Coppages, our next-door neighbors, have new puppies. Their dog had a litter of what Dad calls "Curbstone Setters." I see Dad talk to Mr. Coppage, and the next thing I know Dad says, "We're gettin' us a dog, soon as he's old enough, that is." I feel like whistling again, a new song like the one H. had, a song fit for a new puppy just like H.'s song fit his new job.

A few long weeks of asking Dad when the puppy would be ready and the day finally comes. Dad walks into the house holding him like a newborn baby. It's funny the way Dad looks at that puppy with soft, mushy eyes.

"What 'a we gonna call him?" I ask.

"Well, he looks like a 'Pooch' to me," Dad says.

Mother gives Pooch a quick pet then rolls her eyes. Delma squeals with happiness and yells, "Kin I hold him, kin I?"

"Yeah, but ya gotta be real gentle now 'cause he's still a baby."

"I know," she says.

Dad's eyes get mushy-looking again, but only for a second. Delma puts Pooch down on the floor, and we all watch him take a shit on the kitchen floor. After he's done, he takes a sniff at it.

"Oh, fer cryin' out loud," says Mother.

"Maybe he's lookin' fer a penny," I say and laugh at my joke. Then I think about how Ma says "ba'll movement" and start laughing more.

Dad grabs some newsprint to clean the "ba'll movement" up with. I pick up Pooch and get several puppy licks on my face.

"Cono, don't let him lick ye on the mouth!"

"My mouth was closed, Mother."

She sighs and says, "Well, don't lick yer lips, then." I wipe my mouth with the back of my hand just to be on the side of safe.

"Is he gonna do that all the time?" asks Delma wrinkling up her nose kernel.

"Ya train him, Sis," says Dad. "Ya take him out ever so often 'til he gets the idea."

"When's he gonna get the idee?" she asks, holding her nose.

"Might take a while. Gotta be patient with pups."

"Kin we start now? Kin Cono and me take him outside?"

"I s'pose. But watch over him like a hawk."

Delma and me chase Pooch around the yard. He nips at Delma's ankles.

"Cut that out, Pooch!" she says, stopping now to pick him up.

"He sure is a cute little thang, ain't he, Cono?"

"Sure is," I say, scratching him behind the ears.

"Dad ain't gonna hit him fer being bad, is he?"

"Nah. Dad likes dogs." Besides, he only hits me.

Then we go back to playing chase.

It's funny, but getting our Pooch is like getting a new pair of shoes and fresh bread for the whole family. He's white with a few brown spots, even one over his eye like he's wearing an eye patch. Just watching Pooch do silly puppy things, like shake his head back and forth or bark at flies, makes the whole world look brand-new, like the world was born and we finally got to bring it home to live with us.

Cono, Age 7

CHAPTER 15

100 Miles to Temple

DAD MIGHT HAVE been able to kill wild animals, but he doesn't let anyone mess with his dog. I don't know who loves that dog more: Dad or Delma or me. Mother, on the other hand, helps take care of him, but she's not as smitten as the rest of us. Dad protects that dog like he's the winning hand in a game of dominoes. Hell, if Dad were on this train right now he'd have Pooch perched in his lap like a baby.

One early morning Dad headed out the door saying, "I'm takin' Pooch into town to buy him a little breakfast." He stuck his pistol in the back of his khaki pants like always and took Pooch to the café for some bacon and eggs.

A few hours later he came home madder than a hornet and more than a few sheets to the wind. When Mother asked him what had happened, he said he'd been walking home on the side of the road with Pooch ahead of him. A Model A car passed Dad and aimed itself straight at Pooch, trying to run him over.

"Good Lord! What'd ye do?" Mother asked.

"I shot out the back of his car, is what." Pooch was protected by Dad, the man with the big paws.

One Thanksgiving when we lived in the Tourist Court, we had enough food for Mother to make a real meal, but it was Pooch who landed on Plymouth Rock. We didn't have money to buy a turkey, but somehow Mother got hold of an old hen to cook. She baked it for most of the morning, even making cornbread dressing to go with it, which, for her, was like pulling a cart full of lead. She set the food on the kitchen table to let it cool while we all went to the drugstore to get Dad his medicine. Seeing as how it was Thanksgiving, the drugstore was closed, and Dad had to rely on his refrigerated liquid medicine to make it through the day.

When we got back home, Dad opened the door and what we saw made my mother want to spit cactus needles. There on our kitchen table laid scattered bones where our chicken used to be and only half of what used to be a whole pan of dressing.

We looked around the corner into the bedroom. Lying on Mother and Dad's bed, head on a pillow and wearing a smile that stretched from Rotan to Sweetwater, was Pooch. We were the three bears coming home to find out that our porridge had been eaten, not by a little blonde-haired girl but by a Curbstone Setter with an eye patch.

Pooch's smile disappeared when he caught sight of Mother, spitting fire from her eyeballs, coming at him with a big broom in her hand. Once those straw bristles touched his butt he was out the door lickety-split.

We ate the leftover dressing and the pinto beans, which had

been saved from the thieving by sitting on top of the stove. Mother's teeth were so clenched with madness I'm still not sure how she got anything into her mouth. Dad, on the other hand, was trying not to laugh, and he looked like he was enjoying every bite of the limited portions.

"Ain't it surprisin' how full we can get without eatin' meat?" Dad says, stuffing more beans into his mouth, his eyes pushed into a squint by his smiling cheeks.

"It ain't funny, Wayne," Mother says.

We all stayed quiet for a bit so Dad could concentrate on keeping his food in and his laugh from coming out. Then he mumbled out loud, "Guess we're not saving any leftovers for Pooch."

I couldn't help it. I had to stick my head under the table and hold my breath to try to keep my own laugh from spewing across the table.

Dad leaned back in his chair, pushed his plate away, patted his belly, and said, "I ate so much I think I got a little *pooch*." That's all it took. My sides started to split right along with Dad's. Delma giggled, and Mother, although she tried to hide it, was starting a grin all her own.

Pooch didn't show up until later that night, when everything was calm again and the chicken and dressing had settled nicely in his belly.

Even though we had beans, cornbread, and dressing for Thanksgiving, it was Pooch who really celebrated the feast of the pilgrims. And I think because of that, Pooch had given us a rare gift around the supper table: laughter.

⊰ ✯ ⊱

H. Govan is still the water boy for the Yellowhammers. Not only that, he taught Rotan, Texas, a thing or two about at least one colored folk. When some of his players went off to fight in WWII, it was H. who wrote to them, told them that "Everything was gonna be alright." Almost all my life I've heard my kinfolk say, "The cream in the pitcher always rises to the top." I think they must have been talking about H. Govan. I saw him as often as I could. Gene and I found time to go to the Yellowhammers' games. Mr. H. would tell us about the plays, explain what was happening. He filled my mind with thoughts about the way the world could be, separate from my family life. Those who said coloreds would act nice and steal from you were wrong; acting nice means being nice.

I made it through my first year of grammar school. Nobody kicked me out after all. In fact, the teachers didn't like Tommy Burns any more than I did. They probably thought he deserved a good blade in his thigh.

But after only one month of second grade, just when I was feeling comfortable, Dad came up with another lame-brained idea.

Elnora, Wayne, and Pooch

CHAPTER 16

A Shiny Mirror

1935–36

"ELNORA, WE'RE LEAVING. We're moving in the morning."

"Where we movin' to, Wayne?" she asks while swatting a fly with her dishtowel.

"South Bend."

"What're ye gonna do there?" she says, sitting down and moving a strand of black hair out of her eyes.

"Work on a pipeline." He pulls off his shoes, arches his back, and sits down with her at the kitchen table.

"What're ye gonna do with the business?"

"I gave it to Blackie."

"Ye jes' give it to him?"

"Yep. And everything in it. Now anything that don't fit in that car, jus' leave it or throw it away." Dad's good about giving things away. I've seen him give away a pair of shoes, tools, food, and now he was giving away the business.

"Dad?" I ask, standing in the doorway where they can see me. "Are we gonna take Pooch?"

"Why, a' course. He's part of the family, ain't he?" *Good*, I think. *I sure don't want to have to figure out how to put Pooch in my box of specials.*

I watch Dad walk out of the room before we can ask any more questions.

I don't want to leave my friends, but Dad tells me he's gonna help me hunt and trap. Besides, I reckon Dad needs to change his shoes every now and then, just like H.

The very next day I grab Delma's hand and my box of specials and get into Dad's borrowed car. Somehow we make it the hundred miles from Rotan to South Bend without Dad wrecking the car. When we get there, we see the house Dad rented. It's about two hundred yards from the Brazos River. It leans sideways, and inside we see high-water marks where the river had once invited itself in and stayed a while. But today, the river is steady, moving slowly ahead—just like I guess we're doing.

It's been a week now and we're pretty much settled in. The sun is getting lower to the evening ground, and I go outside to see Dad picking burrs from a sticker plant, what we call "porcupine eggs," off of Pooch. Dad seems happy, like he usually does when something's new.

"Cono, let's you and me take Pooch down to the river and I'll teach ya a few things about trappin'."

"OK," I say, happy as a pig in slop.

As we walk down to the Brazos, Dad starts singing "Down in

the Valley." It's a song I've heard him sing ever so often, so I ask, "Why ye singin' that song, Dad?"

"Ah, I guess 'cause it makes me feel better when the arthritis sets in."

"Has it set in?"

"Yeah, it's set in. But I've seen worse."

So we sing the rest of the song down to the river. "Down in the valley, valley so low, hang your head over, hear the wind blow. Hear the wind blow, dear, hear the wind blow, hang your head over, hear the wind blow."

We get to the river and Dad starts putting his trap together. Pooch starts barking up ahead. Dad stops and looks down the stream at Pooch and says, "Cono, I bet Pooch has cornered something. Go see what it is."

I run up to Pooch, and sure enough, he's trapped something.

"It's a possum, Dad," I yell.

"Well, pull him off and come back here."

After Pooch has calmed down, Dad says, "See this here mirror?" I saw him grab the small hand mirror on the way out the house but didn't want to say anything. Too many questions and his dander flares up into a stream of meanness.

"Yes sir."

"Well, a coon's jus' like a woman. If it sees something shiny it has to go over and touch it."

He sets that mirror in the center of the trap and puts the trap on a low spot in the river. And then we watch and wait as the sun starts to disappear.

Sure enough, a big old coon goes over to it and touches that shiny mirror. That was the last shiny thing that coon ever saw.

Dad shows me how to skin it and we take it home for mother to fry up. Nobody except for Dad likes it. Coon steak is tough and stringy, and I thought that chewing on a piece of leather would have been more appetizing.

Dad prefers to trap skunks since they bring in more money than a coon, especially if there's more black fur than white. Once when Dad was cleaning one I said, "That shor does stink, don't it?"

"Not for eighty cents a pelt it don't."

At least we didn't have to sink our teeth into skunk meat.

Dad teaches me about fishing, how to bait the line, how deep to put it, when to pull it up after you feel the nibble. We take our poles and throw our lines into the Brazos River, catch a few perch, and clean them fit enough for Mother's skillet. The best part is watching my Dad eat those fish. He can pick up a whole perch like it was a corn on the cob and gnaw around the bones until all that's left is a perfect skeleton. When I'm done with mine, it looks like it's been ripped apart by a feral cat.

The next day Dad tells me there's a heap of wood that needs to be chopped, and that I'm old enough to learn. He brings the axe and a smooth rock and starts my lesson.

"First thing to know is a dull blade is your worst enemy. It'll jus' bounce off the wood and right into your shinbone. So ya always keep yer blade sharpened! Sometimes a blade will get bends and cracks in it. If that happens, ya have ta hammer them out. I don't see any here," he says, looking at the blade.

"Ya have to secure the axe up against something, like these here two logs." He wedges the axe, blade up, between the two logs. "Now make sure it's good 'n tight in there or when ya start filin' you'll cut yer finger plumb off. This here's a whetstone, and ya file the blade like this here to make it sharp." He spits on the blade then starts filing it up and down.

"Why'd ye spit on it, Dad?"

"It needs a little moisture on it before ya start. Oil's best, but we don't have none."

He files a little more and says, "Cono, run in and get a piece of paper. We'll check ta see if it's sharp enough."

I run inside to hear Delma ask if I will help her wash Pooch. "Can't, Sis. I'm havin' a lesson on axe choppin'!" I run back out with a piece of paper and hand it to Dad.

"Let's give 'er a try," he says and then slices the edge of the paper across the blade. Sure enough, that blade cut the edge of the paper easier than a pair of scissors. "Now this here's a sharp axe," he says. "Think ya know how to do it?"

"Yes sir!" I say.

"Now, when yer done choppin', always put the axe back in its cover. That'll help keep it sharp. And never leave it in the rain or it'll rust. Then you'll have ta spend twice as long sharpenin' it."

"Dad?"

"An' don't never use the other side as a hammer or go sticking the blade in the dirt."

"OK. Dad?"

"What is it?" Dad gets his hair ruffled when I ask too many questions. But this question needs to be asked.

"How do I chop the wood?"

Dad straightens up and shows me how to hold the axe with my hands apart, pull it over my shoulder, and swing it down towards the wood with my hands coming back together.

"Kin I try it?"

"Go ahead. But don't cut yer damn foot off the first try."

The axe was heavy, but I wanted to show off, so I came down on that log as hard as I could. A tiny chunk flew off.

"You'll have to go harder if ya don't wanna spend all day out here. That there was like tryin' ta light a cigarette without a spark."

"OK."

"Keep practicin'. I'm gonna go wash Pooch."

I practiced for a good hour until my arms burned something awful. I was wore out. But I didn't cut my damn foot off. I was starting to feel strong. Every day, I get a little better and a little stronger.

Today there's plenty of wood stacked up for a big night's supper cooked on our stove; if, that is, we had something besides beans to cook. I look out the window and see Dad staggering and limping back to the house, carrying a six-pack of Pearl. He walks in the door and straight over to me and grabs me by the collar.

"What'd I tell ya about puttin' that cover back on that axe?" Then he shoves me to the floor with a single push.

The next morning I wake up to look for Pooch. I find him on the front porch next to Dad, who's sound asleep and still dressed in the clothes from the day before. I get Mother and watch her walk out to the front porch.

"Wayne, what're ye doin' out here? Get up. Yer late fer work."

He stirs a bit. Then sits up to rub his eyes. I stay clear of him as he goes inside, changes clothes, and leaves.

About an hour passes and Dad's home again.

"Ye got fired didn't ye?" Mother asks. He ignores her and goes to his room slamming the door behind him.

Pa says, "If ye don't like someone, it's because ye don't know him well enough." I've known Dad for eight years now. I wonder how long it'll be 'til I know him well enough.

The next day I chop wood to try to make things better. I chop wood so Dad will be happy when he gets home from wherever he went. I do everything I'm supposed to do when chopping wood: spitting, sharpening, and covering.

I know the newness of South Bend has started to wear off my dad like sunbaked skin. I feel it in my bones.

CHAPTER 17

99 Miles to Temple

WHILE DAD WORKED the pipeline in South Bend, we stayed long enough for me to see parts of my second grade. One morning I got up, looked out the window, and saw that the Brazos River was within fifty yards of our house. There hadn't been raindrop one the night before, so it didn't make much sense. I couldn't believe my eyes. I figured that unless our house moved during the night, our old friend, the Brazos River, was climbing towards us, stalking us like a predator.

Turns out it had rained, a real gully washer upstream. The water had escaped the banks and was planning on paying us a visit. Dad eyed the water stains up on our ceiling and decided he didn't like our living arrangements. We left the next day so we wouldn't have to suck air from the corner of the ceiling like a drowning mule. Somehow it strikes me as silly, being chased away by a river. But I know my dad doesn't trust the weather one iota.

I found out later that there was a hot spring just outside of South Bend. The Mexican laborers discovered the springs before we got there and said it cured their ails. The Stoval Hot Springs became the place to be, and now I know the real reason we went there. If Dad was hurting he'd go to the springs and hope for a miracle.

It didn't work. He only got meaner by the day. While we were packing up to leave South Bend, Mother was ailing something awful. She had doubled over in pain from the ache in her belly. Dad told her we didn't have time for her to be sick, that we had to get going before the river reached us.

"Ye know I ain't sick," she said.

"Well, if you were feeling that bad, you'd be in bed."

I told Mother to stay put, that I would do all the lifting. I did. I packed and lifted the suitcases and trunk into the car. And when I was done with that, Dad watched as I helped my mother into the front seat.

To this day, I'm still not sure why my mother's belly was aching. But I have my ideas.

I don't remember much about my second grade, the first or the second part. Maybe because most of the learning I got was from Dad. Still, I kept thinking that the axe he taught me to use was going to be my new best friend. Later I would picture myself slamming that axe down on something else—a slam so hard that the spark could light a cigarette clear to Oklahoma.

Even back then, when Dad just stood there not helping my mother when she was ailing, I figured my axe wasn't the only thing with bends and wrinkles that needed a good hammering.

Delma with Pooch and Cono in South Bend

CHAPTER 18

Mouths, with and without Teeth

1936

WE DRIVE THAT old car back to Ma and Pa's, so I can finish second grade in Ranger and so we can have another free place to stay. When we drove over that little hill, I knew I was close to Ma and Pa and Polo, to calmness and routine, and my throat got lumpy again. When we arrived, everything was pretty much the same: same house, same Polo. But Pa was different. His teeth were gone.

Dad's high-tailed it again, off to New Mexico to do more trapping. I feel good, him not being here, cause now it's just me and Pa sharing a piece of Ma's famous peach cobbler. Everything's "copacetic."

"Pa, what happened to yer teeth?" I ask, enjoying the sweet, doughy crust of the cobbler.

"Cono, now I'll tell ye. My teeth started to achin' and smellin' so bad that I figured I needed to take 'em out, harvest 'em like an overripe crop."

"All of 'em? Ye pulled all of 'em?"

"Shor did. I got myself a pair 'a pliers, sat there on the front porch, and pulled out the ones that were botherin' me the most. The good ones I had left felt funny bein' in there without company, so I jes' took them out too."

"Damn!" I say. "They don't stink no more?"

Pa laughs. "Ain't nothing left te sniff."

"He's an old coot's what he is," yells Ma from the kitchen, overhearing the story.

"I'm surprised ye noticed, Ma," he yells back. "Ye cain't see two feet without yer glasses."

"Don't ye fret none about it," he says back to me, gumming out his words. "Ever since them holes healed up I kin eat a steak jes' like ever' body else. I chew a little longer's all. And my whistlin's gone to hell in a hand basket."

"Let's hear," I say. He puckers and blows and when nothing but air comes out we both have to laugh.

"Ye don't have te brush no more either?"

"Naw, jes' rinse an' spit." That didn't sound too bad to me.

But Pa looked skinnier to me. His trousers were bunched up around his waist so much that without those "gallasses" attached to them, I knew they'd fall plumb off.

Pa goes back to the field, gee and hawing the mules left and right and up and down, while I go over to put the reins on Polo. I think about how Polo still has every one of his teeth when I take off riding him like a wild Indian.

Polo and I keep going until we get to Connolly Creek to see if my cousins are there. Sure enough, Harold and Darryl Brewer are hooting and hollering, swinging off the old rope still attached to the old tree that hangs over the water. I stand on the edge of the creek watching them swing off the rope and into the cool water. It sure looks fun.

"C'mon in, Cono," yells Harold, the older one.

"He don't know how to swim," mutters Darryl.

"Aw hell, any ol' pissant can swim."

I watch Harold as he climbs out of the creek. He walks up to me, his hands on his hips, and says, "Ye ready fer yer first lesson, Cono?"

"OK."

Harold picks me up and at the same time says, "Now ye swim, 'cause if you drown, I'll be in a heap 'a trouble when we get home."

He tosses me in the air like he was flicking a marble. I make a good splash. My head goes under water, and I start to feel real bad for my kinfolk. Everybody knows a fella can't survive without air. I open my eyes to try to get my bearings. My feet had hit the bottom and stirred up the murky mud, and that's all I can see in the water.

I imagine drowning and how Dad would feel sorry that he hit me all the time. He would say, "I sure wish I would 'a given that boy more attention." But just as I'm thinking that, my feet touch the bottom again and I stand up, popping my head out of the water like a turtle. As I'm coughing up murky water, Harold says, "Damn, Cono! Ye gotta hold yer breath, fer Pete's sake."

The main thing is, I made it through my first swim lesson. I decide right then and there that next time I'll be more prepared. Now when I can, I ride Polo to the creek and practice putting my head under the water and holding my breath. I count to ten, then to fifteen, and keep practicing until I can get up to at least thirty before I let myself come back up for air. I'll show them. I'll swim better than my cousins all put together.

The summer ends and it's time to move back to Rotan. I want to jump up and down on a spring of happy, but I don't let anybody know that's what I'm feeling. I don't want Ma and Pa to think I don't like it here, 'cause I do. I love hearing the train whistles and the boxcars chugging down the track. I love watching Pa smile without any teeth. I just want to see Gene again.

Delma is supposed to start first grade, and Mother and Dad say that Rotan has a better school than Ranger. They haven't met Mrs. Berry, is what I'm thinking.

⊰ ★ ⊱

Back in Rotan we move into Fleming's Tourist Court. Dad doesn't have any money left from working on the pipeline or from trapping in New Mexico, so we can't rent a house of our own. The Tourist Court has community showers that sometimes you have to stand in line for. That doesn't bother me none since the line is sometimes four people long. If I don't feel like showering, I just tell Mother, "I stood in line for hours and started to fall down from bein' plumb tuckered out."

"Jes' go te bed then," she says, which suits me just fine. I hate standing in line with nothing to do but scratch myself.

We have a screen on our front door that has more holes in it than a fishnet. Even with the screen door closed it seems like the Tourist Court must have put up a Vacancy sign for flying bugs. Dad comes home for supper and sees all them flies having a party. He swats at them with his arms flinging, as if he's shooing buzzards away from dying bones.

"Elnora, can't ya get rid of them flies?" She ignores him, and we sit down for supper.

"Cono, give yer sister some 'a yer potatoes. Ya took too many," he says.

"Don't want no more," Delma says quietly looking down at her plate. I look back up at Dad to see if he heard her and changed his mind.

"Go on, do as I tell ye." I scoop some of my potatoes onto Delma's plate and watch her sigh. I know what she's thinking. She's thinking she's full as a tick and doesn't want any more food. After stabbing the little potato, she points the loaded fork up to her mouth and nibbles at it like a perch playing with a worm it's not interested in. When Dad's not looking, Mother gives Pooch one of Delma's potatoes. He sees her patting Pooch's head.

"Don't do that, fer cryin' out loud!"

"Do what?"

"Pat his head like that. Everybody knows pattin' a dog on the head will give him a headache."

"Never knew that," she says.

"Ain't surprised ya don't know. Just don't do it!" Mother looks down and picks at her food.

Anybody that walked by would be able to hear our forks scraping along our plates, since none of us are talking. That's the way it usually is during our suppertimes. In fact, if we could catch each word that came out of our mouths, while the four of us were eating, there wouldn't be enough to fill a soup bowl. And if we were counting on words for our nourishment, well then, we'd starve plumb to death. Conversation can be just as troublesome as not having any money.

Suppertimes were different when we lived with Aunt Nolie. By the time I'd pushed my chair away from the table, I was close to being deaf from all her carrying on. I liked that. She always gave me something new to think about before I went to bed.

A loud knock on our door makes me jump an inch out of my chair and interrupts my thinking. A gruff voice yells, "L. E.?"

I stare at Dad wondering what he's gonna do, since we all know that Mr. L. E. Wright lives next door. Dad doesn't say one word. He just keeps right on eating, ignoring him like he does the rest of us.

We slow down a bit on our chewing. Delma peeks up at me with her big brown eyes and I just shrug my shoulders.

"L. E., open the door or I'll kick the damn thing in!" Finally, in a voice calm as a cucumber, Dad says, "Just a minute."

Dad's voice is steady, but I can see something in his eyes that tells me he's fit to be tied that his supper had been interrupted and his boiled potatoes are about to get cold.

He nudges his plate and silverware ahead of him real slow-like, wipes his mouth with his napkin, walks over to the door, and opens it. I can see this big man standing in our doorway, just like I can see his big truck parked right behind him.

Without nary a word, my dad clenches his fist and punches the truck driver right in the face, knocking him fifteen feet flat on his back, like he was an arrow being shot out of a bow. While that man lay there stiff as a board, my dad finally says in that cucumber voice, "L. E. lives next door." Dad closes the door, comes back to the table, and goes on with his supper.

Mother just sits there, stirring her food around on her plate like a nervous cat. Delma and I sit quiet. But all that empty sound doesn't keep me from thinking, *Dad sure can hit*. And when that thought settled in a bit, I went on with my supper. Inside, I felt a storm brewing. It probably felt so good for Dad to hit someone, that he doesn't want to stop.

⊣ ★ ⊢

The next morning Mother says, "Cono, Delma, hep me out here. We're gonna have us a fly drive."

"What's a fly drive, Mother?" asks Delma.

"It's like we're herdin' cattle through hard land." She ties dish clothes around our faces so we look like bandits. Then she gives us old rags to use to scoot out the intruders.

"I'm gonna open both these here doors. We'll shoo 'em in one an' out the other'n."

We herd those flies from the front door to the back and right out of Fleming's Tourist Court.

"H'yaw!" I yell, slapping those flies out the back door.

"H'yaw!" yells Delma. That's when Mother laughs— belly-like, not just pretend. I like it when she does that. When Mother laughs, it's like the whole world stops to listen. The unfamiliar sound of it plays a happy *loud* in our ears.

I get to see Gene again the next day, and we pick up right where we'd left off before I'd gone to South Bend.

"C'mon, Cono, let's go see a fight."

"Who's fightin'?"

"Jessie Perkins. There's a empty lot 'crost from his house, and he has a fight all planned out there. We gotta be the boxing ring."

I don't know what he's talking about, being a boxing ring, but I follow him to an empty lot where a crowd of kids have gathered. Gene points Jessie out to me, and I think that someday I want to look like him. He's not real tall, but he's got muscles all over his arms that make me look down at mine. I reckon mine are hiding somewhere under my skin and just haven't had a chance to pop up like Jessie's have. Maybe someday they'll pop out like Joe Louis's.

Gene introduces me to two kids he knows, Fred and Donny Allridge, who I've never met before. I size them up for a bit. They have smiles on their faces when they meet me, and Fred even pats me on the shoulder. They're older than me, but they don't glare at me like I'm a nothing like Tommy Burns had. We might just get on fine.

Us kids make a circle like a boxing ring, and I'm part of the rope. Jessie and this other kid I don't know get in the middle of our ring and start circling around each other. Jessie lands the first punch with nothing but bare knuckles and hard spit. If they get too close to our ring, we just push them back into the center.

They trade hits for over an hour, punching, taking it, punching, taking it. Yes sir, I want to be just like Jessie, because when the fight's over our boxing ring votes Jessie the winner.

"Now that was somethin'!" I tell Gene. "They kept goin' for pert near an hour."

"Why 'a course they did, Cono. Boys in Rotan never give up."

Now I remember why I like Gene so much.

Jessie is walking away towards his house when I ask him if I can follow him for a bit.

"Sure," he says, "I jus' gotta clean up's all." I walk him home and watch him wash off his scuffed and bloodied face.

"That sure was some good fightin'," I say. He smiles.

"Where'd ye learn to do that anyway?"

"I ain't sure," he says, drying off his face. "I jus' know that I like it."

"How old 'er ye anyway?"

"Fourteen, going on fifteen."

"Ye gonna be a boxer?"

"Naw, I'm gonna join the army."

I bet he'll do real good in the army, fighting for us Americans.

⇥ ★ ⇤

A few days later, Gene is teaching me how to play checkers. He lets me be red, and I learn about jumping and kinging. I remember Grady's checkerboard, and I think that next time I might just ask him for a game. We could sit outside at his checker table and watch the rich people go in and come out of the Gholson Hotel.

"Cono, there's a new kid in town. He's got two pairs 'a boxing gloves."

"Who is he?" I ask, moving my checker to a new square.

"We call him 'Oklahoma' 'cause that's where he's moved from."

"Can I box with him?"

"He's a little bigger 'n you are."

"Don't matter. Everybody's bigger than me, 'cept you." Being small doesn't seem to bother Gene one iota. He knows how to stand real tall with his short legs.

Gene gets us together at the open lot. Of course, I put on Oklahoma's old pair, the ones with the black, cracked leather and torn laces. It doesn't matter that they're old. They feel good on my hands, strong and powerful, like I could reach down and pick up the whole town.

"Ready to box?" he asks.

"Ready," I say. I try to remember the punches Aunt Nolie has taught me, the ones my Dad used to clobber the Tombstone.

Oklahoma and me start out in the center of the lot, without any ring this time, but with boxing gloves on our third-grade hands. He comes at me full force. I swing my arms like windmills trying to get a hold of something. He circles around me, trying to get my attention, which he does alright; right on my mouth. I can feel with my tongue that a piece of my tooth is missing. The fight lasts a whole minute. He beat the tar outta me.

"Ya OK, Cono?" asks Oklahoma.

"Sure," I say, even though I got dog tired after one minute. "Jes' lost a piece 'a my tooth's all." I bend down to try to find it.

Gene looks in my mouth to see my broken tooth and says, "Cono, ye ain't gonna find that tiny piece of tooth, not in this dirt 'n weeds. Why're' ya lookin' fer it anyhow?"

"Ya gonna try to glue it back on or somethin'?" laughs Oklahoma. I just shrug my shoulders and stop looking. I don't want to tell them that I wanted to save it for my box of specials.

When Oklahoma has his back turned, I tear off a piece of the worn lace from my borrowed glove and stick it in my pocket. That'll have to do.

I'm no Jessie Perkins, that's for sure. But at least now I can say that I've worn real boxing gloves and felt the goodness in them. And I have a broken tooth to prove it. Getting a beating in checkers is one thing. Getting a real beating is different.

I get home and show Mother my tooth.

"Don't worry none 'bout it, Cono. When ye grow, yer tooth'll grow right along with ye and that little chip won't even show." That's what I was afraid of.

Fighting in Rotan is like breathing. Sometimes we divide into two teams and plan a day when we'll have a combat. Of course, nobody wants to be the Germans, so we just say the teams are called "Americans One" and "Americans Two." I'm on the Americans

One team. Gene and I fill up sandbags for a week and store up good throwing rocks.

On the day of the war, Gene and I fill up his wagon with sandbags and rocks, and his old mare pulls us to the deserted barn right outside of town. Some of us stay on the ground and take the hits from the kids who throw rocks down out of the window. But a few of us American Ones have already climbed up on the roof of the barn and start throwing sandbags on the heads of the window throwers. Damn, they were surprised at being hit from above. Being tall and above everybody else is the winning ticket, probably because it was unexpected. It was Gene who'd thought up the idea. He knows how to trick people with the unexpected. That's something I want to learn too.

After it was over, nobody can agree on who's won. My team won, whether the other team says so or not.

Fighting and wrestling with my friends is one of the things I like to do best. Pooch watches over me when I'm fighting. If I'm on top everything's OK by him. But if the other kid gets lucky enough to get on top, Pooch grabs him by the neck and pulls him.

Pooch is like Polo to me now. I can talk to him about anything, like my sandbags of troubles. Even throwing them off a barn won't help.

Polo

CHAPTER 19

Bank Robbers

1936

MOTHER HAS DELMA all dressed up in a cute little blue-checkered dress with a bow tied in the back.

"Where'd ye get that nice dress, Delma Jean?"

"From Mrs. Gallagher, one 'a her daughter's outgrown it, and now I get it! I'm goin' ta school, Cono!"

"I know. And I'm goin' with ye." I look at the bottom of my shoes and tell Mother about the holes on the bottom.

"There's holes in the bottom 'a yer shoes?" I nod.

Dad looks up from his paper and coffee and says, "Stick a wad 'a paper in 'em then."

"OK." But I don't do it. I think that a wad of paper inside would feel worse than dirt and pebbles.

I hold Delma's little hand and we walk together, just her and me, to a world she doesn't yet know about.

"Everythin's gonna be fine, Sis. But if it ain't, you jes' let me know, and I'll solve the problem right quick."

"OK, Cono," she says. And I walk her to her classroom. I watch her slowly stroll in, and I feel proud as a parent.

I don't pay any mind to what's happening in my schoolroom. I'm mostly thinking about Delma, going home to play with Pooch, and seeing if there's a boxing match to get in on.

But I do pay attention when this new little fella walks in. His mother says, "OK, honey bee, you have a real good day at school now, ya hear?"

"OK, Ma."

"I love ye now," she says.

"I know, Ma." His name is Ervin Clay Carter, and he's come to school with powder on his face. He's a nice enough fella, but I keep thinking that his mother forgot he was a boy.

Before long I had to be in a play with Ervin Clay, Nancy Lou Roberts, and Norma Lou Dry. We had to put on silly clothes, wear stupid wigs, and put powder on our faces, just so we could dance the "Minuet." I thought, *At least Ervin Clay Carter's used to wearing powder*. Norma Lou was as happy as a pig in mud. Her mother had even made her a new dress so she looked like Martha Washington. But for me, I couldn't wait to wipe that crap off my face. The whole experience was the stupidest thing I've ever done, and I'd just as soon not think about it anymore.

By the end of September, the cicadas are still chirping loud like we're in the heat of summer. Dad goes off for a while to drink and play dominoes. He probably went to "down in the valley" to sing off his troubles somewhere.

He's much better at playing dominoes than owning a whole domino hall. When he draws his hand from the bone yard, he picks all seven dominoes up in one palm, reads them like he's reading a book, and lays them face down back on the table. Some say he memorizes his hand the very first time and never has to look at them again before picking them out for play. Those same folks say he "hustles" the dominoes by making people think he can't play, but after they bet, Dad rakes in all the money. But we don't see any raked in money, just a few coins here and there to keep us from starving.

Me, I just like stacking up those dotted rectangle blocks in different ways or putting them in a row and watching one knock down the others. That doesn't cost us one red cent.

Delma and I come home from school and can't find Mother anywhere. She's always home when we come home from school, so we start to get a little worried until we see her talking to our Tourist Court neighbor on her front porch.

Miss Essie stoops over her cane and is at least a hundred years old if she's a day. "C'mon ov'r here, kids, I wanna tell ye what I jes' tol' yer mother," she says, using her cane like a big hand to wave us over. We sit on her step and look up at the old lady sitting in her wobbly porch chair.

"Well, my nephew took me into Sweetwater t'day, ya know, ta do a little shoppin'?" *Oh sweet Jesus*, I think. *I have to hear a shopping story.*

"Well, I was at the Five-and-Dime, and I got in line to pay for the odds and ends I'd picked up, ye know, like a new hair bonnet, a few necessary toiletries. What else did I get, now?" She looks up at the sky like she's waiting for Jesus to remind her. Delma and me look up too but we don't hear any loud voice coming from Heaven. That doesn't surprise me none.

"Oh, some of that sweet-smelling toilet water they sell up by the front counter. What's it called again, Elnora?" This time she doesn't look up. Mother shakes her head back and forth to say she doesn't know, while I take my mind to anywhere but shopping in Sweetwater with Miss Essie.

She grunts as she stands up from her chair. So I think she's forgotten and is going inside and I can get on with my day, but she keeps going.

"Then I see this gal in front 'a me with a stack 'a clothes piled up on the counter, 'nuff fer three families, mind ye, *three* families. Well, the clerk starts ringin' up them clothes but the gal says—now listen to this children—the gal says, 'I ain't payin'. Jes' put 'em in a bag. I'm Bonnie Parker.' Kin ye imagine? I was standing right next to Bonnie Parker herself. I could 'a been kilt right then and there, right then and there." Then she fans the heat and fear off herself and sits down in her rickety porch chair like she's about to faint.

"Bonnie Parker?" I say. "Like Bonnie and Clyde Parker?"

"One 'n the same."

"Who's Bonnie and Clyde Parker?" Delma asks.

"Barrow," Mother says. "Clyde Barrow."

"Who's Bonnie and Clyde Barrow?" she asks again.

"Never ye mind, Delma," says Mother.

"I'll tell ye later," I whisper to Sis.

But Miss Essie says, "Killers, that's what they are. Natural born killers." She keeps fanning like she's trying to air herself away from being dead.

I sat there thinking on what it would be like to meet Bonnie and Clyde. All the kids talk about them, and sometimes, when our parents don't know, we pretend we're holding up banks just like they do.

The sun is setting as the wind starts to pick up, making whirl-winds in the dust. Mother walks out into the street and stares up to the sky. I follow her and see strange-looking clouds that start on the ground and go up instead of lying in the sky like they're supposed to.

"Miss Essie, yer nephew gonna be home soon?" I hear Mother ask.

"Should be home any time now. Why ye ask?"

"'Cause I think we're 'bout to have ourselves a sandstorm."

"Oh, Lordy, what a day! First a brush with death and now a sandstorm!"

We watch Mother get Miss Essie settled back in her house. Delma comes out to the street and stands beside me. We see low clouds off in the distance, the color of sand and dust, and they're heading our way.

We get back to our place, and Mother tells us to hurry and put towels under the door and more around the windows. She finishes up the supper on the stove and puts the food on the table just as the sand starts swirling outside our windows. "Damn," she says, watching our once clean laundry blow all over the clothesline.

"Cono, get Pooch inside." Pooch was standing at the door whining like a newborn pup. Pooch hates storms as much as Dad does.

Mother grabs an old white sheet from the cupboard and throws it over the food like she's putting a blanket over her cold children instead of keeping the beans and fresh cornbread from the lonely and gritty dry dust of the Depression.

"Git under here," she says, pointing under the table. "A storm's a'comin'." She smiles like she's already won a game of checkers.

Delma and I giggle and crawl under the table with Mother. Pooch tries to get under the table with us but there's no room for all of him. He has to settle for putting his head under the table and keeping his butt out on the wooden floor.

Mother's not talking much; she just sits under that little kitchen table and smiles her pretty smile at us. It's not that she's scared. I've never seen her act scared of anything except for Dad.

Delma and I giggle again. I knew right then and there that life was a whole lot more fun when Dad wasn't around, and a whole lot easier. Dad's a sandstorm all on his own.

After the first thirty minutes of sitting, our bellies start to rumble, and Delma and I start to complain.

"Ye don't want yer beans and cornbread te taste like dirt, do ye?" Mother asks. So instead of bellyaching, we sit under that covered table for another half an hour talking about Bonnie and Clyde and Delma's school day, listening to the wind blowing, knowing that the sand was swirling outside but our food was covered up on top of us.

When the wind finally dies down, we crawl back out from under the table to see the job the towels didn't do. There are too many cracks in the walls to keep out a West Texas sandstorm.

Mother takes the sheet off the table, and we eat. It's the best meal I've ever eaten. It's the calm after an exciting storm of a day.

It wasn't the first sandstorm we'd seen either. That old sand would sneak right on in like ghost spirits, and when it finally settled, Mother would spend the rest of the day sweeping up the remains. Oftentimes, I blow so much sand out my nose that I could make a sandcastle. Sometimes I put a handkerchief over my face pretending I'm on a cattle drive. I imagine there's also a good felt cowboy hat sitting on the top of my head, the kind that stays on real tight when the wind blows. But this sandstorm was different. It was mixed with under-the-table stories of real bank robbers.

The next day, about suppertime, Dad comes home from drinking and domino playing. Pooch jumps up on him, and Dad rubs Pooch's head and takes a lick on his chin. Mother doesn't ask him where he was during the storm, but I can picture him in somebody's basement curled up like a baby. Wherever he was, I'm glad he wasn't with us. I can't imagine how the four of us would have fit under that table and not killed each other.

"Where's my clean clothes, Elnora?"

"Sand got to 'em. I'll wash 'em again tomorree," Mother says, painting her long nails with her red polish.

"Why the hell didn't ya wash 'em today? Ya been spending all day painting yer nails?"

"No. I was cleanin' sand outta here all day."

Dad clenched his fist and his jaw at the same time. "Show me a woman with long nails, and I'll show ya a lazy woman." Mother ignores his comment but finishes up, putting the lid back on.

"Damn that shit stinks," he says, staring at the polish bottle. "Ya'll go on to bed now," he tells Delma and me.

"But it ain't—"

"I said git to bed!"

"It's early, Wayne—"

"I'm havin' company, Elnora. You need to go on too. I'm havin' a business meetin'."

Delma and I go to our room, and she has no trouble falling asleep. For me it's just too early and my body and head want more things to do.

After a little while, I hear men's voices come in through our door. I hear Dad tell them to sit down at the table. I hear the sound of coffee brewing on the stove.

"I don't want any part of it, Earl," says Dad.

"But Marshal Dry will be in on it, and he'll make sure we get in and out of there without a hitch, ain't that right, J. D.?"

Then I knew who was sitting at my dinner table, the very table I'd sat under just the night before. It was Mr. J. D. Eckles himself, the outlaw from Ranger, and Joe and Earl Adams, the outlaws from Rotan. I peek out of the little hole in my door and get to see pieces of their faces.

J. D. says, "Williams Drugstore is across from the bank. When we're done with that, I can back up my truck and load up the narcotics."

Now I know what they're planning to do. They're planning to rob our town's bank, the bank where H. works. I picture H. just doing his job, cleaning and sweeping, when men come in with guns ready to shoot. I don't like it. Not one iota.

All the while J. D.'s talking his eyes are roaming around the room like horseflies searching for a place to land. I've heard from the kids around the schoolyard that J. D. Eckles can never look anyone in the eye. Maybe he thinks his eyes are the windows into hell, and if he accidentally locks his onto somebody else's they'd hold him in those fiery pits forever. Nobody ever sees him smile, never. I guess unless he's strung upside down from a tree, he'll always look like he's frowning.

Dad leans over the table, points his eyebrows up to the ceiling, and says real serious-like, "There's a bounty of five thousand dollars if ya kill a bank robber, and these are hard times. So if Dry is in on it, he'll kill ya jus' for the bounty. But if ya do go through with it, I'd appreciate it if ye didn't hit the drugstore. Mr. Williams has been real good to us when I was sick and all. He let me have medicine I couldn't afford. Never pressed me on it. Fact is I still owe him." Dad twirls his pointer finger around his thumb over and over again like he's trying to wipe off something sticky. For whatever reason, he does that a lot.

Everything's quiet for a minute. J. D. glances in the direction of the Adams boys, and they stare back at him.

"OK, Wayne, we won't hit the drugstore."

"'Preciate it," Dad says.

Joe sits there silent, like there's something that wasn't sitting quite right on his mind. Earl says to his brother, "Joe, you keep puckerin' like that, pretty soon your face'll match your asshole."

I hear them chuckle, everyone except Joe. I hear the slurping up of coffee. Then, as much as I try to stay awake, I crawl back into bed and fall asleep.

⊰ ★ ⊱

The next morning I wake up and get ready for school. On the way, I grab Delma's hand a little harder than usual and pull her along.

"Why we walkin' so fast, Cono?"

"Jes' ready to get to school's all." We get to her classroom, and I'm still thinking about Bonnie and Clyde, but mostly I'm thinking about the bank robbers that had been in my own house—the house where Mother lives, where Delma lives, where I live. And I'm thinking about the bank where H. works. I don't want to play bank robbers anymore.

At recess I'm telling Gene about the robbers when Delma runs up to me slobbering tears and says, "Cono, he-he-he slapped me!"

"Who?" I ask, feeling my blood start to boil.

"Him. Over there!" and she points to a kid with curly blonde hair who looks a little on the mad side. I scope him out real quick. Even though this kid is two years younger than me, I'm not any bigger. I decide it's alright to go off on him in order to teach this bully a lesson. Delma looks on while I pin him down and start punching him.

"Cono, Cono," he says while trying to block my punches. "She started it!"

"What?" I ask, stopping my fist up in the air before it comes back down.

"She started it, Cono. She kicked me in the shin."

"What do ye mean she kicked ye?" Then it occurred to me. Delma's favorite weapon was her shoes, and her favorite target was a shin. I stop hitting him, but I get right in his face and say, "Next time, if ye hit my little sister I'll come find ye. I don't care if she hits ye first. I'll find ye." I stand up, brush the dust off my pants, and help him up.

I grab Delma's hand and walk her away from the kid I'd punched, the one who was only trying to protect himself.

"Delma, did ye start it like he said?" I ask.

"He called me a name, Cono, so I had to kick him."

"What'd he call ye?"

She mumbles, "He kept on sayin', 'Delma Jean's a stringy bean.'"

"A what?" I ask 'cause I really can't understand her.

"A stringy bean!" she yells.

I have to turn my head away from her and bite down hard on my tongue so she can't see that I'm about to spit laughter from the schoolyard to the next county. Damn, a stringy bean. I sure wish I would've thought of that one.

I turn back around and say, "Sis, you know that if ye hit some-body it's their own fairness ta hit ye back. Now, ta hit somebody jes''cause they've called ye a name, well I reckon it depends."

"What'd ye mean, Cono?"

"Well, what I mean is this. Could you by any chance a'tall be a stringy bean?" I have to turn my face away from her again.

She stops like she's thinking about it for a second, like she's picturing herself in a bowl being served at suppertime.

"Well, no," she says.

"Then, as long as ye know yer not a stringy bean, then it don't really matter what somebody calls ye, does it?"

"Guess not."

"OK, now let me have a look at ye jes' te make sure."

I eye her up and down and say, "Ye look jes' fine to me, but if ye start turnin' green, Delma Jean, ye let me know."

She likes my rhyme. She looks up at me with those big brown eyes and gives me a toothy grin.

"OK, Cono. I will."

"Delma, it's best ye keep them kicks to yerself. I don't wanna beat somebody up 'less I have te."

I reach over and grab her nose between my fingers, show her my thumb, and say, "Got her nose!"

"Cut that out, Cono. I'm too big fer that game."

"Ye gonna kick me?"

She lets out a big breath of air, grabs my hand this time, and says, "Let's go home, Cono."

"Good idee," I say. "'Cause all this talk about food has made me hungry."

I grin at my own little joke, and then, after we had walked a little ways I say, "Delma Jean?"

"Yeah?" Then I tell her something Ike's told me before. At the time, it didn't make no sense. Now I think his words are starting to add up.

"If I tell ye a rooster wears a pistol jes' look under its wing," I say.

"What rooster?"

"Any rooster." And I leave it at that. She'll have to figure that one out on her own just like I did.

We walk the rest of the way, and my mind goes back to H. Govan. I don't want him to get hurt for no reason. I look up at the sky and think to myself, "Please don't let H. get in the crossfire." But, of course, I don't hear anything back.

CHAPTER 20

92 Miles to Temple

I HAVE SOME distant relatives living in Springlake, up in the panhandle. Years back, Mrs. Clayton looked out her kitchen window and saw a stalled car up the road with a man leaning over the engine and a woman walking towards her house. Mr. Clayton opened the door for the woman and asked if she needed help. "No, jes' a jug 'a water. I'll take it out there myself," she said. The Claytons kept watching the couple from their distant window.

The man poured the water into the overheated engine, left the jug by the side of the road, and drove off.

"Well I'll be," said Mr. Clayton. "That there was Bonnie and Clyde!"

J. D. Eckles and Joe and Earl Adams never did rob that bank. A month later, Marshal Dry killed Joe on the street across from the very bank they wanted to rob and near the same drugstore they agreed not to hit. Joe must have told the marshal they weren't going to do the bank deal so Dry killed him where he stood.

About two or three weeks after that, Earl Adams killed Gazzard Davis not thirty feet away from where his brother was killed. As it turned out, Gazzard Davis was Gene's uncle and was known for being a tushhog, a real badass. Gene told me once that his Uncle Gazzard had ripped a gun away from a Texas Ranger so fast that the Ranger never even saw it coming. Shortly thereafter Earl died of a heart attack.

That left J. D. Eckles. J. D. died in Ranger shortly after from a heart attack. Pretty Boy Floyd no longer had to worry about being blamed for some of J. D.'s killings like he often was. There was a lot of dying that month. But thankfully, H. Govan kept on living.

Jailbirds and lawbreakers wouldn't be strangers in my house. In fact, before long, they'd be living under the same roof as me. But that would come later.

⊣ ★ ⊢

It was almost Christmas, and we were up at the ranch visiting Ike when Uncle Sid, Ike's brother, drove up in his brand-new Chevrolet. Uncle Sid lives in New Mexico, has his own ranch, and cowboys up just as good as Ike, but Uncle Sid makes a lot more money.

Delma and I ran out to meet Uncle Sid. He rubbed my head and picked up Delma and twirled her around. After reaching into his back pocket, he pulled out his fine leather wallet.

"Here ye go, kids. Merry Christmas!" In our palms he laid two unwrinkled, fresh-from-the-mint one-dollar bills. Delma and me had never been handed a whole dollar bill. I remember smelling the paper of those bills and wondering if a five-dollar bill or even a ten-dollar bill smelled any better. *If they did, then surely*, I thought, *the hundred-dollar bill would probably smell the best, maybe like vanilla ice cream with warm chocolate syrup poured over the top.*

When we got back into town, we spent a few nickels on ice cream cones, two scoops each. We'd never had two scoops. Delma and I were having fun licking our ice cream cones until she started bragging that even though my ice cream was almost gone, she still had some left. When I had nothing else to show for it but a stain on my shirt, Delma said to me real calm and sassy-like, "Cono, ye done *already?*"

"Yeah."

"Well, I still got *mine!*"

I didn't like the way she was bragging so I said, "Yeah, and most of it's on your *face!*"

She kicked dirt onto my shoes, which made me laugh. And, of course, that made her even madder, so I shouldn't have been surprised when she kicked me in the shin with her girly shoes.

I ran off from her. She probably would have caught me, except she didn't want to risk dropping the rest of her ice cream.

Even though she was skinnier than a post, she called herself "short and pleasantly plump." We all knew better, of course. It was the Gallaghers, our bootlegging friends, who called her "Spider" since her two legs carried her as fast as eight would have.

Anyhow, if I had known then what the next few months would be like, I never would have spent any of that money on an ice cream cone no matter how good it tasted. I was just about to turn eight years old when I noticed that everything started looking small, dusty, and picked over. I don't really know how to explain what happened to the part of me that had always felt that, no matter what, everything would be OK. That part was gone. The hunger had driven it away.

We had our Christmas while we were still living in the Tourist Court. We never had a tree and that year wasn't any different. What was different was that our meals became less and less filling and more and more scant.

On Christmas morning, Delma got a doll and a dress. I got a new football and a new green pullover sweater. I don't remember Mom or Dad giving each other anything that Christmas or any Christmas before. That holiday was bad enough, but when Delma got so sick, was even worse.

CHAPTER 21

Scarlet Fever and a Medium Onion

1937

FIRST THING I do is go outside to give my new football a try. Gene wasn't home; he was up in Roby visiting his grandparents, so I thought I'd just go ahead and practice my kicking. On the first kick, my football lands on the eaves of the Tourist Court, popping all the air out of my ball. One of my two presents is already gone only a few hours after I get it.

The first day school starts back up my teacher tells us to come up to the front of the room one by one and tell everyone what we got for Christmas. Some kids got chocolate and shoes and toys.

When it's my turn I walk up to the front of the class, look down at my green sweater, and say, "I got this here sweater fer Christmas."

Some stupid kid in the back of the class says, "Sit down, Cono! We've already seen yer sweater!" I want to tell them about my football, but then I'd have to explain about busting it after my first kick. I've been cut through enough for one day.

⊰ ★ ⊱

It's January now and Delma is so sick I start to worry. Her throat is real sore and her fever is so high that Mother keeps pacing around wringing her hands like she's trying to unscrew them from her wrists.

When the doctor finally shows up, he says that Delma's come down with the scarlet fever and that we can't go out of the house for a month. Then he puts a note on our door that tells all the passersby the same thing.

Dad's real sick too but his is different. His sickness is his pain that won't let him get out of bed. We're prisoners in our own home, least that's what it feels like.

For a week, the whole house feels pain of one kind or another. Delma's in one bed crying, Dad's moaning and cussing in his. But the only sickness Mother and I feel is a mean rumbling in our bellies from lack of food. Since Dad's been bedridden, we don't have any gambling money to spend on groceries.

For the longest time, I watch Mother sit at our Tourist Court kitchen table propping her head in her hands as if it was gonna fall off if she let go. When she stands up, she looks so skinny I think that if she turns sideways, she'll disappear. She starts looking through the kitchen cabinets. At first there isn't one dang thing to eat—no cans, no stale bread, not even salt or pepper. Finally, in the last cabinet, all by itself, is a medium-size onion. She takes it out, holds it in both her hands, and stares at it like she's thinking a roast is fixing to pop out of it. At least that's what I'm imagining, and my mouth gets all watery. I picture some potatoes next to it and one of Ma's hard biscuits. My head's feeling kinda swimmy-like, and I don't know if I have enough get-up-and-go to lift a fork even if there were a real meal in front of me. I want to sit with Pa again, on the breezy side of his house, and eat cheese and crackers. I want things to be copacetic.

Mother peels that onion real slow, like it's a prized Hereford being slaughtered for steak. She slices it up just as slowly as she'd peeled it. She puts it in a skillet and adds a little water, looks at it, and adds more water. As it heats, it smells like supper might just show up after all.

Mother walks a cup of the onion soup to Dad and then to Delma. I sit at the kitchen table waiting for my turn.

"Here ye go, Cono," she says quietly, not looking in my eyes. The onion soup doesn't taste like onion or even warm water. It tastes like cold hunger seasoned with poor and sprinkled with fear. And the stuff that settled on the bottom of the cup? That's anger. I drink it anyway. I feel like a devil's claw, stacked up and falling back down on my own self. It's like being slapped without even having a hand laid on me. Maybe it's because the slap I feel is on the inside instead of on the outside, like a burning slap on my face that's just as uninvited.

"Why'd she'd get so sick, Mother," I ask, breaking up the silence. "Is it 'cause she didn't cover up her hiney when she went to bed?" Ma's always saying that "If ye don't cover up yer hiney at night then yer sure te get a cold."

"She doesn't have a cold, Cono. It's worse than that."

We finish our skinny soup, and Mother goes on to bed.

I'm sleeping on a blanket in the main room so I won't catch Delma's scarlet fever. I know I'm not supposed to, but I want to sneak in to check on her.

I go into the kitchen and grab a pot from the cupboard. I put the pot on my head like I used to when she was little. It had always made her laugh. I sneak into Mother and Dad's room, opening the door slowly so they won't hear me. "Pooch," I whisper. He gets up and follows me into Delma's room, staring at me and wondering why I have a pot on my head.

"Cono?" she says turning towards me. "Ye got a pot on yer head," she whispers.

"I sure do."

"It's too small," she says, the word matching her voice.

"Reckon I need to go back te the store and trade it in fer one that fits," I say, trying to make her laugh.

"OK," she smiles. "Cono, my throat hurts."

"I know. It'll get better. Jes' go to sleep, now." She nods and turns her little brown-haired head away from me.

I stare at her weakness, at her missing spunkiness. I want her to jump up and kick me hard on my shin. How can she get better if she doesn't have anything more than a cup of watery soup? I decide to give her what I can.

Before I know it she's sound asleep, and a little drool slides out of the corner of her mouth. I take the silly pot off my head and tell Pooch, "Ye stay here with Delma tonight. She needs ye more 'n Dad."

I don't know much about Jesus God, but I lay my head on my pillow, my belly just as empty as our kitchen cupboards, and I pray, "Lord, please don't let my baby sister die. And if I live 'til mornin', I will do everything in my power to make sure my family will never go hungry no matter what I half ta do. Amen."

And I mean it too.

CHAPTER 22

89 Miles to Temple

A YOUNG, TOWHEADED boy is walking up and down the aisle carrying a tray of sandwiches. I buy myself a ham and cheese and a bottle of Dr. Pepper and give him an extra nickel for his trouble. I remember being a kid and doing the same thing once, but instead of selling sandwiches on a train, I sold them on a bus.

I unwrap the sandwich from its foil and take a few bites, realizing it's a tad stale, but it's food, and a whole helluva lot better than skinny onion soup. Truth being told, now every time I have a decent meal I say to myself, "I sure hope the poor people are doing alright."

Delma didn't die. Every day she got stronger and stronger and more and more like her old self again. Dad stayed about the same, hardly ever getting up outta bed. After the quarantine sign was pulled off our door and our prison sentence was over, Aunt Nolie moved to Rotan and rescued us once again. This time she wasn't alone. She'd gotten herself a new husband by the name of Red Griffice. Back then I thought he was called "Red" since the name matched the color of his face after a few beers.

Bootlegging was their main business. I'm not sure who learned from who, but our neighbors, the Rushings and the Gallaghers, were bootleggers too. Mr. Gallagher owned a gas station off the side of the road, but only one or two times do I remember him only having gas in those pumps. It was annoying for the out-of-town customers who pulled up for petrol but found the tanks to be empty. The bigger problem was Sheriff P. V. Hail. Whenever he pulled up to the "gas station," Mr. Gallagher would say things like, "Ah hell, P. V., ya know how things are. Can ya believe that I'm still waitin' on that delivery? I got plenty of RC Cola. Can I get one for ye? It's on the house as always."

After a while, P. V. would finally leave, Mr. Gallagher would wipe his forehead and recheck his supply of beer and whiskey. Nobody in Rotan knew where he hid it.

When Aunt Nolie and Red would drive up to Sweetwater to stock up on their booze, it was only P. V. they had to watch out for as they crossed that county line from wet to dry. I even heard that on Sundays somebody from town went to church and sold "eggs" to the Amen-ers. The "eggs" came either in tall bottles or short ones.

A couple of times Aunt Nolie and Red drove up to Sweetwater for something aside from booze. They'd scope out the folks who looked like they had a jingle in their pockets and follow them into a bar. Red would buy them a round of drinks, talk some kind of bullshit, and act drunker than Cooter Brown. Then he'd "accidentally" spill the man's beer on the ground. He'd apologize, of course, and say his good-byes and stumble out the door. That's when Aunt Nolie would make her dramatic appearance. Like she told me, she'd dress up "all woman" and would slip and fall down right there on the floor before anyone had a chance to clean up the spill. She'd lie there and whine and whimper and ask how she was gonna pay for the doctor bill. And since she was a widow with four kids and "ironed clothes" for a living, she asked how was she gonna make ends meet for the next few weeks until she got better.

Before long she'd have a five-dollar bill in her hand, ten if she was lucky. And when that money was gone? There was always something or someone else to do.

Now, that wasn't a real honest thing to do, but I do believe that sometimes we do what we have to do to in order to keep from starving. On my last leave, I ended up telling Ike what I'd been doing to rise above the pennies.

Shortly after arriving in San Antone, I went to town and bought some switchblades, knucks, and other crap that I thought I could sell for a profit to those little green-behind-the-ear boys who were still thinking about sucking on their mothers' tits. I went into our classroom, and when the instructor wasn't around, I sold everything I'd bought, and for a good profit, too. I even told those boys that if they needed help knowing how to use those weapons just to let me know and I'd teach them—for a little fee of course.

About a day later, some fella came in and said, "Dennis, the lieutenant wants to see you." I walk in and salute, and he says, "Soldier, what were you doing selling those knives and knucks?"

I had to think real quick-like so I said, "Sir, I didn't want 'em anymore, didn't need 'em anymore. I just wanted to get rid of them."

He sized me up better than I could've done myself, smiled, and said, "I don't want to ever see you in here again."

"No sir," I said, and I haven't seen him since. But it didn't stop me from still wanting to do something extra on the other side of the army air force paycheck. Before long, another opportunity invited itself over. I was made responsible for mashing the brass cans that bombardier and pilot wings come in. I looked in them before I started mashing them, and I'll be damned if there still weren't wings stuck to the bottom of some of those cans.

I looked in every one of those cans with the eye of a person who had starved before, who had tasted hunger, but had learned to keep it as a memory pinched between cheek and gum like chewing tobacco. I plucked those pins out and shined them up real good with a blitz cloth until they looked brand-new. I took them to class, and again, when the instructor wasn't around, I asked, "Who wants to be a bombardier? A pilot?"

I remember Dad telling me a long time ago that if a girl sees something shiny, she'd just have to go over and touch it. So I knew it really didn't matter if they wanted to be a pilot or bombardier. What mattered to those boys was going out for a little R & R, because if girls got sight of those shiny pins, those boys would be happy for a whole night and maybe more. Now that I think on it, I should have sold them for more than a dollar apiece.

I also knew that a unit of boys was about to be shipped over to Japan. I bought all the fake diamond rings I could find at the five-and-dime store, went back to the barracks, and told those boys the same thing. Today, thanks to me, I bet there's a lot of gals over in the Pacific wearing fake rings on their fingers.

No more onion soup for this man. The money in my pocket is finally mine. Pulling out my wallet I count twenty dollars and change. Nobody's stealing this money from me.

Maybe I'll buy Ike a beer when I get back.

Cono

CHAPTER 23

Garden Seeds and a Jackass

1937

I DON'T THINK Dad minds our new living arrangements since he gets free beer from Aunt Nolie and Red's bootlegging business. Aunt Nolie and Red stay on one side of the house, the four of us stay on the other side, and the bootlegging business stays in front.

Aunt Nolie is the best bootlegger there is. She runs around like a cranberry merchant most of the time, hardly ever sitting still. I asked Aunt Nolie why we're called bootleggers, and she said it's because bootleggers used to carry their flask of whiskey on the inside of their boots. She must carry hers somewheres else.

Dad drinks up most of her profits. I don't think she cares for that, but she knows he's sick with his pain. I like it just fine. He keeps his hands off me and doesn't have enough energy to yell at Mother, at least not as loud.

A West Texas spring has arrived. It's warm out and buttercups and prairie lace are growing next to the tall grasses and around the cactus. We have all the next week off from school for Easter break, and I got nothing but springtime.

Delma and Mother have gone to the store to pick up a few things, and since Gene's out of town again, sitting on the front porch is all I've come up with to do.

Aunt Nolie and Red drive up to the house in their pickup truck and start uncovering and unloading the Sweetwater liquor they bought—another day of not getting caught by P. V. Hail.

"Cono, give us a hand, will ye?" asks Red. Guess I have something to do.

I get up and help carry the Pearl beers and whiskey into the house. Aunt Nolie has her hands full too when she says, "Cono, I got ye something today."

"Yeah?"

"Cono!" I hear Dad yell.

I go into his room to hear him ask, "Are they home?"

"Yes sir."

"Bring me a couple 'a beers then."

After I get Dad settled in with his "pain medicine," I go back out to Aunt Nolie's side of the house.

"Yeah?" I ask again.

"I got ye some garden seeds."

"What in tarnation fer?"

"'Cause you and me 'r gonna walk around Rotan today 'n sell 'em so ye kin have a little money for that guitar ye been wantin'."

I can't believe it, but she remembered what I'd told her and Red a few weeks back, the story about Dickie, how he'd bought that donkey instead of school supplies and how he played the fiddle. Then I told her that if I had myself a real guitar, I'd teach myself how to play it and maybe make a few dollars entertaining folks with "Home on the Range" and a couple of Bob Wills or Gene Autry songs. I figured that all I needed was three dollars and fifty cents to buy one. I thought I'd just been daydreaming out loud, but she'd caught my dream and was pulling me closer and closer to it.

"Well, I'm ready whenever you are!"

Aunt Nolie and me take off walking all over Rotan. We sell those little seeds for twenty cents a packet to any folks who feel they could grow a little something in our West Texas Depression dirt. I had a real job. I'd become an honorable seed seller.

I go to bed happy. It had been a real good honest day's work. We'd sold three dollars and twenty cents' worth of those little seed packets, and after tomorrow's sell day, I know I'm just one step closer to having me a brand-new guitar.

I wrap my money in a dish towel, tie it up with a string, and put it in my box of specials that I keep hidden under my bed. Nothing like an honest day's work to make a feller wore out. I put my head on my pillow and go straight to sleep.

The first thing I do next morning after waking up is pull out my cigar box. My other specials are in there: my devil's claw, toothbrush, Tiger, my pocketknife, my piece of boxing glove lace, my penny from Great Uncle Will. But my dish towel of money isn't there. I leave my room and find Aunt Nolie sitting at the kitchen table eating a biscuit.

"It's gone!" I say.

"What's gone, Cono?"

"My money fer my geetar. It's all gone. It ain't where I put it!"

CHAPTER 24

79 Miles to Temple

BACK IN SAN Antone, Vargo and I shared the same barracks and—
most of the time—the same sense of humor. He was a big man,
a real blowhard from Philadelphia. He reminded me of Tarzan,
except instead of wearing a loincloth, he'd always wear a plain
white T-shirt, a pair of fatigues, and a baseball cap to cover up his
almost shaved head. He didn't care much for hair, and he cared
even less for rules and regulations. Vargo was anything but "standard issue."

Not many folks in the army know me by my Ike-given name.
Sometimes they call me by my second name, which is "Ray," but
usually they just call me "Dennis." Not Vargo.

"C'mon, Tex," he'd mumble. He was the master of the mumble, but I learned how to understand him like some folks learn a
foreign language.

"Let's go to the movies."

"Hell, Vargo, ye know I don't spend no money for a picture show."

"Don't need money."

"Well, I don't think they're gonna let us inside just because of your good looks unless ye were countin' on mine."

He grinned and said, "We'd die first, Tex. C'mon."

"What are we fixin' to do? Steal an old woman's purse or something?"

"It's a pocketbook."

"A what?"

"It's called a 'pocketbook,' not a 'purse.'"

"I've never heard such a thing. You Yanks make up the craziest words fer something so simple," I said as we kept on walking to the theater.

When we got to the picture show, where *Abilene Town* was playing, there was a snake of a line waiting to get in. Even a couple of generals were in line, all striped up and ready to sit down.

"Follow me," he says.

We walked around the theater and found the back door. Vargo jimmied the door open, peeked inside, and said, "Let's go."

We got seats right in the front and center and had time to settle in for a few minutes before the line was let in. I turned around to see the generals trying to be satisfied with their seats in the back of the theater.

We watched the show, which wasn't all that good since it was about Abilene, Kansas, and not Abilene, Texas. But it was better than a hard kick in the ass. And it was free. Thanks to Vargo, so was the swimming pool, and the roller rink. Now I'm a helluva good swimmer. But skating?

"I ain't going skating," I told him on the day he came up with that smart idea.

"Scared?" he asked.

"No. I just didn't grow up with wheels under my feet like you did. I grew up with stirrups under 'em and a horse under my butt."

I tried anyway. Vargo put those skates on and it was the funniest thing I ever saw: Tarzan on skates wearing a T-shirt and fatigues, speeding around the wooden floor like a real goofball.

I watched for a few minutes before getting my size ten and a half skates from the counter. Sitting on the bench, I put those rolling shoes on feet meant for boots. I must have laced them skates up for half an hour.

Vargo had already gone miles around that rink before I'd even had a chance to stand up. When I finally did, I held on to the side railings and stepped onto that floor from hell. My legs were strong and my balance good from boxing, but before I could even get squared off, the skates took me down faster than a Joe Louis left hook. I was embarrassed, sure enough, lying there like a sack of feed.

I sat up feeling dumbfounded, out of control, and even more out of my element. All the skaters were swarming around me, circling me like a bunch of buzzards. Then this sweet little girl—probably all of eight years old—skated over to me and said in her tiny voice, "Can I help you up, Mister?"

She stuck out her tiny little hand, and I still think that, maybe, that one moment was one of the nicest things any stranger had ever done for me.

"No, hon', that's OK," I said, suddenly missing my little sister. "I think I can make it."

An eight-year-old girl had tried to save me. Ain't that something?

I didn't even try to get back to the bench on those skates. I didn't even try to stand up. I sat right there in the middle of the busy floor of rolling people and took those goddamn things off my feet. My skating days were over.

Vargo laughed all the way back on our bus ride to the barracks.

"Sure had fun, Tex."

"Sure 'm glad," I mumbled back.

After a few minutes on the bus, when the agitation had settled down, I asked, "Vargo, what are ye plannin' to do after ye get outta the service?"

"Own a parking lot," he said without taking a second to blink. "Going to take the nickels and have someone else park the cars."

That's a perfect job for Vargo. He wouldn't have to work a lick. All he'd have to do is collect the money and go back up north to ice-skate and watch picture shows for free.

Yep, that was a perfect job for Vargo. I didn't tell him what I wanted to do after the army because I didn't know. I still don't. The only thing that settles in my mind is getting up every morning in Ike's skin and running a ranch. Owning one would be even better.

I knew that Vargo wasn't a rules and regs man, not at all the military type. He must have bucked every system all over Pennsylvania until he finally had to try a new state. Why the military in Texas I had no idea. I didn't get the chance to ask.

Soon after our next free movie, Vargo walked past a lieutenant colonel without saluting. The lieutenant colonel stopped him and said, "Soldier, don't you ever salute?"

"Yes sir," says Vargo.

"Go report to the captain."

"Yes sir." But he didn't go report to the captain.

A few days later the same lieutenant colonel walks past Vargo.

"Soldier, don't you ever salute?"

"Yes sir," says Vargo.

"This time, I'm taking you to the captain."

After they all had their come-to-Jesus meeting, Vargo was put on 104 punishment—manual labor—and given a mower to push for the next few hours. And when the few hours had passed and I hadn't seen hide nor hair of Vargo, I decided to go check on him. Damn if I didn't find him sound asleep in our barracks at two in the afternoon.

"Vargo, where's the mower?" I asked.

"I sold it."

Now, I knew I'd sold things on the side, but I never considered selling something that belonged to the U.S. Army.

"Vargo," I said, "yer gonna be in a heap 'a trouble."

It wasn't any surprise to me that they called him in just so they could ship him out. I saw him walking down the stairs carrying two big drawstring duffle bags.

"Glad to see you, Tex! Mind carrying this one to the bus stop for me?" he asked, pointing to one of his duffle bugs.

"Not at all, Vargo. Jes' hate to see ye go."

We got to the bus stop, where I handed him his duffle bag.

"Thanks, Tex. I hate to go too. But if you ever get to Philly, come see me."

"I'll sure do it. If you ever make it back to these parts, I'll show you how to ride a horse."

He laughed and mumbled, "Butt wasn't made for that."

I shook his hand and watched as Vargo got on the bus and pulled away.

As I walked back, I thought about what a character he was, always marching to his own drummer. I like that in a fella, someone who knows what he wants and doesn't worry too much about what other people think, just like my grandfather Ike.

I returned to my barracks to discover that my trunk was open. I looked inside. Except for one pair of wraps, my trunk was almost empty.

"Well kiss a fat man's ass," I said loud enough to be heard the next barracks over. My good friend Vargo had stripped me out of most of my boxing gear. My new six-ounce kickers, my robe, my other wraps—all gone.

"But the worst part about the whole ordeal?" I told Colonel Posey later that day. "I carried and loaded my own boxing gear onto a bus headed for Philadelphia!" We both got a good laugh out of that one.

Truth be told, I liked ol' Vargo. He was one of a kind. I like picturing him right now, sitting at his parking lot collecting nickels during the day and sneaking into a picture show at night.

But some thieving I just can't tolerate.

CHAPTER 25

Sunshine on a Jackass

1937

AUNT NOLIE GETS a funny look on her face that makes me have to say, "Where's Red?"

"He's left already, hightailed it out of here early this morning." She said it almost like she was asking a question to herself. Then I had no doubt who had done stole my money. It was Aunt Nolie's no-account husband. Yesterday they'd spent all their money buying bootlegged liquor. Until a few customers came by today, they wouldn't 'a had a nickel towards taking a piss.

Aunt Nolie is madder than a hornet. She didn't come right out and say so, but I know she's thinking the same thing I am 'cause she slams her breakfast plate in the sink. I go outside and slam my fist into a tree.

For the last couple of days since then I haven't talked much to anybody, not even Delma. I wasn't mean to her or anything; I just kept telling her that I didn't feel much like playing. Even Pooch was lucky to get a pat on the head. And every time Uncle Red has walked past me I can't even look into his thieving eyes.

Mother and Delma have taken Dad to the doctor. Mother's tired of seeing him in bed all the time, and I think Dad's finally got tired of it too. I'm tossing up Gene's football, the one he lent me before visiting his kinfolk in Roby. Uncle No-Account comes up to me and says, "Cono, let's you and me go to Sweetwater and I'll buy you a donkey."

Aunt Nolie must have read him the riot act and was sticking up for me. I thought about it for a minute, about how I really wanted a guitar, but I figured that a donkey would at least put me right up there with Dickey Dennis.

"OK," I say. Aunt Nolie walks us to the truck and waves us down the street.

No-Account and me drive towards Sweetwater not saying a whole lot, unless his jabbering about anything that helps leave his stealing guilt at home counts as a real conversation. Then I see them, up ahead on the right.

"There they are, Uncle Red!" I point to a field where five donkeys are grazing.

"Uh-huh, OK. We'll git 'em on our way back."

"Uh-huh, OK," I say. Yeah, and there ain't no pistol under *your* rooster's wing.

We get to Sweetwater and he parks his truck in front of a beer joint named the Lucky Star Bar.

"C'mon, Cono," says No-Account. "Let's you and me go inside and wet our whistle."

I think to myself, *the only donkey in here is the jackass I'm stupid enough to be walking behind.*

I should have known he was a jackass the time Aunt Nolie told me I could sleep with her and not squirmy Delma since Red was going to be "out and about" all night. Both of us were sound asleep, that is, until No-Account came home three sheets to the wind. I heard him stumble in and fumble around his bedroom until he found his bed. Next thing I knew, I was on the floor and he was lying on my spot on the bed.

In my sleepy stupor, I grabbed a throw pillow, stuck it under my head, and tried to go back to sleep. Instead of hearing the sound of sleep, I heard moans and groans. Their bed started thumping like a cyclone was tearing down a barn, and then instead of hearing wind howling through the window, all I could hear was Uncle No-Account grunting. That's when it dawned on me what they were doing.

In my baby days, I'd seen a bull standing on two legs hanging on to the back end of a cow. "What's that?" I asked Ike. He laughed and said, "Well, Cono, I reckon ye'll know 'bout that soon 'nough."

There'd been a bull on top of Aunt Nolie and now he was sitting on a bar stool kissing the woman next to him smack-dab on her red lips.

"Cono, this here's Sunshine."

I know that song "You are my Sunshine, my only Sunshine." I figure that song was named after her. She has short blonde hair and looks like she hadn't missed a meal in a while. Not that she's fat, but she has more meat on her bones than most gals I see.

"Well hello there, Cono," she says giving me a little wink.

"Hello," I say, turning back to look at No-Account and giving him my best "you're a no-account" stare.

"Cono," he says, "ye go on over there and sit at an empty table, and I'll get ye a sody pop. Sunshine and me are gonna talk some business fer a minute."

No-Account gives Sunshine a pinch on her round butt and she lets out a stupid-sounding noise that's something between a squeal and a giggle.

Sitting there by myself doesn't stop me from staring, disgusted-like, at their carryings-on. She whispers in his ear, he gives her a little smooch; he whispers in her ear, she lets out another hare-brained giggle. I get so fed up my belly starts to twist around and I think I might just puke. Standing up I say, "I'm gonna wait in the truck." And that's what I do.

I look around the truck, but I don't see any rope. That sorry son of a bitch never intended to buy me a donkey.

I watch people go in and come out and think about the loser I'm with, the jackass full of bullcorn. My hard-earned-honest-day's-work-seed-selling money had gone straight towards something to do with that blonde-haired giggly eye-winker named "Sunshine."

No-Account finally gets back into the truck and starts jawing again about more things that don't make no sense. The difference is this time he's swerving around the road like a drunk man, which he is.

"Damn," he says when we almost go off the road. "What was that in the street?"

I don't answer. Even Dad could drive better than this. I just keep sitting and feeling like a stool pigeon, a stool pigeon that has to hold on to the door handle just in case it needs to jump out.

He seems to have forgotten about buying me that donkey since we've driven past the donkey field for the second time. I look over at him. He's got a shit-eating grin on his face that tells me his mind is sitting on something else. Wink, wink.

That grin flipped over real quick when we got home.

"Where ye been so long, and where's that donkey?" screams Aunt Nolie.

"Couldn't get one today," he says.

Aunt Nolie looks at the mad on my face and yells, "What the hell were ye doin' then?"

No-Account whistles himself into the other room and ignores her.

"Cono, where ya'll been?" she asks, her tone a little softer now.

"We went to Sweetwater to the Lucky Star beer joint."

"Why didn't ye get a donkey?"

"He wouldn't stop fer one," I tell her. Then I add more of the honest truth. "Red had some beers and started kissin' on Sunshine."

"He was, was he?"

"Yep."

"C'mon, Cono. I'm gonna get my pistol, and I'm gonna drive right back over there and shoot that no-good hussy."

"Ye know who she is?"

"Everybody in Sweetwater knows that slut."

I decide right then and there that another ride to Sweetwater to shoot Sunshine didn't make no nevermind to me. I don't have nothin' to strum and nothin' to ride on anyhow.

After Aunt Nolie gets her gun, we're back in the truck. She puts on some kinda girly scarf and ties it under her chin. Then she takes out her lipstick, looks in the rearview mirror, and smears it on her lips. I guess Ike was right that time he told me that ladies are real competitive, that they dress up not for the men folk but to look better than the other ladies. Aunt Nolie must want to look good when she shoots No-Account's girlfriend.

Here I go again, on the way back to Sweetwater. Not to get a donkey but to shoot Sunshine, my only Sunshine.

Driving down the highway, Aunt Nolie doesn't talk much, at least not with her mouth. She clutches that steering wheel like she's about to squeeze all the Texas sand and grit out of it, and that's a whole conversation in itself.

We finally get to Sweetwater and park in front of the Lucky Star Bar.

"Cono, ye wait right here."

"OK," I say, since I've already met the woman who's about to be shot anyway.

I sit in the car, again. I watch the people come and go, again, except this time, the ones that had been going were coming and the ones that had been coming were now going. I wait for the sound of a gunshot, the sound I've become familiar with when I hunt with my dad. I wait alright, 'cause there's nothing else for me to do.

I hear unfamiliar folks talking and yelling at each another. I hear a dog bark and a couple of horns honking. So far I haven't heard no gunshot. I wait some more.

I look in the rearview mirror. Finally I see Aunt Nolie walking real fast towards the truck. Ah, Jesus, she's gone and done it. After the sheriff puts her in jail, I'll have to find myself a ride back to Rotan.

She gets back in the truck, mad still glued to her face. She slams the door and says, "She wadn't there."

"OK," I say.

We start our drive back to Rotan. I use that quiet to keep thinking that maybe when we get home she'll still put that pistol to good use on No-Account. But I know better. A third husband might be hard to find. So I just stare out the window and wonder if those little seeds I'd sold have started sprouting in the gardens around Rotan. Then I picture me, Cono of Cono, Texas, riding on his new donkey, inviting street musicians over to my house for supper. I join in with them playing "Home on the Range" on my new guitar.

But picturing it was as close as I was gonna git. Nolie didn't get her revenge, and I didn't get my new guitar. And I didn't get my donkey, neither. All gone, just like Pa's teeth.

When I get back, maybe I'll use that hammer on No-Account and watch his eyeballs twitch.

CHAPTER 26

68 Miles to Temple

EVEN THOUGH I didn't get a donkey or a new guitar, I knew Aunt Nolie was in my corner, wiping off my brow between rounds and telling me to "Get up!" at the same time. I've since learned how to "get up" from many of the folks around West Texas. In that rugged terrain, if you don't stand your ground you'll be bitten into hard, chewed on for a long time, and finally spit out just like Granny Dennis's snuff. You don't give up in West Texas; you get up.

It's strange the ways people stick up for others and how they don't. Sometimes they do it with yelling words, soft words, or even no words at all. Sometimes they do it by fighting, like Punk Squares did. But most of the time the people in your corner just tell you to suck it up and go back at it. That's what I've learned to do.

On that no-account day I did get a good reminder of what Ike taught me later on. Never trust anybody but your own self. I'd decided that from then on I was going to protect my hard-earned money, hold on to it real tight in one hand and clutch the handle of my axe even tighter in the other. An honest day's pay should be just that, and nobody—nobody—should ever take that away from you.

Cono boxing for the army

CHAPTER 27

A Bird in a Storm

1937

ALTHOUGH I THOUGHT about it many a time, I've made it through half of the summer without killing No-Account. So has Aunt Nolie for that matter. They seem to be back to some kind of normal, which for them probably means bed grunting. Dad was told by his doctor last spring about another hot pool that might help his arthritis. He left a few weeks ago saying he was "gonna give it a go." No-Account left a few hours ago to pick him up.

I see No-Account's truck pull up in the driveway. He walks through the door supporting a man under his arm who looks nothing like my dad. He weighs little more than a baby bird. Ninety pounds is what they say he is now. Skinny as a rail, not worth a grain of salt, and not strong enough to lift a hand on me. He's barely strong enough to lift a word.

"God in Heaven, Wayne," says Mother. "Didn't they feed ye there?"

"Wadn't hungry," he says, barely a whisper. Even though it's only four o'clock in the afternoon, No-Account puts Dad in bed.

Delma and I are outside playing Kick the Can when a stranger walks up. He looks like a hobo I'd pictured early on, the ones that went from place to place with never any real idea of where they were going. His shirt pocket is torn almost in half, making it hard for his pack of cigarettes to stay put. His pants ride up too high from his ankles and too low for his butt. Although the hair on his head seems to stay in place, the hairs on his chin are scraggly, hanging at different lengths. But resting above those chin hairs sits a nice smile. He doesn't look like someone who would eat a little boy.

"Yer folks home?" he asks. This poor fella stinks to high heaven.

"Yes sir," I say. "In the house." I follow him in to see what kind of business he's carrying.

"Cono, ye met Mr. Reynolds yet?" asks Mother.

He sticks out a calloused hand, offers it to me, and says, "Wort Reynolds, a pleasure."

"Wort's a friend of yer dad's from way back. They went te school together."

"Oh," I say.

"Shor em sorry yer Dad's sick. He's a good fella."

"Yes sir," I say, wondering if he's talking about the same man.

Aunt Nolie brings Mr. Reynolds a cold beer. No-Account slaps her butt as she walks past him.

"Cut that out, Red!" she says, sticking out her butt and rubbing it in circles just to make him laugh.

Wort has himself a few of our bootlegged beers, discounted

since he's a friend and all. We all sit around the front bootlegging room and they talk a bit about times being hard. Wort says he's going on to Clyde, Texas, gonna try to find work there. I like Mr. Reynolds, but I feel sorry for him. Now I recognize his smell. It's not just from sweat but from being poor, like he doesn't have but half a penny to his name.

Dad doesn't get to visit much with his old friend since he seems to be withering away in his free bed. That hot springs didn't help him one iota.

Aunt Nolie offers Wort a couch to sleep on for the night, and before long, he's snoring to beat the band. Probably the best night's sleep he's had in a while.

Morning rolls around and the wind starts howling like a thousand coyotes.

"Best be gettin' along," says Wort, looking up at the sky. "Need te beat that storm."

"Well here, then," says Aunt Nolie. "Take a few biscuits with ye."

Wort walks into Dad's room to say good-bye, and even though I can't hear what they're saying, I see that Wort is walking out of my dad's room stuffing a five-dollar bill in his pants pocket.

"Now ye take care 'a yerself," says Aunt Nolie. "Stop on by anytime, anytime a'tall."

"Shor will. And thanks again fer yer hospitality. "Elnora," he says, nodding in Mother's direction. Mother holds up a hand in front of her to say good-bye. We walk out with Wort and watch him walk towards the railroad tracks to hop on a train to Clyde, Texas.

The wind is picking up, blowing Texas dirt in our eyes. We all look up to the sky and decide to start paying those clouds a little more respect. They're pearly gray and making pictures quicker than you can figure out what they're pictures of.

"Ya'll get in the cellar," says No-Account. "I'll get Wayne." I watched as Red picked up my ninety-pound dad and carried him step-by-step down the cellar stairs.

"Don't forget Pooch," says Dad, his eyes flitting back and forth. "He hates storms ya know."

Sitting in that storm cellar for at least an hour I got a good look at my Uncle Red. I know what he did, carrying Dad like a baby, was a real nice thing. I also know that Dad didn't like it one bit.

⊨ ★ ⊨

Aunt Nolie and Red are taking me on a little vacation. Their friends, the Underwoods, have boys around my age. And even though the Underwoods have a place in Rotan, they also have a ranch in Jayton. Two places to live, don't that beat all? Dad's starting to feel better every day, but he, Mother, and Delma stay home.

Mr. Underwood picks us up, and I swear that at his ten miles an hour I'm gonna grow old and gray before we even get there. They tell me I'm going on a cattle drive. It'll be my first one, and I feel like I'm about to jump out of my britches with excitement.

We finally get there, and we see that Mrs. Underwood has made us a stack of pancakes. "Eat up now," she says, "an' take the rest with ya." Aunt Nolie and Red borrow Mr. Underwood's car and leave me there.

"We're gonna go on a little road trip, Cono. We'll be back in a few days. Have fun now, ye hear?"

Like Dad, Aunt Nolie and Red aren't one bit interested in cattle drives. They'd rather make their money by bootlegging and tricking folks out of their money. Mr. Underwood and his boys pack up for our cattle drive and lead me out to the barn. They put me on a black Shetland pony and we ride off into the day to circle cattle.

The first night we sit around the campfire and eat more pancakes.

Mr. Underwood says, "So, Cono, what do ya like ta do in Rotan?"

I swallow my dry pancake and say, "I like te play checkers with my friend Gene."

"We have a checkerboard at the house," says Lucky, the oldest one. "We'll have to play when we get back, see how good ya are."

I nod. "I like to box too."

"Aren't ya kinda young to be boxin'?" asks Lucky.

"Naw, anybody can box. Ye jes' have te know yer punches is all."

"What punches?" asks Ben, who's a year younger than me.

"Jabs, uppercuts, straight rights, hooks."

"Who taught ya that, yer dad?"

"Naw, he was too busy boxing himself, winning matches. And 'course huntin' and trappin' like Dan'el Boone."

"Who then?" asks Lucky.

"Who then what?" I ask.

"Who taught ya how ta box?"

"Aunt Nolie."

Lucky laughs and says, "Yer aunt taught ya how to fight? Doesn't she fight like a girl?"

I stare at him. He's grinning and making fun of me, and I don't like it.

"Now Lucky, you've never met Nola," says Mr. Underwood. "She's a real go-getter, she is."

"Sure is," I smile. I want to tell them about her packing a pistol to shoot Sunshine, but I don't. I'm not real sure Mr. Underwood would like his kids to hear about that.

"Win any fights?" asks Ben.

I don't want to tell them I'd lost my first and only fight so I just say, "I boxed with a kid named Oklahoma. Got my tooth chipped 'n everything."

"Let's see," Ben says. I pull down my lower lip and show him my tooth. He leans closer, squinting and wrinkling up his nose to get a good look.

"Hmm."

We keep on gnawing our pancakes until my belly feels like it's about to blow up. I sure hope they brought something else to eat. I don't think I can stomach one more round piece of fried batter for the rest of my life.

The second day and into the night, Lucky and Ben tell me a bit about themselves. Lucky makes good grades, and Ben's got himself a real bow and arrow.

"My daddy taught me how ta use it," he says like he's bragging. "Ya have ta be real strong to pull that arrow all the way back, ya know. I can show ya if ya want."

"Hmm," I say. I think it would be better for me to play checkers when we get back.

"We got ourselves a slingshot too," says Lucky.

"Yeah, Lucky can sling a rock and hit an armadillo right 'tween the eyes."

"I like slingshots too," I say, even though I don't have one.

Lucky and Ben think Kick the Can is boring. They're too busy shooting arrows and hitting animals between the eyes with slingshots.

"My dad's a domino player," I say.

"Do ya play with him?" asks Ben.

"Naw, he just does it fer work."

"Work? That's his work?" asks Lucky.

"Sure is. He's a domino hustler. Can beat anybody in town and gets paid for it and all." Mr. Underwood snickers, and I think it's about time for me to shut my trap. I'm tired of talking to these boys anyhow.

We settle into our camp for the last night. I watch carefully as Lucky builds another perfect fire. I roll out my bag and realize how sore my butt is from all the riding. My black Shetland is a good horse, but she can't hold a candle to Polo.

Mr. Underwood surprises me by pulling out some dried beef. He opens up a can of beans and puts them on the fire. Finally, no goddamn pancakes. We eat quietly, me enjoying every bite. Then we hear thunder.

"Sounds like a storm's comin' our way, boys. Let's hunker down a little closer to those trees over there."

"What about the fire, Daddy?" asks Ben.

"We'll kick'er out in the mornin' 'less the rain beats us to it."

I know that if Dad and Pooch were here right now they'd be shivering in their paws looking for a storm cellar.

We move our bags under a group of trees, and as soon as I start to doze off, I hear, "Wake up, boys, look at that!" Mr. Underwood points to the cattle herd, and there in front of me is something so unbelievable that I think I must still be asleep. Blue lightning was sparking off the cows' horns, one to the next like a streak of electricity running across a wire on a telephone pole. It didn't hurt the cows any, just made them moo a bit louder. It made me think about other things I haven't seen yet. It made me think that this was just the kind of story Gene would like to hear. It's the first thing I'm gonna tell him when I get back.

It's my last night at the Underwoods' and we're back at their house giving our butts a little rest. Aunt Nolie and Red are coming back in the morning.

"Cono, how 'bout that game 'a checkers?" asks Lucky.

It's not even a match. In the first ten minutes, my black checkers are dead off the board while all he's got left are kings. I play Ben next and grab the red ones. I beat him just about as quick as Lucky beat me and think I can sleep good tonight.

"I'm gonna hit the sack, boys," says Mr. Underwood.

"I'm with ya, Daddy," says Mrs. Underwood. "You boys go ta bed soon now, ya hear?" I'm ready to hit the sack too. But as soon as their folks close their bedroom door, Lucky points out the window and says, "Cono, see that pond o'r yonder?"

"Yeah."

"That's where all the snipe are."

"What're snipe?" I ask.

"Well, they're kinda hard to explain. Only one person at a time can try to catch 'em 'cause they can sense when they're being ganged up on. Go on, see if you can catch one. Take yer hat and sit by the pond real still-like. When ya see one flyin' in the air or coming down for a drink, snag it with yer hat."

I'm staring out the window for a second when he says, "Well, are ya up for it or are ya too tuckered out?"

"It's real fun, Cono," says Ben. "They can't hurt none. They don't have any teeth or nothin'."

"OK," I say and start walking out the door.

"And Cono," whispers Lucky, "take off yer shoes so they cain't hear ya comin'."

I walk my bare feet over thorns and stickers down to the pond and take my hat off, sitting real still like I'm supposed to. I wait. My feet are getting eaten up by skeeters, and I try real hard not to scratch or swat them away so the snipe won't notice I'm here. Sometimes, though, I have to ease my hand down real slow and scratch anyway, the itch growing too big to ignore.

Sitting here with my hat in my hand, stickers in my feet and skeeter bumps all up and down my legs, makes me think that a bed right now would be a whole lot better. But I don't want to give up. I really want to catch one of them snipe, a big one too. I don't want to go back in and tell those boys that I'm a no-good hunter. So I wait some more.

The lightning bugs are everywhere, hundreds of them. Now that's what I like to catch. If I just had me a see-through jar I could catch all of them and show off my lightning bug talent. But I don't have a jar.

Maybe the snipe are afraid of lightning bugs. Lucky and Ben forgot to tell me if snipe are smart or dumb, brave or chicken, and I forgot to ask. I wait for almost an hour when I look up at the house and see those boys looking out their lighted kitchen window. They're laughing their fool heads off.

That's when I figured out that catching a snipe was something that was never gonna happen, with me or anyone else. I wanted Jessie Perkins to meet Lucky right about now. Jessie'd finish him off so quick he wouldn't have a chance to make another good grade.

Maybe I can get Delma to try to snipe hunting. I go to sleep with a grin on my face just thinking about it.

CHAPTER 28

A Stop in Austin

THE TRAIN'S JUST idling now, waiting for more passengers to get off and some to get on. I've never been to our state capital before, except for inside a train, but someday I plan to visit, maybe introduce myself to a few lawmakers. While I'm there, I might as well knock on Governor Stevenson's door just to see how big and important he really is. I'll have to save that for another time. Temple business is first.

It's funny, looking back and seeing how I tried to make my dad something he wasn't, something bigger. I should have just said, "He's a worthless, no-good father." But I didn't.

Aunt Nolie and Red came back to the Underwoods the next morning. They made an offer on Mr. Underwood's car and ended up buying it. Come to find out, that was the whole reason we went there in the first place.

Driving home I told them about pancakes and blue lightning and snipe hunting.

"Cono, ye didn't know about snipe?"

"Nobody ever told me there wadn't such a thing."

"Well, maybe ye jes' weren't looking in the right place," said Red, full of serious. My eyebrows squeezed together, confused, until I saw Aunt Nolie laugh.

"No such thing as a snipe," I said again.

Then I asked Aunt Nolie how Lucky got his name. "Is it because he makes good grades?" I asked.

"No, it ain't because 'a that."

"'Cause he can hit animals 'tween the eyes with a slingshot?"

"No. His real name is Samuel. Everybody started callin' him 'Lucky' when he was four. He got on a renegade horse that threw 'em off backward. Head hit a rock. Nathan said that when he ran over to him, he thought he was dead. His eyes half-open, staring into nowhere. And blood? So much of it poured outta that kid's head that Nathan said he started sobbin' and thinkin' 'bout where to bury him. He carried him home, and when the doctor came, he bandaged up Samuel's head and just shook his own head back and forth. The doctor thought that if Samuel did wake up, he'd probably be a turnip. But after four days, Lucky woke up and asked what was fer supper.

Mr. Reynolds wasn't so lucky. We got home to hear the news. A cyclone had hit the town of Clyde. It killed at least fourteen people, destroyed dozens of homes and other buildings, including the school. The newspaper said that a freight train on the Texas and Pacific Railroad was split plumb in two, the boxcars thrown all around like a bunch of toys. It said there was a transient on that train who had to be identified by his fingerprints since his head was gone. It said the man was from Ranger, Texas. It said his name was Ben Allen Wort Reynolds.

So that cyclone ran straight through Clyde, Texas, grabbed Wort's head, and kept right on going. I guess he didn't beat that storm after all. Instead, the storm beat him. A real nice fella that man was. I can't help thinking what would have happened if he'd lived. Would he ever have made something of himself? At least back then, Lucky was on the right track.

Dad giving Wort that money was a gesture of kindness we rarely saw. He was charitable with other folks.

I think back to when I told H. about Tommy Burns being so mean and how he said, "Little Dennis, there's good in everybody."

"What about Bonnie and Clyde? There's good in them?" I had asked.

"Jus' have ta look a little deeper into them I s'pose." So I'm looking a little deeper into Dad.

When people like Dad, they really like him and will do anything for him. Even the outlaw J. D. Eckles didn't rob the drugstore when Dad asked him not to.

On occasion, Dad even has a good sense of humor. Once when we still lived in Rotan, one of his friends had a domino hall, and being summertime it was hotter than hell. Dad lent him his big oscillating fan. His friend said, "Wayne, whenever ye need it, jes' come get it."

"I will," he said.

So sure enough, on a day just as hot, Dad walked into the domino hall, straight past all the players, unplugged the fan, and started walking towards the door with it. They all just stared at him, sweat running down their faces. Dad didn't say a word until he got to the door. Then he turned around, looked at his friend, and said with a straight face, "That's what happens when ye don't pay the bill." Of course, his friend laughed and got the humor, but those other poor suckers wondered where their breeze had blown off to.

Dad had picked up his fan when he needed it just like he said he would. He can be a man of his word, and I think, most of the time, he really likes it when he is. Other times, I think he just keeps boxing his own self into a corner that he can't get out of.

⊨ ★ ⊯

I didn't think Delma would ever forgive me for taking her on a snipe hunt. When I came back from the Underwoods', I told her to grab a paper bag and I'd help her hunt for snipe. When she was at the front of the house, I'd run to the back and yell, "Delma, they're back here. Quick!"

When she'd run around the back, I'd say, "Aw, ye jes' missed one."

We did that back and forth until Aunt Nolie came out and said, "Delma, ye couldn't get even one?" And then she laughed her ass off. I guess there's always a time in snipe hunting when you know, even without being told, that there's no such thing. It took two days for Delma to talk to me again and a good week before I stopped laughing.

After summer ended, it was about time to start fourth grade. If I'd thought I hated Dad before then, I didn't know a damn thing. My insides started seeping hatred out my pores until they became so clogged I started attempting to fight back. But I was still a kid.

Soon I'll be in that ring with him, and I'll be the one putting him in the corner, shining *his* shoes.

CHAPTER 29

A Threat to Cut a Head Off and a Peek at God Jesus

1937–38

SINCE DAD'S FEELING better, we're back at the Tourist Court, and for the time being, done with mooching off Aunt Nolie and No-Account. The Tourist Court is close to Gene, so that's the good thing. I told him first thing about the blue lightning, and at first he didn't believe me. His dad's a straight shooter, so when Gene asked him, he said, "Blue lightning? Few folks ever get to see that. Tell Cono he's real lucky." Telling Gene about snipe hunting was another thing. "Aw, Cono, ya didn't fall fer that, did ya?"

"Not anymore I don't," I told him.

The bad thing about today is finding out that Mrs. Berry is my fourth-grade teacher. I can't believe it. She's supposed to have moved back to teaching second grade, which made sense to me since she's dumber than a box of hammers. But I guess Principal Pall is dumber than her.

The first day of school I'm sitting in the back hoping she won't see me. But she does. "Cono," she says, "sit on up here in front, where I can keep 'n eye on you-uh." I hate it when she says "you-uh," like it's two words instead of one.

Mrs. Berry doesn't like anything I do. She doesn't like the way I look, the way I walk, the way I smell, the way I put on my shoes. Well I don't like her neither. She stares at me from the corner of her crinkled-up eyes, just to find something else she doesn't like.

"Cono, you're pressin' down too hard with that pencil, you're gonna break it." "Cono, I can barely read what you're writing, it looks invisible." "Cono, you-uh got something to say or don't ya?" She thinks that she's higher and mightier than God Jesus himself. She walks with her nose so far up in the air that if she were a turkey, she'd drown. Turkeys do that. They're so stupid that if it starts raining they look up to see what's dropping on them and sniff! That's all it takes. They plumb drown in a drop of rain. You'd think they would have caught on after a while, seeing their loved ones plop down dead after looking up, and that would give them a clue. But no way. They ever look up just to see the pretty stars? Nah. They only look up when it's raining. Sniff! Dead. The only thing dumber than a turkey is the man that owns them, and he's about as sharp as one of Gene's marbles. Just like Mrs. Berry and Principal Pall.

Recess finally rolls around and I don't have to look at her mean face for twenty whole minutes. I find Gene outside and I tell him, "So, when she asked me if I had somethin' te say, ye know what I told her?"

"What?" says Gene.

"I said, 'Yes ma'am. Yer crazier 'n a bat and look ten times worse. What kinda teacher are ye anyhow? Ye don't teach us nothin' 'cept how to act like a horse's ass. Ye teach us how stupid we are, but the more I'm in your class the more stupid *you* get. Why don't ye just retire and beat rugs for a livin' instead 'a kids. What gives ye the right is what I wanna know?'"

Gene stares at me like I'm the crazy one. Then I laugh.

"Ah, hell, Cono, ya didn't say none of that. Shoot, if ya did ya wouldn't be able to sit here 'cause yer butt would be blistered."

We laugh a bit, catching up on our summer until we see a fight break out.

"Well, if it ain't Tommy Burns," says Gene, looking across the play yard.

"I thought he was supposed to be in sixth grade now," I say.

"Nah, he's in my grade, so I guess you've about caught up with him." We laugh some more and decide to watch the fight.

He's whuppin' up on a kid we call "Arty Bamma" when Mrs. Berry runs up to him and says, "Get off of him, Tommy."

"Jes't a minute," says Tommy, still punching.

"Tommy, you-uh get off 'a him this second."

"Jes't a minute," he says again. I hated the way he said that.

I can't for the life of me understand why she doesn't just slap him on the back of his head like she'd done mine that time. I think she's afraid of him; all the teachers are. That's probably why they didn't care when I stuck that pocketknife in him when I was in first grade. They wished they could have done it.

After school, Gene comes over and says, "Cono, I got somethin' te tell ya."

"Yeah?"

"I know why Mrs. Berry doesn't like ya."

"How ye know?"

"I told my dad about how mean she is to ya. And he says, 'Probably since Wayne hit that man in the chair four times 'for he could git up.'"

"So?"

"That man was her brother-in-law."

So, Mrs. Berry hates me because of what my dad had done to that man several years back. It doesn't make me hate her any less. It makes me hate Dad even more. I want to go home and tell Dad about what I'd learned, about how poorly I'm treated at school because of him. But I know what he'd say. He'd say something like, "Cono, what I did ain't none 'a yer concern, so I don't want ya ever to talk about it again." Then he'd probably slap me to make sure I was paying attention. Or he'd say, "So? Yer gettin' ta be a big enough boy. You can take care 'a yerself." Then he'd turn around and walk away, making me feel stupid again.

The only time I can remember Dad sticking up for me was when he told Delma not to look in my cigar box of specials.

⊨ ★ ⊨

Me, Gene, and the Allridge brothers have gotten used to walking the railroad tracks. The tracks stop at the cattle yard switching station, which is a good place to stop our own tracks. We pick lamb's-quarter weed since it's free and all and take it back to our mothers to boil for supper.

The switching station is also where we go to watch the cattle buyers. We talk about where we've been and where we plan to go. Donny says, "Jes' put me in a big city like Houston so I kin see more than ten folks at a time. Then I'll sign up with the navy and get te ride in a big boat and travel around the world."

"I'll swannin', Donny," Fred says. "If ye got on a boat, you'd get sick as a dog an' hafta come running home to yer mommy. Ye can't even ride two miles in a car without pukin'." Donny throws a rock towards him, and Fred says, "Besides, ye kin keep all them strangers te yerself. I like it here jes' fine."

"Then what're ye gonna do te make money?" I ask.

"Hell, I don't know. I ain't grown yet," he says, sticking another Tootsie Roll into his mouth. I know that Fred would just as soon stay here and play checkers with his cousins and wait for his "mommy" to yell, "Supper's ready."

"What about you, Cono? What're you gonna do?" asks Donny. I shrug my shoulders. I stare at those railroad tracks, see how the ties are lined up one after the other as far as I can see.

⊰ ★ ⊱

It's Sunday. Revival time at the Baptist church. I don't like it much, but the Allridge boys have invited me and the punch and cookies are good—that is, if I can hold my patience until the end when all the Amen-ing is done.

I stuff those cookies into my mouth two at a time. "Gracious me, Cono," says Mrs. Allridge, "looks like you ain't eaten anything for a month."

Almost every time I get to one of those revivals, the grown-ups say, "Cono, don't you want to be saved?"

"From what?" I say.

"Why the Devil hisself," they say, and then they add a bunch of amens to go along with it.

Unless they're thinking about Dad being the Devil, I just say, "No thank you."

"But what are you waitin for? We could baptize you right now and all your sins would be forgiven and you would have eternal life."

As far as sinning goes, I guess I've done my fair share of it. Amen.

"What's 'eternal' mean?" I ask.

"Well, it means you'll live forever with Jesus right next to you."

I picture Jesus standing right next to me while I'm thunk, thunk, thunkin' on a woodpile forever and ever into eternity, and it doesn't appeal to me one iota. Last year when we lived with Aunt Nolie, I didn't have much chopping to do. But now I have to chop all the time. Chop, chop, chop to make sure Mother has enough wood for the cookstove at the Tourist Court. Chop, chop, chop so Dad won't lay into me.

Anyway, I've heard stories about how some churches take a poor person's last dime so they can put more gold up by the Jesus statue. Then, a penniless old woman with only one shoe and five starving children crawls away with her head all covered up, as if she's ashamed of being broke. It doesn't make no sense to me whatsoever. It seems to me that Jesus would want you to keep most of your money so you don't have to starve and die and can at least make it to church to pray. What gets me is watching them churchgoers and knowing that they talk all big about Jesus, but when they get home, they just keep doing their sinning anyway, like they'd forgotten every word they'd learned. Maybe all you have to do is say you believe in Jesus and then you'll be saved no matter how you act. But what do I know? I ain't been saved yet.

H. Govan is different. He's a religious man who doesn't talk about being religious. In fact, he rarely talks about Jesus at all. You can tell by the way he treats people that he knows Jesus real well. Maybe not talking about Jesus so much and not making others feel like heathens is one sure way to let folks know that Jesus can live inside you peacefully. Not like those folks who yell on the outside about Jesus and end up pissing everybody off. Anyway, Mr. H., he treats everyone with respect even if, in my opinion, they ain't deserving of it, like he does my dad.

Pa grew up being a member of Church of Christ, but Ma grew up being a Baptist. Pa says that Baptists are all just a bunch of "Camel Lights." Ma used to tell me, "Thar ain't nothin' wrong with readin' the Bible, Cono." Maybe I'll read it someday and find out more about "An eye for an eye" and "Turn the other cheek," like they mentioned at the revival while I was praying for my punch and cookies. I reckon they're saying that "Turn the other cheek" means if Dad slaps me on my right cheek side, I should turn my head so he can hit the left one too, and "An eye for an eye" means if somebody pulls out your eye, you can turn around and pluck out one of theirs. Ma's a good, God-loving woman who always tells me, "Cono, ain't no sense in not bein' polite." But I don't think plucking out someone's eyeball is a very polite thing to do.

Like I said, religion makes no sense to me whatsoever.

⊰ ★ ⊱

I was right. Mr. Pall, our principal, is dumber than dirt. Yesterday I saw him trying to fit boxes into his car. He had to load and unload the cardboard so many times to make them all fit, it was like he couldn't figure out if he was coming or going. He's what my dad would call "an educated idiot."

I see Mr. Pall staring out his office window watching the All-ridge boys and me. All we're doing is walking around the school-yard waiting for school to start, but the way he's staring at us makes me wonder if they've passed a new law or something that says kids can't go to school too early and just hang around, 'cause we were at school early just hanging around.

"Cono, come in here," yells Mr. Pall from his window.

He said it like he's tougher than a pair of old leather boots, probably because he used to be some kinda wrestler or something. He isn't nearly as tough as Dad, who last week had beaten a man unconscious on Main Street just because the man spouted off to him. I walk into his office, where's he's sitting behind his desk looking puffed up with importance.

"Cono, were you smoking in the schoolyard?"

"No sir, I wadn't."

"Were the Allridge boys smoking?" I think, *Why didn't ye just call them in here like you've done me?* but I don't say that. Maybe it was Mr. Pall's brother-in-law, who Dad had beaten up last week.

"I have no idee, sir," I say. "I reckon you oughta ask them."

His right eye stares a hole in my left eyeball. His left one kinda wanders around on its own, like it's been punched one too many times. Maybe he grunts with Mrs. Berry on occasion.

He opens up his desk drawer and pulls out a rubber hose. He thumps it on the desk a few times and says, "Well, I need to whip you with this hose."

I stare back into his bad eye with both of my good ones and say, "Go ahead, sir. But I jes' half to tell ye that my daddy said if you ever laid a hand on me, he'd have to come up here and whup you." I say it real nice, though.

He sits real quiet in his principal's chair, like he's picturing himself drawing a crowd on Main Street while my dad beats the tar outta his one good eye. While he was chewing on that idea like a piece of gum, I was busy staring at him, thinking that his front teeth stick out so far he could eat an apple through a keyhole. After that picture in my mind, I'm not scared one little bit.

Finally, he says, "Git on outta here, Cono."

"Yes sir," I say, 'cause there's no sense in not being polite.

At lunchtime I'm eating my sandwich, minding my own business, when Tommy scopes me out and says, "Cono, what'cha got fer lunch?"

Even though he's five times bigger than me I say, "It don't make no difference 'cause you ain't getting none of it."

"Cono, you shouldn't 'a stuck that knife in me that time."

I look up at him with a face as serious as Dad's and say, "Tommy, if ye mess with me in any way, shape 'r form, I'll cut your head plumb off with the same pocketknife I used before."

And just as I'm picturing his dead body without a head like Wort Reynolds, Tommy Burns walks away.

School's out for the day, and it was another discouraging one. I grab Delma's hand and start walking back home, now having a little time to think about what happened.

The Allridge boys had been smoking like a bunch a chimney stacks, but I ain't one to rat on somebody else when it's none of my business. And, I like to think that Dad would beat the tar outta Mr. Pall if he laid a hand on me. But Dad never said that. If Dad ever finds out that I lied I might as well curl up in a ball and prepare myself—or maybe just grab my axe.

Lying isn't always a bad thing. Sometimes we have to lie in order to protect ourselves and the people we care about.

An "eye for an eye" is what I did today. Maybe that part of the Bible makes sense after all.

CHAPTER 30

69 Miles to Temple

DAD TRIED TO help me once during that fourth-grade year. I wanted to fight like Joe Louis, but of course, I couldn't.

Almost every day of that year Hicks Boy came by the house, grabbed my ears, and whupped me good. He was several years older and several years bigger. I didn't have any beef with him, so back then I just figured he was mad that he didn't have a proper first name. Even his own dad called him Hicks Boy. Once there was a rumor that his first name was Francis, so maybe that's why he was always so mad.

Anyway, my Dad finally figured out that Hicks Boy was beating me on a regular basis, so he said to me, "Cono, here's what ya do. Every time ya see him, ya go out and ya hit him first. If yer in school and he's gettin' a drink 'a water at the water fountain, when he turns 'round, ya hit him. Now, don't hit him whiles he's drinkin', but hit him as soon as he turns 'round. Pretty soon, he'll quit fightin' with ya."

Well, Hicks Boy would come by, I'd jump on him, and he'd whup me. At school when he got a drink of water, he'd turn around, and I'd hit him, and he'd whup me again. By the end of the year, Hicks Boy came up to me and said, "Cono, lets us be friends. There ain't no reason for you and me to fight no more." "OK," I told him, since there's no sense in not being polite. Hicks Boy couldn't beat me now, no matter how big he is.

A few weeks ago, I got to use some of the boxing and survival skills I'd learned growing up and, truth being told, I enjoyed every minute of it. A captain in charge came in to see me about a problem he was having. He said, "We've got a cooks' barracks that no one can control. Can you go over there and straighten that barracks out?"

"My way?" I asked, taking another sip of PX coffee.

"Yes, Sergeant, your way, and I'll not bother you none."

The problem was, when bulletins were put up in those barracks, those boys would tear them down before they read them. If they were told to fall out, maybe they'd stumble out or maybe they wouldn't come out at all. The only thing that was steady about that group was the fact that they were all cooks, but other than that they weren't steady at all.

I went straight over there and called them all together.

"I'm just gonna tell you this one time," I said. "If anything goes up on that board it stays there. You don't touch it. When I tell you to 'fall out' in the morning, you fall out and you fall out right then."

Hutch was the most calm of the group and seemed like he wouldn't mind a little order himself, so I turned to him and said, "Hutch, you're gonna be the bay chief."

The next morning I walked into the cooks' barracks at 0400,

hearing nothing but a bunch of air sucking from all the snoring going on. Then I yelled, "Fall out!" Those boys did fairly good at getting up considering they weren't used to welcoming the sun to the morning. But there's one in every crowd who thinks he's too tough to follow the rules. This guy's name was Johnson, a former merchant marine with big old biceps who thought he could fight a circular saw and come out ahead. He pulled the cover over his head. That son of a bitch had ignored me.

Everyone was watching me, so I knew I had an impression to make. I walked over and said, "Well aren't you smart?" Then I took that cot and flipped it right in the middle of him.

He stood up, towering over me like a big gorilla, stared down at me, and drew back. Now, the thing about big ol' boys like Johnson is that they might have a lot of muscle and power, but for a lightweight-class like me, they move like molasses. When he drew his big arm back, my fist landed square on his chin before his pea brain could register what hit him. He dropped like a loose button, out cold.

When Johnson started to stir a bit, he looked at me with surprise and reached up to feel his mouth, like he was making sure all his teeth were still there.

"It's OK," I told him. "I know a couple of folks without any teeth at all and they can still eat almost anything; jes' takes a little longer is all."

He sat there glaring at me, and I kept talking.

"And if you keep puckerin' like that, pretty soon your face is gonna match your asshole. Now get up!" I said, worthy of Earl Adams. Everybody laughed except for Johnson. I guess he didn't think it was funny. But he did stand up and, so far, Johnson and the rest of the guys in the cooks' barracks have been looking at me in a different light. I don't count on Johnson looking down on me ever again. Besides, he couldn't fight the gnats off his butt.

I suppose the fighting instinct was born into me, like red is born into a beet. Maybe it's because I was fighting in first grade, the time I stuck that pocketknife into the thigh of Tommy Burns. Or maybe I'd learned from the best. I've made up for Oklahoma and Hicks Boy. Now I'm more like Jessie Perkins.

Sometimes the fight's over before the bell rings, but not always.

Cono's boxing gloves

CHAPTER 31

Fur Coats and Handcuffs

1938

THE GALLAGHERS LIVE next door to us. Dorothy is about my age, and as girls go, she's right up there on top. She's really more like a boy than a girl anyhow. Lottie is Dorothy's mother, and I like her a lot too, even though she's got no teeth and is uglier than home-made soap.

Dorothy's got an older sister, Genevieve, and a little brother called "Spurt." He's a real pistol. Delma likes playing with him. She likes to practice her mothering skills on him like what Aunt Nolie does to us since she doesn't have any kids.

The Gallaghers are over at our house drinking up Aunt Nolie's beer, and Spurt hears a sound that none of the rest of us caught on to.

"What's that?" he says.

"What's what?" says Mr. Gallagher.

The little feller walks over to the closet, opens the door, and slams it real fast.

"What is it?" Dad asks.

In his best three-year-old grown-up voice he says, "It's a goddamn booger!" Everybody laughed, especially Delma and me. We thought our innards were gonna split open.

"I think that boy's been shot with a Victrola needle," says Dad.

I go outside to chop wood and hear Dorothy say, "C'mon, Cono. Let's you and me go walk around town."

"What fer?" I ask.

"Jes' fer fun."

"OK, but I gotta finish up here first. If I don't, Dad'll knock me upside the head with a *tar* tool, out like Lottie's eye."

"My mother might not have all her teeth but she's still got both her eyes."

"Not Lottie your mother. Another Lottie."

"Who you talkin' about, Cono?"

"It's just a sayin', fer cryin' out loud. Heard it all my life."

"Hmm," she says and sits down on a nearby stump and watches me swing my axe.

"Ye ever gonna get married, Cono?"

"Hell, I don't know, haven't even thought on it."

"Well, I think yer' too ugly to take a wife."

I laugh and say, "Well, you ain't exactly Miss Texas neither." Then we both laugh.

"Are ya about done?"

"What's yer hurry?"

"Bored I guess. Haven't done nothin' fun all day."

"Ye expect te have fun every day?"

"Sure I do, don't you?"

I put the axe back under the awning of the Tourist Court and start walking into town with Dorothy, who's walking next to me trying to untangle the mess in her hair.

"Look up ahead there, Cono!"

"What?"

"A calf walking down Main Street!"

Sure enough there's a little Hereford calf wandering around like it's window-shopping for jewelry or a new hat. Other folks are laughing and pointing as they watch that calf take a stroll down Main Street. Dorothy and me get the same idea.

"Let's get her!" I say.

"OK, but what're we gonna do with her after we've caught her?"

"Hell, we'll sell her to the highest bidder, maybe start our careers as cattlemen!" Even though Cono, Texas, means I'd be a rich man who owns the whole town, I still want to be a rancher just like Ike. Best to get a head start on things.

We take off real slow towards that calf, and when I get close enough, I spring off my feet to grab her and land flat on my face in the dirt. Then Dorothy does the same thing.

"She's a tough little booger," pants Dorothy.

"Shor is."

We try for most of an hour to catch that damn calf, but all we have to show for it is dirt in our hair and ears, even between our teeth. We laid there in the dirt laughing and panting so hard that Dorothy had to keep jabbing me in the ribs with her elbow like she was trying to remind me how funny it was.

We start our walk back home when Dorothy says, "We'll get her next time."

"Yeah, next time we'll bring a rope."

"Yeah, and maybe somethin' fer her ta eat."

"Like what? Left over lamb's-quarter?"

"That'll do fer starters."

"Well, she can sure have my portion. I hate that crap."

"It ain't so bad when ya get used to it, Cono."

"I'm used to it all right. Still don't like it. That calf can have all she wants as far as I'm concerned."

When I get home, Mother takes one look at me and says, "Cono, ye git to the showers right now! It don't matter how long the line is, ye wait in it 'til ye come back clean as a whistle." This time, I do as I'm told.

⊨ ★ ⊨

Yesterday was the best day ever. Hardley Saddler rolled up in his wagon, pitched a tent, and started up his Medicine Ahow. He told us about his elixirs and about how, if we bought them, they could treat most of our ailments. If he had an elixir for meanness, I would have bought a bottle right then and there, mixed it into a Pearl beer, and taken it straight home.

Hardley Saddler had all kinds of shows to see and games to play. Dorothy and me grabbed a couple of big slices of watermelon that were lying off to the side of the food tent and started to walk off to see one of the contests.

"Hey, you kids!" yelled a man behind the table.

"What?" Dorothy said turning around. "My mother done paid for these," she lied through her teeth. She stared at him like he'd just thrown a punch at her. He waved us away making a face.

One of the games was a contest to see who could hammer their one big nail the fastest into the wooden board. This contest was only open to girls since there were other contests open for boys.

"Hey, look who's enterin' the contest," said Dorothy, spitting a watermelon seed at my face. I spat one back and saw Aunt Nolie and Genevieve stepping up to the boards. Then Dorothy and me started a contest all our own, seeing how far we could spit the watermelon seeds. Damn, that girl can spit. I bet she's had lots of practice.

Besides Aunt Nolie and Genevieve there were five other ladies lined up at the board. The whistle blew and there they were, those gals pounding their nails in such a hurry you would've thought they were putting up a church roof to keep Jesus dry before a storm. We were all cheerin' and a hollerin' for our favorite girl, and wouldn't you know it? I was still picturing Freezer's eyeballs twitching and Aunt Nolie hammering something else.

Aunt Nolie got real close to winning, her face dripping with girl sweat. But Genevieve, Dorothy's older sister, slammed that nail in quicker than a racehorse coming out the gate.

After Genevieve was declared the winner, I couldn't believe what the first prize was. Genevieve had won herself a brand-new, over-the-knee fur coat. Even the folks who had rooted for someone else to win were hooting and clapping that at least one person in Rotan now owns a new fur coat.

I spent most of the night thinking about the Medicine Show. When I wake up, I peek out the window and see Lottie, Genevieve's mother, standing outside her Tourist Court cabin, a cigarette dangling from her bottom lip and her feet barefoot in the snow. She looks over and waves to me like she does every morning. But on this particular day, she waves to me like she was the Queen of England, standing there wearing nothing but a toothless grin and a brand-new over-the-knee fur coat.

At school all we can talk about at school is Hardley Saddler's Medicine Show. For two days, everybody has been sharing their own stories about what they saw, did, or heard. Me seeing Lottie standing on her front porch was the funniest of all.

As we're walking home from school that afternoon, Delma says, "I shor am hungry, Cono."

"Didn't ye eat yer lunch?"

"Yeah, but I gave Sally Burns half my sandwich."

I was thinking about her older brother, so I said, "How come? She didn't threaten ye did she?"

"No, but she didn't have anything fer lunch. Not even a cracker." Maybe Tommy and his sister are even more poor than we are.

"We're almost home anyhow. Maybe we still got some lamb's-quarter left over from dinner."

"That ain't funny, Cono. Ye know how I hate lambs squatter!"

"Lamb's-quarter," I corrected.

"Whatever, I hate it."

We round the corner to our street to see Mother standing on the front porch waiting for us. We race to the steps, stopping in front of her.

"Kids, I got somethin' te tell ye."

"What, Mamma?" pants Delma.

"Yer Dad's in jail."

CHAPTER 32

65 Miles to Temple

I'VE NEVER BEEN to jail nor do I plan to ever go. Growing up, sometimes I felt like I was in jail just from living under the same roof as Dad. I can't imagine being all boxed in like that. I'd think the roof was coming down to cover me up.

When I found out about what Sheriff P. V. Hail had done, it made me outright mad. Not because of my Dad but because of Ike. It wasn't until Dad's jail time that I found out about something else that happened to Ike long before.

P. V. had caught Ike staggering around Rotan like a drunk man, which he was. Ike wasn't hurting anybody. He was just bleeding his lizard on Main Street. Instead of arresting Ike and putting him in the jailhouse to sleep it off, he beat the shit out of him first. I hated hearing that. I hated hearing that anyone could treat my grandfather with such little respect. I think P. V. did it because he suffered from small man's disease. He was so short he could have made a good butt doctor.

Dad had been drinking coffee in Rotan's café trying to sober up a bit before he came home. After the waitress brought him his sugar, she said, "I'll be right back with a spoon."

"Don't need no spoon," Dad said. Then he reached into the back of his britches, brought out his pistol, and started stirring his coffee with it.

Needless to say, that waitress called the sheriff. When Dad walked outta that café, P. V. was pointing his own gun straight up at Dad's forehead.

Dad was smart enough not to put up a fight. Instead, he put up his hands and told him where the gun was. P. V. took the gun and then took his time patting Dad down. Then P. V. got real low, like he was checking Dad's ankles, but he was really getting down out of the line of fire. That's when Dad noticed one of P. V.'s deputies standing behind a truck about a hundred feet away, crosshairing a rifle straight at him. If Dad had wanted to he could have plucked up his gun and killed them both before they'd had time to blink. Instead, Dad just nodded at the deputy and smiled as if to say, "If ya planned on ambushin' me, ya shoulda hidden yourself a little better."

Ike and Dad hinted that it might have been a setup, but they weren't real sure why. Maybe it was something to do with Aunt Nolie's bootlegging, or maybe something a little closer to home?

CHAPTER 33

Jail Time and a Longer Sentence

1938

DAD HAS BEEN in the Roby jailhouse, our county seat, for one night now. He has one more night to go. Tonight, the Rushings have invited all of us to go into Roby, not to see Dad but to take Mother to a dance. Mother loves to dance. She's all gussied up, even wearing her best shoes. Delma and me get to tag along and go to a picture show. We all get into the Rushings' shiny red pickup truck and head off to Roby. Delma and me laugh and giggle 'cause we're out of jail instead of in one.

"That's where yer Dad is," says Mother as we follow behind her clicking shoes towards the theater. She points to the three-story building with bars on the windows.

"What's he doin' in there, Mamma?" asks Delma.

"Not much to do in there but think. Shor hope that's what he's doin'."

Mr. Rushing hands Delma and me a dollar bill each, more

than enough for two tickets, popcorn, and sodas. I feel like a rich man riding high on a hog. "Ya'll have a good time now," he says.

"Thank ye, Mr. Rushing," I say.

"Yeah, thank ye, Mr. Rushing," copies Delma.

"Now when the picture show's over, ya'll wait right outside 'til we come git ye," says Mother.

Delma and me walk straight into the Roby Theater right next to the jailhouse.

⋈ ★ ⋈

The Land Beyond the Law was about a man who becomes a sheriff when his father is killed by rustlers. The whole time I'm sitting in those nice theater chairs, I keep thinking it would be just as much fun to be sitting in front of the jailhouse, making up stories about what Dad was doing in jail, kinda like how Gene made up stories about Mrs. Berry. I do it anyway, trying to watch the picture show at the same time. I picture Dad banging on the cell bars with a tin cup yelling, "Let me outta here, you sons a bitches!" I picture him arching his back trying to make it pop and asking for his Pearl medicine. I picture him playing dominoes with his cellmate and betting him our rent money.

When the show's over, we stand outside to wait for Mother and the Rushings. Delma points over to the jailhouse and whispers, "Cono, now what's he doin' in there?"

"Bangin' on his cell bars with a tin cup and askin' fer Pearl beer."

"He is?"

"I dunno, maybe," I say. "But don't worry, they won't let him out 'til he gets better and learns his lesson." Of course, I'm probably expecting a little too much from the judicial system of Fisher County.

We ride back home the same way we'd come, in that shiny red pickup truck. Mother's giggling with Mrs. Rushing like she's had a few beers too. She sounds happy tonight.

"Whew," she says, "My dogs shor are barkin'." Mother pulls off her fancy shoes and starts rubbing her feet.

"Did ye dance, Mamma?" asks Delma.

"I shor did. I danced and danced. Gonna sleep good tonight, I reckon."

"Who'd ye dance with?" I ask.

"Anybody that would ask me, so I danced the whole night," she giggled.

"Yep, everybody asked her," says a smiling Mr. Rushing. "Yer mother's a good dancer too."

"Ain't that good, but it doesn't matter. I like it. Felt free as a bird," she says, still rubbing her feet.

"Even though it hurts?" asks Delma.

"Doesn't hurt while yer dancin', only hurts when ye stop. Ye don't even think about yer feet when they're movin' 'round a dance floor."

"Does Daddy ever dance with ye?" asks Delma.

"Umph, that'd be the day. He doesn't like it. Hurts his back, I reckon."

"But why won't he dance with ye if ye like it so much?"

"That's a whole nuther story," she says and stops talking to look out the window.

I don't think I've ever heard Mother talk so much at one time. She was all happy down to her aching toes until Delma had to bring Dad into the conversation. I hope she sleeps real good and peaceful tonight and dreams she's dancing on the moon.

The sunlight coming in my window gets me up and moving. I'm already chopping wood with my newly sharpened axe when

Dad gets out of a stranger's car and thanks him for the ride. I guess his jail time is over and ours has started up again. He walks straight over to me and says, "Why was your mother in Roby last night?"

He'd seen us, sure enough. While Sis and I were watching rustlers being shot or hung, Dad was looking out his barred windows and pondering what his wife was doing walking past him in her dancing shoes. I don't answer. I just keep swinging my axe.

"Son," he says again, "I asked ya a question. Why was your mother in Roby?"

I stop chopping long enough to turn towards him, but I'm holding my axe tight in both hands.

"I ain't telling ye nothin'. It ain't none 'a my business."

He starts a fire in his eyes, looks down at my sharp axe and back to my own eyes that stay unflinching and ready. *Here's my chance*, I think to myself. *Let Slewfoot limp towards me just once, and I'll be ready.*

I think he'd been a little sat on in that jail, like he didn't feel like such a tushhog anymore. Maybe he was just tired from all that banging with his tin cup. All I know is this. We lock eyes for a bit and then he turns away from me and walks into the house. I keep chopping wood.

I put the cover on my axe and walk back into the house. Dad is gone, and Delma is playing with Pooch outside. I walk in to see Mother sitting at the kitchen table, her hands covering her face.

"What's the matter?"

"Nothin', Cono, jes' tired is all." But her eyes are swollen and red.

Dad doesn't come home until the sun has set. Nobody talks, not even Delma or Mother, since Dad can take a word and turn it into a civil war. I go to bed and hear Ike's voice and the sound of coffees being stirred.

"Wayne, I told ya he'd find a reason to git ta get ya."

"Ah hell, he thinks he's tougher 'n a woodhauler's ass is all."

"I'm dead serious now, Wayne. I think he's keepin' an eye on all the bootleggers around here, but for whatever reason, 'specially for anyone connected to you. Some things jus' don't add up's all I'm sayin'."

I listen to the continuing sound of coffee being slurped.

"Anyhow," Ike says, "you know what they say."

"What's that?"

"There ain't nothin' worse than bein' woken up in the middle 'a the night to the feelin' 'a yer balls bein' squeezed and hearin' the sound of a pocketknife bein' opened up at the same time."

That's when I sum up something on my own; I ain't the only one looking over his own shoulder. We're in the land beyond the law.

⊰ ★ ⊱

The spring has come and gone, and today I wake up happy. Today is the last day of school and we get to go to Ranger and see Ma and Pa. But I'm also happy that today is the last time I'll have to lay my eyes or ears on old Mrs. Head-Thumping Berry.

Instead, I go in to school only to hear, "Cono, I'm not gonna pass you-uh on to fifth grade. You-uh need another year of fourth."

I just got my own jail sentence.

CHAPTER 34

Spewing Up a Storm of a Different Kind

1938

WE PACK UP all our stuff and get ready to leave. I run over to say bye to Gene, telling him I'll see him again at the beginning of the school year.

"Ya want me ta pay Mrs. Berry a few visits while yer gone? Ya know, offer to feed her twenty-seven cats 'r somethin'?"

"You bet," I say, still knowing that, like always, Gene's got my back.

"Well, guess I'll be seeing ya after the summer then."

"After the summer," I say, then I hit him on the shoulder so he can hit me back.

I finally get to see Ma and Pa again after a long drive and that throat-lumpy hill. Ma's still skinner than a post, and Pa still has no teeth. I'm trying not to think on next school year since it doesn't do any good no how.

For the last few days, I've been riding on Polo and settling in a bit. My cousins Harold and Darryl have come over to welcome us back. I don't know why it is, but whenever we're living with somebody else—Aunt Nolie or Ma and Pa—Dad's a little easier on us. So, when Harold asks me to go mess around with them, Dad says, "Go on, then."

Me, Harold, and Darryl and a couple of their friends spend most of the day at Connelly Creek. I swim like a fish and jump off that rope like nobody's business.

"It was me that taught ye how to swim, 'member, Cono?" asks Harold.

"Yeah, and there ain't no flies in a kitchen," I tell him.

The Texas sun dries us off while Harold starts talking about girls.

"Them titties are soft as a stack 'a warm pancakes," he says, "with a pink pat of butter right in the middle!" I think he's pretending to know a whole lot more about girls than what he does. I think he's just showing off.

So, it's all new to me when Harold says, "OK, boys," pointing to a rock on the ground, "there's the target. When I say 'go,' start the spewin' contest."

Now, I've heard of peeing contests since I've done them before. I'm good at it too, 'cause I can wait all day before I have to bleed my lizard. But these boys do something different. They pull their pants down to their knees, and on the count of three, they spit in their hands and start pumping their wieners. It doesn't take me too long to figure out what they're doing. It ain't pee they're trying to spew out the farthest.

They're all grimacing and pumping, sometimes slow, sometimes fast until one of them whoops and hollers first. The other ones don't stop, though. They keep on going like there's a second and third place. I just watch, knowing that I'll have to think about spewing on my own time. Like when I'm alone somewhere.

Today is a good summer day in Ranger, Texas. Ma and Mother have made a fine dinner of roast and mashed potatoes. I sit at the table eating more than my fair share, thinking how good my belly feels. I watch Mother fix another plate and cover it up with a dish towel.

"Cono," she says, "take this plate to yer Dad at the domino hall." The domino hall in Ranger is a good two miles from here, so I have to tell my belly that, instead of a rest, it'll have to settle in for a walk.

By the time I get there, I'm sweating up a storm. I walk up the hot metal steps of the domino hall and straight through the door and see billows of cigar smoke circling the heads of domino players like dirty halos. I find the table Dad's sitting at.

"Mother said to bring yer lunch."

"Cono, you been smokin'?" he asks.

"No sir, I don't smoke."

"Don't lie to me," he says. I gawk at him for a minute not believing my ears and then, before I know it, he reaches over and slaps me across the face in front of God and everyone.

I want to say something, but any words I think about saying are stuck in the sting on my face and the embarrassment under my skin. The roast beef and potatoes start to feel like they want me to taste them all over again.

If I wanted to smoke, I would, and that's all there is to it. All I'd have to do is just grab a little tobacco off Mother and Dad since they both look like they're on fire most of the time.

I turn around and walk the two miles back to Ma and Pa's,

feeling even hotter than before. Now I want to spew something, rattle snake venom into that son of a bitch's neck. My shirt is covered in sweat, a sweat that drips down my loose pants and down my butt crack.

I go back to my room, lie on my bed, and decide I don't want to talk to anybody, not one soul, maybe never again. Mother asks me what's wrong, why I'm not out messing around. "Nothing's wrong," I say. "Not one goddamn thing." She looks at me but I turn away, trying to get my belly to behave itself.

CHAPTER 35

36 Miles to Temple

THIS TRAIN'S JUST passed through Georgetown, another fella who got a town named after him.

The only thing I can think of about that time in the domino hall was that Dad hated cigar smoke and maybe wanted to make a point to all those cigar-smoking domino players. Or maybe he was craving his habit of slapping me, since he never lays a hand on me in front of Ma or Pa. But, more than likely, he was losing his ass in the gambling business of that day. Don't matter, though. What he did was wrong. I knew it back then, and I know it now. A normal person would have at least offered up a "Thank you" after having a hot meal delivered to them.

I still haven't taken up the habit of smoking, but maybe when I get to Temple it will be a good time to start. I'll start a storm all on my own, the kind he's afraid of. I'll grab one of Dad's cigarettes off the coffee table, light it up in front of him, and say, "Damn, I've always liked these."

Better yet, I'll stop off and buy a big fat cigar, light it up, and say, "Dad, ye ready to spar yet? Come and get me, you son of a bitch."

CHAPTER 36

Pedaling Forward and Standing Up

1938

AUNT EVA AND her husband, Roy, have shown up with a present just for me. Costing him three dollars and fifty cents, Roy has built me a bike made from scraps he's found. I stare at it not believing my own eyes. It's not the prettiest thing I've seen, rusty in some parts and bent in others. But it's my very first bike. When Mother says, "Cono, what ye say?" I say what I feel.

"Shor do 'preciate ye, Uncle Roy."

"My pleasure, Cono," he says back. "Now, ye have any idee how te ride one 'a these things?"

"I tried once," I say, fibbing just a bit. Some of the boxing ring kids in Rotan had themselves bikes, but I never asked to ride one. I figured they would have offered if they'd wanted me to. But I had stood over one once, felt the handlebars under my palms and the seat touching my butt.

I had seen friends on bikes, racing around each other, ramming their front tires together until they fell over laughing. I could only smile at their fun, like getting close enough to touch it but never getting the feel of it. Like a guitar.

"Well, let's you and me take a few lessons."

After a few falls and lessons, the day of practice pays off. I'm an official bike rider. Sure wish Uncle Roy had been around to teach me how to use a toothbrush and to tie my shoes. He's a real good teacher.

Later that night my arms, legs, and butt are shouting a few cuss words at me. But I don't care. The soreness was all worth it. Pa and I sit on the front porch, watching the day spill away, and I ask, "Pa, ye ever ride a bike?"

"Nah, never really rode one," he says. "Tried to once, but my spurs got tangled up in the spokes."

I laugh at the picture he'd just put in my head: Pa wearing spurs while riding a bike. Then when he starts hee-hawing a mouthful empty of teeth, I laugh even harder.

I spend over a month riding that bike, taking Delma on rides, her on the seat and me standing up pedaling. Every so often I remember to ride on Polo, who looks jealous that I'm riding something with wheels. I don't ever want Polo to feel left out. I know that feeling and I don't like it.

Day by day and part by part, my new homemade bicycle starts to fall apart. Now all I have left is a handlebar, and since it's too big to put in my box of specials, I'll just have to remember that I had it. I will, too. Between Polo and my bike, I didn't have much time to be thinking about doing fourth grade all over again with that teacher from hell.

It's August now and hotter than a piece of coal held in the

right hand of a two-year-old. Mr. Hager, Pa's neighbor, is over, and I hear him say, "Jim, I need someone to drive my hay rake. Who'd be the youngest 'a yer bunch?"

"That'd be Cono," I hear Pa say. "Cono, c'mon over here and meet Mr. Hager."

We shake hands and he tells me what he needs done, to drive his Spanish mule on a hay rake. Without thinking on it twice I say, "OK sir, I'll do it."

"Fine. I'll pay ye fifty cents a day."

Money in my pocket is what I'm thinking. I don't even know what I'll do with that money since a guitar or a donkey don't appeal to me no more. I'll think of something.

After Mr. Hager leaves, Pa says, "Cono, be careful with him now. He's got a reputation of being a no-pay."

I think about working as a seed seller and not getting anything to show for it. Still, I want another try at making an honest living. Besides, it's not like I have any other offers.

In the heat of August, I sweat up and down Mr. Hager's fields, driving his hay rake. Now I know why he wanted someone young. His Spanish mule's back is all caved in from being skinny and overworked, so at least somebody little like me won't kill him. I drive that hay rake for fifteen days, and now Mr. Hager owes me seven dollars and fifty cents. I store up his poor mule and say, "I'm all done, Mr. Hager."

"OK, Cono. I'll see ye later then, and I'll pay ye."

"OK," I say, my empty pockets itching to be scratched.

Two whole weeks have gone by and I haven't seen hide nor hair of that money or of Mr. Hager.

"If I knew where Mr. Hager was I'd go git my money," I tell Pa while he saddles up his horse.

Pa gums out, "Well, I don't know about gettin' your money, Cono, but I do know where Mr. Hager's at."

"Where?" I squint.

"He's up at the American Legion playin' dominos. Ye know, right yonder above Joe Harn's drugstore."

"Sure I know," I say. I sure do know alright. That's where Dad slapped me in front of all those domino players.

I take off walking the two miles back to town, and the longer and hotter I get, the madder I am.

What seems like a hundred years later, I walk up those familiar metal stairs on the outside of the building with sweat just pouring off my head like I was a water spigot. I open the door and see three tables of domino players. Sure enough, Mr. Hager is sitting at one of them, wearing a cowboy hat and puffing on a big fat cigar. He watches me walk towards him, seeing my face all sweaty with mad. He leans backwards, balancing himself on the back two legs of his chair, which makes his potbelly stick out even further.

"Cono, what're ye doing here?"

"I came to git my money, sir."

Over the sound of dominoes being shuffled on scratched-up wooden tables and grown men hee-hawing over my statement, Mr. Hager says, "Well, what if I don't wanna give it to ye right now?" His eyeballs sit on mine like they're digging in to make a permanent home. I stare back just as hard.

His domino friends notice that I haven't even flinched or cracked a smile. They stop laughing. Everything gets real quiet. I wait. I brace my left hand on the table for leverage and say, "Then I'll have te fight ye fer it right now."

Mr. Hager smiles with one side of his mouth and holds on to his cigar with the other half. He takes a big puff on his cigar and blows it right towards my face. I don't even cough. I want to, but I don't. I just keep staring at him.

Mr. Hager puts all four chair legs back down on the floor where they're supposed to be in the first place. He sticks a hand in his pocket and I think he might shoot me in front of his friends just to show how tough he is. Instead of a pistol, he pulls out exactly seven dollars and fifty cents.

"There ye go, son," he says, grinning like it's all been another game. He lays the money in my sweaty, outstretched hand.

"'Preciate it," I say, since there's no sense in not being polite.

Then I turn around and go back down those metal stairs with a spring in my step, an ease on my mind, and hard-earned money in my pocket. I'm walking in tall cotton. Going home I feel a cool breeze on my back.

As I walk closer to Ma and Pa's, I realize there was a valuable lesson in there somewheres. Maybe one lesson is knowing that if my dad had a reputation for being tough that he had passed it on to me.

It felt good to make my own money, but how many people do I have to fight to keep it? I was reminded yet again that I was the only one I could really trust and to never count on nobody but my own self.

CHAPTER 37

26 Miles to Temple

I NEVER SPENT that money on myself. Since we were fixing to move back to Rotan I gave it to Mother. Whenever I could, I gave her any money I earned so she could hide it away from Dad. She called it our "safety cushion." Neither one of us wanted to take the chance of having another onion soup night.

What I didn't know at the time was that we weren't gonna be on our own in Rotan, and all that summer's worry about spending a whole nuther lifetime in Mrs. Berry's class again was for nothing. We were on our way to living at the ranch with Ike. The only disappointment I had about the new change of events was that unless I got into town, I wouldn't get to see Gene very often.

I also didn't know that the beginning of that summer of 1938, when Gene had shoulder-punched me good-bye, was the last time I'd ever see him.

Jim Dennis, my great-grandfather, bought the ranch in 1904.

When he decided to retire to a simpler life than cowboying, he told Ike he could run the place. Great Grandpa Dennis took Granny Dennis and moved to town.

Jim's recountings of his younger days were filled with pioneering stories and Indian raids. "After the Civil War, the country was full of unbranded cattle and it was customary for cowmen to brand everythin' in sight. We sorta tapered off, though, when the cattle brandin' law went into force. In the free branding days, there was grass enough for all, and plenty of cattle, but the cattle had small market value. In 1881 fencing became general, and free pasture was a thing of the past," he told us great grandkids. "I remember the days when Fort Griffin was a boomtown. The center of buffalo hide and bone business. Hunters outfitted their parties at Fort Griffin and brought their hides and bones there to be sold. When the buffalo were all killed and the Indians had been put on the reservations, Fort Griffin's businessmen moved to Albany and the old fort was soon a ghost town."

Great Grandpa Dennis also told us that doctors were few and far between, but not many people got sick. "Couldn't afford to get down with doctors twenty-five miles away. There weren't any dentists, and teeth seemed to last nearly as long as the folks did. Maybe the pioneer diet of beans, syrup, bread, meat, and coffee wadn't so bad after all."

When Jim and Granny Dennis first got married, they moved to Nolan County and spent twenty years on Bitter Creek. Their first ranch home was a dugout, twelve feet square. I didn't know it in 1938, but Delma, Mother, Dad, and me would be living in a dugout before too long.

God almighty, they had a total of twelve kids. I can only imagine Granny Dennis raising those kids, taking a break every so often to sit on the front porch to chew her tobacco and spit it back out into her brass spittoon—*"Ping!"*—like she probably did when Dad kidnapped Delma that time. "Now Wayne, *ping,* she belongs with her mother, *ping.* Ye take her back right now, *ping."*

Their son Henry died in 1898. And Boxley died in 1918 while serving with the American Expeditionary Force in France. That left James, Sid, Maggie, Ike, Bertie, Lawrence, Thurmond, Florine, and the twins, Raymond and Rubie. Uncle Sid is ranching in New Mexico; Uncle Thurmond is the foreman of the Martin ranch; Uncle Raymond ranches too. While the other kids were off doing other things, thirty-two hundred acres of pure Texas sat in the capable hands of Ike.

The ranch sits at the base of Double Mountain about fifteen miles outside of Rotan, just past the Clear Fork of the Brazos River. Mesquite trees, scrub brush, and red dirt were pure and raw Texas. In 1941 the land that spoke to itself and made the people who lived there a little stronger would be out of our hands and in the hands of the famous football player Mr. Sammy Baugh. But I didn't know that then. All I knew in 1938 was that I'd get to be with Ike and not with Mrs. Berry, and at the time, that was all that mattered.

Ike gave us the foreman's house to live in while he stayed in the main house. Ike still wasn't remarried and said he wasn't ever going to make that mistake again. But he wasn't lonely. He had ladies to his left, right, in front, and behind. Maybe it's because his birthday is February fourteenth and he was destined to be a lover.

One of those lover ladies was Miss Bandy of the Bandy ranch, who was smitten over Ike. One time Ike and Miss Bandy had been out on a date and came to pick me up from the ranch and take me to town. Ike was driving a stick shift '37 pickup truck, and Miss

Bandy, trying to make room for me, scooched almost right on top of that shifter.

Ike started driving, shifting those gears, shifting then playing with her knee; shifting, then playing with her thigh. "I sure can't see why anyone in the world would want one 'a them cars with the gear shift up high on the steerin' wheel," he said. She giggled, and I looked out the window so they wouldn't see the funny showing on my face too.

From all his various gals, there's one who still sticks around. Mary worked on the adjacent property at the Kennedys'. She's as plain as a door but as sweet as strawberry jam. Every so often, I'd see her ride off the Kennedys' property and onto ours to "clean" Ike's house. Even then I knew what she was really cleaning.

I smile when I watch Ike. It doesn't matter if he's breaking a horse or branding a steer, he's the best there is. He always wears a button-down shirt with a front pocket so he can keep his tobacco safe inside. He tucks his shirt into his trousers, pulls on his boots, and he's ready for the day. His face and arms have almost turned into leather, like his saddle has bled right into his skin.

Except for Dad being there, it was quiet on the ranch. I no longer could hear oil jacks pumping. The cows mooing and the wind blowing was all I needed. It was "home on the range."

Dad went back to hustling domino money, gambling in poker, and setting traps to earn us a little more money.

I started my second fourth grade while we lived on the ranch. The yellow school bus came every morning to pick up Delma and me. Every morning, I held her hand until we got to the bus stop, where I had to shoo Pooch and Zexie back towards the house. Zexie belonged to the ranch, and I guess all the cowhands took care of her. She and Pooch got along real well, played together,

even. That was a good thing since Pooch had (and still has) a reputation of not taking any crap off another dog. I guess he learned
from the best.

When the bus showed up, we'd ride the one and a half miles
to the Wright School. It was the "right" school for me, that's for
damn sure. I felt like I could learn something there, almost like
I was itching to be taught something from the man I took an
instant liking to: Mr. Sam Green. Even though the schoolhouse
was a small two-room building, Mr. Green seemed to make the
whole place bigger. He encouraged me, told me that I could do
that arithmetic if I just set my mind to it. He told me that about
grammar lessons too. He had my back, not at all like Mrs. Berry,
who'd hurt mine. In my book, he was right up there close to H.
Govan. He taught me that some teachers could be good and fair,
firm but not mean—even kind. I needed some kindness back then.
There wasn't much to go around.

alls Raids by Indians

ould walk all over Fort
an hour back in 1879," says
nis of Rotan, who is proud
been in the cattle business
his 83 years. One of his
s to the Fort Worth mar-
a sizable herd was made in
1,000 big 3 and 4 year old
The cattle were gathered
North Concho Country and
to Fort Worth require
days, Dennis recalls. Whil
e hunting buyers in Fort
e cattle were herded on
e, there being no stock-

Harris of Fort Worth, who
part of the cattle, Branch
d Charlie Bucklin of Colo-
and Jim Hinton of Roby
ers who made the trip 61
, Dennis says.
ecalls Indian Raids.
pioneer days stories go
h further than those of the
ails, however. He was
Bosque County in 1857, and
ood memories are filled
es of buffalo hunts and In-

Mr. and Mrs J. F. Dennis of
Rotan, who have been West
Texas ranch folk for their 60
years of married life.

sold. When the buffalo were all
killed and the Indians had been
put on the reservation in Indian

Jim and Granny Dennis, Cono's great-grandparents

CHAPTER 38

Balls

1938–39

FALL ROUNDUP MEANS cutting time for the cattle, the ones that are doomed the moment they're born with balls instead of udders. I watch Ike and the other cowhands snip those wannabe bulls right back into cowdom. Their eyes get real wide and their moos real loud. I bet they don't feel very home on the range about now. Their balls are thrown into a bucket. We follow Ike back to the foreman's house, the bucket of balls swinging from his arm.

"Elnora, I brought ya a heap 'a mountain oysters," says Ike as he hands her the bucket of warm, bloody balls. "Fry these up for us, will ya?"

Mother stares in the bucket, turns one side of her lip up, and rolls her eyes. I don't think this is what Mother had in mind for dinner.

We all sit down at the kitchen table, even Dad, who didn't

want anything to do with the cutting. She's done it alright. She's fried them up and brings them to the table.

It takes me a while, but I make myself eat two since they come in pairs anyway. They're a little on the tough and grizzly side, but I pretend they're chicken gizzards. I can't stop thinking about what he was doing now that a couple of his parts are missing.

Delma won't even try hers. She has a look of fear on her face like someone's gonna notice that all she's eating is cornbread and butter.

The last fork is set down and my quiet mother stands up from the table and says to Ike, "Don't you *never* bring those to me again!" Everybody laughs, including Dad and me.

"And Cono," she says, "ye get out that wash tub and bathe up."

"But Mother—"

"Makes no difference what yer about te say," Mother says interrupting me. "I don't want anything in this house that smells like cow balls." We're still laughing as we watch her storm off to the bedroom, a walk I've seen Aunt Nolie take many a time.

Damn, a bath already. Except for tonight my bath is always on Saturday night—whether I need it or not.

Ike comes to the foreman's house to eat supper with us every now and again, and not just for mountain oysters. I like it when he does. He eats like a magician. He holds one fork in one hand and a knife in the other and somehow makes his knife and fork dance around the plate like boxing partners aiming at the same target. Sometimes I just have to sit still and watch. I try to figure out how he does it, kinda like how I learned to tie my shoes or brush my teeth. It's a magic show. But me? I just pick up my fork with my right hand and end up eating like everybody else: stab potato, put in mouth; scoop peas up onto fork—sometimes having to use my other hand to pile them on—stick in mouth. Maybe Ike gets some of his magic from his Cherokee side and I don't have enough Indian in me to make the knife and fork do doodley-squat, except stuff in food.

⊣ ★ ⊢

Ike's come over for supper. It's not even Thanksgiving, but Mother has made a meal fit for kings: roast beef, cornbread, and mushy pinto beans, just the way we like them. She's even made my favorite dessert, a fresh-baked apple pie.

Slowly, Ike takes off his cowboy hat and carefully hangs it on the nail by the door. He takes as good a care of his hat as he does his livestock. I've heard him say many times when he goes inside someplace, "Take care 'a that hat, it's worth a whole lot more than what sits underneath it."

"Shor smells good in here, Elnora," he says. "Almost like thar's somethin' in here good enough ta eat."

He rubs the top of my head and picks up Delma and gives her a little squeeze, greeting us like we're the most special people in the whole world. I don't know exactly what Ike thinks of his son, but part of me thinks he's saying to himself, "Damn, he acts like his mean ol' mother, Lizzie."

"Wayne," he says, sticking out his hand to shake.

"Dad," says Dad. "Bring me a beer, Delma." She walks to the icebox and pulls out a can of his liquid painkiller.

"Here, Daddy."

"Thanks, Sis." Dad's in a good mood, and we're going to have a good dinner with Ike and a good apple pie. It's the beginnings of a good night.

We all sit down at the table, and with all the food that starts going into our mouths, there's no room for talk. We chew and watch Ike use his knife and fork. Ike sits at one end of the table and Mother at the other next to Delma. I'm sitting across from Dad.

Ike mounds his beans on top of his cornbread, takes a bite, then chomps off the end of his jalapeno. Sweat is just pouring off his forehead and tears have started to roll down his cheeks.

"Damn, that's good," he says. "A good go for short dough."

We all laugh, even Ike, about how something that hurts so bad can also be so good at the same time.

We finish our meal and Mother takes all the empty plates off the table and replaces them with the little ones made especially for slices of apple pie.

I take my first bite. The crust is the perfect cover for the apples that melt like butter in my mouth. I eat every single bit of my piece. I even lick my pointer finger and use it like a fork just so I can pick up any stray crumbs.

Ike's pie is still sitting there, untouched of course, since everybody knows he'd just as soon be chewing on a piece of mesquite bark than to eat pie. He always says he prefers to get his sugar from a whiskey bottle.

I stare at his piece and see that it's bigger than mine was. The sweet apples ooze out the sides between the top and bottom crust. It's calling me forward, challenging me to come and get it. I slowly reach over and pull Ike's pie in front of me. I stare down at it and wonder if Ike's piece is gonna taste as good as my first.

Dad says nary a word when he reaches across the table and slowly pulls that slice of pie back over to Ike like we're playing a game of checkers. I concentrate, thinking that the next move is mine. I smile and slowly pull that pie towards me thinking I should be kinged.

The hard slap across my face surprises me and drives me half-way out of my chair. What the hell just happened? I don't waste any time. I stand up, knocking my chair over, grab a knife off the table, and swing it under Dad's chin, wanting to cut his head plumb off.

I've made a big mistake. I've missed. He runs around to my side of the table holding a craze of fire where his eyes used to be. He grabs me by my shirt collar, kicking a table leg that snaps off and throws the dishes on the floor. He drags me to the door. I hear it slam shut. We're outside. He's not finished.

Although I feel the fast blows to my head and face, they seem to come at me in slow motion. On the ground I curl up into a ball the best I can.

"Protect yourself at all times!" *Who's saying that? Who's saying that? There's no one else out here!*

"It doesn't matter, put your arms around your head! Protect yourself!"

I do as I'm told. I wrap my elbows over my ears, my hands on top of my head. OK, that's better. It doesn't hurt as much. My eyes are stinging from the sandstorm. No, it's a hailstorm. I can feel big clumps of ice hammering my body.

My ears are ringing. Somewhere Pooch is barking his head off, somewhere close to me. There's so much ringing in my ears, I can't tell for sure where he is. Then I scream really loud, but I know that I'm the only one that can hear. "The first chance I get, I'm gonna kill you!"

My bed is soft. The storm is over, but my body hurts. How did I get into my room? I don't remember. There's a wet washcloth on my forehead. Did Mother help me? Ike? I don't remember.

I hear new voices in the kitchen. "Ye oughta be better to that boy, Wayne, or someday he'll git ya."

Speedy Dale, Ike's neighbor, is the one who said those words. A neighbor has stood up for me. When did he get here? Did he see me on the ground trying to protect myself? Did he smell the air of hatred same as me?

Delma comes into my room, her face leaning in towards mine. Her face has a blotchy redness of its own. I hate it when she cries. Now I'm stirred up with mad all over again.

"Mother says to give this to ye." She hands me a fresh wet cloth that I put over my eyes. I know Mother's not coming in. I know Dad probably said, "It's between me and the boy, Elnora." That's me alright, "The Boy."

"Are ye OK, Cono?" Delma whispers.

"Fine, Sis." I clear my throat a couple of times to let the words sound better. Then I fish out of my throat, "Don't you worry about me none."

I'm starting to settle into my aches, letting them take their place on my skin and in my bones like old familiar friends. My thoughts settle in next and truth being told, they hurt even more.

My father is a worthless, sorry son of a bitch, no better than calves' slobber. I've tried to find reasons to believe otherwise, I really have.

How can a piece of apple pie be so good and so bad at the same time? Maybe it's like Ike's jalapeno, the price for eating one is steep. But at least Ike got a little satisfaction from those hot bites, the taste being worth it.

I think about Hicks Boy, how I never could beat him, and I wonder if it will ever be me who is standing up at the end of a round with my right hand held up by a referee. "And the new boxing champion is Cono Dennis." The crowd cheers.

I will look down at the calves' slobber lying bloodied on the boxing ring canvas. I will spit down on him and say, "There ain't nothin' worse than bein' woken up in the middle 'a the night to the feelin' 'a yer balls bein' squeezed and hearin' the sound of a pocketknife bein' opened up at the same time." Then I will walk away from the ring, the crowd still cheering.

☆ ☆ ☆

The next morning I see that the table has been fixed, and I wonder if it was really broken in the first place. Everything's a little blurry, like sand is in my eyes.

Mother, Dad, and Delma are heading out the door when Mother says, "Cono, we're going into town."

"Get busy on that woodpile," says Dad, not even looking at me.

"There's some eggs on the cookstove, Cono," says Mother. Then they're out the door.

Even though I want to see Gene again, it doesn't make no difference to me that they've left me here. I don't want to be around that son of a bitch anyway.

I'm back to chopping that goddamn wood. But it feels good, real good. I swing my axe high over my head and come down hard. It's quiet out except for the Herefords' moos and the whinnying of the horses. I haven't even seen Ike. He must be in town too.

I chop wood for hours, only taking a quick rest to grab a cheese sandwich from the kitchen. It's late in the afternoon. My arms hurt, but somehow I feel a little lighter on the inside. But only until I hear our car pull up.

Delma yells, "Hey, Cono" and runs into the house.

Mother waves to me and follows her in. Dad's been drinking. He sways his way over to me with a look on his sorry-ass face that says, "Ya best answer this next question the way I wanna here it."

"Where's Zexie?" He didn't ask where Pooch was. He could see him lying in the shade by the house.

"What?" I say, trying to keep my axe swinging in the right direction.

"I said where's Zexie?" he yells.

Unlike Dad, time is standing still and sober, like at the picture show when the film has snapped and nobody knows what to do with themselves. All I know is, I'd been doing what I was told. I was chopping and sharpening, chopping and sharpening all day, the sharpening part being my idea. I have enough wood stacked up to make it through a blizzard.

I say back to him, "I don't know. Haven't seen her. Been chopping wood all day."

"Get the gun," he says. "We'll follow the trap line. See if she got caught up." I run inside and get the single shot .22 off the chest 'a drawers and run to catch up with Dad.

Sure enough, Zexie is lying in the first trap we come to, poor little thing. She's been gnawing on her own leg to get out of that trap. I know I didn't have anything to do with it. Dad set that goddamn trap, not me. I was only doing what I was told.

Dad pulls the trap open and picks her up, cradling her in one arm like a baby. Then he walks over and slaps the living hell out of me with the other. I stumble back, but this time I don't fall. I make myself stand up straight.

Dad sure does like dogs.

He hands me the .22 to carry back and starts walking towards the house. Just as I'm thinking, "Don't turn around you sorry son of a bitch 'cause I'm gonna shoot you in the back of the head," he turns back around, grabs the .22 right out of my hand, and takes the bullets out.

"Here," he says, and hands the pistol back to me.

He doesn't trust me, and I don't trust him. That's about the sum of it.

I know exactly how it feels to be caught in a trap, and I'll be damned if I gotta gnaw off my foot to get out of this one. I also know there's a way to have supper without feeling poisoned. I just have to figure out where that is and which direction I need to go to get there. I'd follow those railroad tracks anywhere about now.

That night, I have a dream. I'm taking a walk when a trap, the size of a bear trap, grabs my leg and holds on to it. I feel the iron around my ankle but it doesn't hurt; it only confuses me. I can't go anywhere. I'm stuck. I sit down to stack up devil's claws. I stare at my trapped leg thinking about the things the trap is going to keep me from doing; how I'm gonna get to school, how I'm gonna eat my supper. An idea shows up and sits on my shoulder like nudging me until I listen. H. Govan is standing in front of me. He says, "Well now, Little Dennis, everything's gonna be alright." The next thing I know and as easy as apple pie is supposed to be, I pull the jaws of the trap apart. Then I stare out into the vastness of West Texas trying to figure out what to do next. The steel itself? It was like putty in my fucking hands.

◄ ★ ►

I get up with the sun and sit on the front porch. I'd rather be going to school today to get away to the ease of Mr. Green and the few friends I have there. But it's Sunday, and I have to make it through another day of staring into Dad's cold face. Another day of figuring out what I'm supposed to do, how to get out of the trap Dad's set.

Just when I feel that things are "discouraging," Ike rides up to me on P. A., his favorite horse, and he's leading another one beside him.

"Cono? Whatcha say we take a little ride?"

"OK," I say, already feeling a little better.

I hoist myself up onto the mare and we take off riding quiet, like there's nothing to ponder except this native land. I watch Ike pull out his tobacco and rolling papers, see his left hand roll the cigarette and his right hand lightly holding on to the reins. He lights up and spits out a piece of tobacco caught up on his lip.

"Ya like it out here, Cono?" says Ike, busting up the silence.

"Shor do, Ike, most the time anyhow."

"Uh-huh."

"Shor am glad I'm at the Wright School. Mr. Green is a real nice fella."

"S'what I hear." Ike pulls the reins on P. A. and stops, staring down at the ground.

"Good sign," he says.

"What is?"

"See all that clover down there?"

"Yeah."

"It's because of the rain we had this fall. Means it'll be a good year fer the cattle."

We keep riding until we get close to the stock pond. Ike mashes on one side of his nose and snorts out snot from the other.

"Damn," he says. "Those dandelion feathers float up my nose ev'ry time this year." Then he continues. "That pond o're yonder?" he says, nodding his head towards the water.

"Yeah."

"That there's yer Great Grandpa Dennis's favorite spot. Used ta ride up on him sometimes, saw him sittin' there starin' at the water like he was waitin' for it ta talk to him."

"Did it?" I ask.

"Prob'ly. Guess that's why he kept goin' back to it."

"Maybe I should sit there sometime."

"Wouldn't do no harm. A little peace 'n quiet kin go a long way for a man." I like that he said that. I like that he can see the man in me.

"Kin I ask ye somethin', Ike?"

"Uh-huh."

"That time P. V. Hail beat the tar outta ye on Main Street? Did ye wanna kill 'em?"

"P. V.? Nah. He was jes' doin' his job's all."

"But it wadn't right. He shouldn't 'a done that."

"Nah, wadn't right. But some folks feel a little too big fer their own britches."

He pauses and says, "Besides, it shor wouldn't 'a been right fer me to kill him. That's a whole nuther thing. He's jes' a pissant's all. Kinda like this here horse I'm ridin'." He reaches down and gives P. A. a couple of pats on his neck.

"Did ye feel sorry fer yerself?"

"Fer what?"

"That you'd been done wrong."

"Why 'a course not. That's called pity. Hell, pityin' yerself don't do no good. Nobody ever got anywhere by pityin' themselves."

"That a fact?"

"Which part?"

"The part that ye really didn't wanna kill him."

"Cono, if I tell ye a rooster wears a pistol—"

"Jes' look under its wing," we finish together.

"That's right," he says.

"Yer a straight shooter, ain't ye, Ike?"

"Only way to be."

I stare up in the cool and clear Texas sky and picture that rooster standing up on our fence post, his wing back like he's ready to draw, saying, "Cock-a-doodle-doo, you sons a bitches. Now get up!" Then I laugh.

"What's so funny?" says Ike.

I tell him about the picture I'd put in my head and he says, "He's prob'ly one 'a P. V.'s deputies." And when he laughs his "hee hee hee" laugh, I laugh even harder.

"Ike," I say, "I believe what ye say, that a rooster's got a pistol under his wing, when ye tell me he does." Not only that, I'm thinking that he's got a six-shooter under there ready to unload.

"Let me tell ye a little somethin', and I want ya ta listen up." He pauses, clicking the left side of his cheek like he's finding the right words, and I wait. I can wait all day if need be just to hear what Ike has to say.

"When it comes right down to it, yer your own best friend. Most the time, ya can't trust anybody but yer own self."

I think I've done figured that out on my own. But I say what I mean. "I trust you, though."

"But trustin' yer own self's even better."

I don't say anything for a while. I'm too busy thinking about being my own best friend, shaking my own hand or playing checkers by myself.

We turn around for a calm, slow walk back to the house, only hearing the rustling of the wind and the sound of eight good horse hooves walking on Texas ranch land. Just before we get back to the barn Ike says, "Cono?"

I turn my head to look over at him. His proud hat almost covers his eyes, but the sun still finds his high cheekbones.

"There's two things in life ya can't hep, 'specially when yer young. One is where ye live."

"And the other 'n?"

"Who yer parents are." That's when I feel a little water collecting in the corners of my eyes.

Yep, the weather in West Texas, with its hailstorms, sandstorms, and cyclones, can pick you up and toss you over the edge. But the funny thing is, the next day the sun comes up as always and Ike shows up with two saddled horses and asks you to go for a ride. Suddenly, there's a little "Home on the Range" to make you feel better.

How do I look at Dad and say, "I can't help it that I'm yer son?"

Ike on his horse

CHAPTER 39

19 Miles to Temple

THIS TRAIN'S GIVING me a headache. I don't get them very often, but when I do, they're doozies. Maybe it's the smell of the engine air blowing into my open window. Maybe it's something else. I sure wish I could sleep, but every railroad tie we pass over is one too many towards Temple, or maybe, one too few.

Truth be told, I did feel sorry for myself, defending my own face from getting slapped by my own father. All the time I was getting slapped around, there was good ol' reliable Pooch, whining and carrying on like he was a soldier on both sides of a war. I know he was telling Dad to cut it out. Dad didn't listen. He kept right on slapping and yelling words I don't remember, not sure I even heard. And every time I tried to stand back up? He knocked me back down.

Ike stood up for me. I know that now. He didn't stop Dad from hitting me; there's a kind of code in that neck of the woods that says, "the business between a father and his son is the business between a father and his son." So, on that horse ride at the ranch, we talked a lot about that apple pie night without even talking about it at all.

That doesn't apply, though, to mothers and sisters, least not in my book. If Delma or Mother need protection? I'll do my damndest to be there. And, as it turned out later, I'd have to protect them both at the same time.

It makes me smile to think that sometimes I needed protection from my own sister. Delma was a real pistol on the ranch too. I couldn't help but to tease her because she was so darn funny when she got mad. I had plenty of bruises on my shins from me teasing her, but this one time, it wasn't my shins that took a shining.

Zexie had made it through her trap ordeal, which at the time gave me hope that I could too. One spring morning, still at the ranch, Delma and me were running around chasing Pooch and Zexie. I caught up to her, grabbed her by the arm, and said in my most concerned voice, "Hey Sis, are you gonna get rid of that spider that lives in your hair or ye gonna keep on feedin' it 'til the cousins show up?"

"Cono! There ain't no spider in my hair!"

"Well, then, what kinda bug legs are those I see stickin' out?"

"Where?"

"Right ch'ere!" I said and tickled her ear with my fingers, screaming "Ahhhh!" at the same time. Then I grabbed her button nose and held out my hand to show her my thumb tucked between my two fingers.

"Cono, I've done told ye I was too big fer that!" she yelled and stomped her little feet in the dirt.

That time, instead of kicking me in the shins, she picked up a stave from the ground and hit me right square between the eyes with it. I remember thinking, "Now she's gone and done it!" She could tell by the look on my red face that I was madder than a hornet.

"Ye better start runnin', Delma Jean, 'cause I'm comin' after ye, and I'm gonna spank ye!"

She ran those deer legs of hers right straight to the outhouse and got there just in time to lock herself in.

"I'm gonna push this outhouse right over on ye, Delma Jean!" I said, banging on the old cedar door.

I stood outside that smelly outhouse, listening for what she was gonna say next. Then I listened some more. When I didn't hear anything, I said, "OK. Well, when ye come out, I'll be right here waitin' for ye. Then ye can see this knot between my eyes that's growin' into a real-life unicorn horn."

I thought for sure she'd come out right then just to see my horn for herself. But she didn't. I tiptoed away and went on about my business.

I pretended that my new horn was a badge of courage, which I guess it was if you had yourself a little sister like Delma. I can't say for sure how long she stayed in there, but she knew that I wouldn't spank her, and of course, I'd never push a stinky old outhouse over with her in it.

Delma showed up for our quiet suppertime more clammed up than usual. I put my elbow on the table and used my left hand to hide the goose egg on my forehead. I didn't want Delma to see it any more than I wanted Mother and Dad to. Then with my right hand, I ate my supper in silence like everybody else. Several times I caught Delma staring between my fingers trying to get a peek at my horn. Later that night, Delma told me she didn't mean to put a horn between my eyes. I told her it didn't matter, that it didn't really hurt anyhow.

By the next morning, my badge of courage was almost completely sucked back into my skull. Even though nobody else could see it, I reckoned it was still in there somewhere. And that's where I decided I'd keep it from then on, next to the other ones I got elsewhere.

⊣ ★ ⊢

It was Mother who told me about Gene dying. Dad had found out when he was in town but gave Mother the job of breaking the news to me.

"Cono," she said, "I got some bad news fer ye."

I thought that maybe we'd have to move away again, away from Ike. Or that Delma was sick again.

"Yer little friend Gene has died, gone to Heaven."

I remember staring at her for the longest time. I remember going to Uncle Joe's funeral, and about hearing that Wort Reynolds went to Heaven without a head.

But this was different. This was *my* friend. This was Gene Davis, who was only a year older than me.

"He went to Roby to the hospital 'cause he had a pain in his side."

I saw Gene and me playing checkers, riding on his mare, making up stories.

"It was a bad appendix, burst before the doctors could git to it."

I thought Dad was right about one thing. Doctors were good-for-nothings. Couldn't fix Dad, couldn't fix Gene.

"Mother?"

"Yeah?"

"When Uncle Joe died, why'd they say 'ashes to ashes'?"

"I ain't real sure, Cono. I think it has te do with the fact that we were born nothin' and go right on back te bein' nothin'."

"So now Gene's jes' nothin?" I asked, getting upset that the world was going to pretend he never existed.

"Nah, he's somethin' alright. He's jes' back to being part of the Texas soil's all."

"That ain't so bad, is it?"

"Nothin' wrong with that."

"But I don't get te see him again?"

"Afraid not, Cono. I'm sorry," she said.

And I still am.

Ike's favorite picture

CHAPTER 40

A Substitute's Not as Good as the Real Thing

1939

I GO INTO my room and pull out my box of specials. There's the old lace from a boxing glove from the time when Gene put together that fight for me. It was my first fight with real gloves.

At school and in front of everybody Mr. Green says, "Cono found out that he's lost a good friend. His name was Gene Davis, and he lived in Rotan. Cono, I just want to tell you how sorry we are."

I nod my head and look down at my desk. Even this kid Mackerel says, "Yeah, Cono. That's a shame." Mackerel reminds me a bit of Gene. He's my age, but he's small like Gene was. Maybe we can be friends.

I don't quite understand it, doesn't make no sense whatsoever that Gene is dead. I want to see him again. I want to laugh with him. I want him to pull me behind his mare in the red wagon. I want to beat him at checkers.

Mr. Green has told me I can do anything I want. He says I can. He says he knows I can. So I decide to write Gene a letter, send it up to God Jesus to give to him. Maybe even read to him, so he doesn't have to do the reading himself. We're supposed to be writing a paper about our life. But I'll write that later, maybe at home so Dad will leave me alone. He hardly ever bothers me when I'm doing schoolwork. Anyway, I know Mr. Green won't mind. I lift the lid of my desk, pull out my paper and pencil, and start to write.

Dear Gene,

I hate it that you're dead and that those stupid doctors in Roby couldn't fix you to save your life. We had more things to do, you and me. More wars to fight with the other boys in the neighborhood and more of our own fights to have just between the two of us, the ones that were so much fun but made us dog tired and bruised afterward. Even though you were just a little older, but a lot littler, you always got the best of me. We never gave up. You'd just say, "Cono, ye tired yet?"

"Yeah," I'd say.

"How bouts you and me stop fightin' for the day?"

"OK," I'd say.

And that's what we'd do. We'd get up, dust off our britches, and stop for the day. But we'd never give up. Boys in Rotan, Texas, never give up. That's what you said.

Don't feel bad about being dead. I think some of us are dead when we're still alive anyway. Or maybe it's just that some of us aren't completely born yet, like we're waiting for a little peace and quiet to show up so we can take our first real breath.

I'm sorry I never made it back to see you. The one time my whole family went into Rotan I couldn't go. I had to stay here and chop wood. I'm sorry I couldn't make you better, and I'm sorry that nobody could take me to visit you in the hospital. Maybe if you had been in there a little longer I could have found a ride. I know you never gave up, so there must have been something else that caught your eye.

Things are growing on me, Gene, and I'm not talking about inches or new hairs. Things are crawling under my skin. I'm feeling antsy and mad and even a little bit not like myself. I wouldn't be a bit surprised if someone were to holler, "Cono!" and I'd just keep going the other direction thinking my name was George or something. My hands clench more often than they used to. My teeth do too. Just the other day I caught myself staring in the bathroom mirror. I was about to brush my teeth, but my jawbones were moving in and out and I realized I was clamping down so hard with my grinders that a toothbrush didn't have a chance to get in to do its job.

I'm writing to you, Gene, fishing all my words outta my truth bucket. And when I'm done? I'll send this letter up to God Jesus, so he can read it to you. Better yet, maybe I'll go someplace real quiet, where nobody else on this earth can hear. And I'll talk real loud, so you can hear me all the way up in Heaven. And if someone else up there happens to hear? It's OK. I know they won't tell anyone since they're dead too. You'll know it's me. I'll be the one flicking marbles with my pocketknife!

I sure wish you could tell me what it's like up there. When I went to the revivals with the Allridge boys, they told me that Jesus has made a room for dead people and you'll get to live there forever with Him. What does your room look like?

I wanna know if you've made any friends and if Jesus lets you wrestle and fight with them like we used to do for fun. The revivalists say that we'll get to meet our loved ones again when we die. But what if I die when I'm a hundred and I get there and you're still only eleven years old? Are you gonna sit on my lap and tell me Jesus stories? Ha-ha. It's good to know that you have a room up there in Heaven, although I'm not sure I believe everything they tell me at those revivals.

Gene, I want to kill my Dad. Send him right up there to Heaven, where maybe you can teach him a few things, like how to be nice

*to me. But then, I guess it would be too
late. Unless he was Jesus, and got alive again
to came back to do something good. That'll
be the day.*

*Anyhow, I sure hope you're real happy up
there. I hope you get to throw the football and play checkers and flick marbles. And
say? If you see my Uncle Joe and our friend
Wort Reynolds, tell them I say, "Hello."*

Your friend,
Cono

P.S.: Wort's the one without the head.

Later that night, I light the lantern and turn my attention to
my schoolwork—the paper I was to write today in class instead of
the letter to Gene. Dad's still out, so I have the quiet to think. I
write about Ma and Pa and Polo. I write about how I hate lamb's-
quarter and how Pooch is always getting caught up in porcupine
eggs. I write about Ike being the best cowboy who ever lived. After
spending a good hour on my paper, I think about what my last
sentence is going to be. I finally decide: "And Gene Davis was my
best friend."

I pull the letter I'd written to Gene out of my pocket and walk
over to the cookstove. I scoop out some ashes. "Ashes to ashes, dust
to dust."

I fold up Gene's letter and put it in my cigar box of specials,
along with my pocketknife, Tiger stick, penny, glove lace, toothbrush top, and devil's claw. Then I add one scoop of ashes. They
might not be Gene's ashes, but it's a good reminder that he's still
here, living in West Texas where he belongs.

The next morning I wake up to find my schoolwork still sitting on the kitchen table. There's a stained ring in the middle of my paper where a beer bottle sits, smearing the words on my paper.

☆

It's real cold out this morning. Winter's almost here and there's a light snow falling on top of Delma and me as we walk to the bus stop. I reach down to hold Delma's hand. It's frozen like an ice cream cone. I keep thinking that maybe my hand will keep hers warm if I keep holding it. Maybe I'm also thinking that her little hand will help the cold in mine.

Me and Delma get to go home for dinner today. Dinner is better than supper since Dad's never here during the noon hour. Mother's made us some sandwiches, and just like always at this time of day, The Light Crust Doughboys come on the radio. We sit at the table gnawing on our ham sandwiches and listen to them sing "Sitting on Top of the World," "Brother Can You Spare a Dime," and "Cattle Serenade." That quiet time, with just the three of us, puts me in better spirits, and I'm almost filled plumb up to my eyeballs in satisfied. Almost. I still can't get Gene out of my head.

"Takes time, Cono," says Mother looking at me. "Jes' takes time's all."

☆

The weather's turning nice again. The warmer air of the beginning of spring is putting little lively steps in the hooves of the horses. The cattle are mooing with happy.

I ask Mackerel if he wants to go with me on a picnic, seeing as how there's no wood to chop and he's been nice to me about Gene and all. I've never gone on a picnic before, but this feels like the right day for it, nothing but fresh air to breathe.

His real name is Lennie McElry, but one of the kids named him "Mackerel" for short. The kids at school think it's funny to say, "Holy Mackerel!" Hubert, Jack, and J. T. are friends too, but now that the school year is more than half over, I'm just now getting to know them a little better.

Mackerel and me grab some crackers and a can of Vienna Sausages and take off walking to find ourselves a picnic spot. "I know jes' the place," I tell him.

We walk the mile to Great Grandpa Dennis's favorite spot by the pond. Nobody else is around except for a few thirsty cows and a few field larks flying around and landing just long enough to drink some water. We sit there for five whole minutes, stacking up all the devil's claws we find. When I tell Mackerel about Great Grandpa Dennis listening for the pond to talk to him, he says, "That's the craziest thing I ever heard."

"I don't think it's crazy. Besides, how do you know it doesn't talk to ye?"

"Water don't talk."

"Well maybe ye ain't been listening."

"Let's just eat."

"Fine by me," I say and watch him open up that can of sausages. I can almost taste them.

"Ow, ow," says Mackerel looking down at the blood on his thumb. Then he starts in on crying.

"What happened?" I ask.

"I cut myself is what," and he keeps right on spewing out tears.

"Oh, fer cryin' out loud. That ain't no reason to cry. Just suck off the blood, and let's have ourselves a picnic."

But Mackerel doesn't stop. He keeps right on crying, and I'm so mad that I punch him on his arm, telling him to stop his bellyaching.

He stands up and sniffles out, "I wanna go home."

"Well go on then! Git!" I say, as I kick at his baby ass to hurry him along.

I watch him run along in the distance, and then I stare down at that can of sausages now tainted with coward's blood. I'm hungry, and I think that maybe I can overlook the coward's blood inside the can if I just wipe it off with my shirttail. Instead, I throw that whole can, wieners and all, as far across West Texas as I can. I keep sitting by the edge of the pond until I decide it's not in the mood for talking today, and I start walking back to the ranch house.

Gene never would have acted like that, like such a baby ass. I should have just taken my own self out for a picnic and sat longer by the pond, giving it a better shake at talking to me. I keep walking and eat the driest cracker that ever laid down across my tongue.

As I get closer to the house, I stare out into the vastness of West Texas. Maybe Mackerel couldn't help crying, like I can't help it that Dad doesn't like me and has to hit me to prove his point. Besides, it's not Mackerel's fault that he's not Gene.

The horizon is pulling my eyeballs to its edge like two setting suns. I'm watching and waiting for the world to unfold, hoping that when I get home it won't unfold on me.

CHAPTER 41

17 Miles to Temple

I DIDN'T KNOW it then, but my time on the ranch was winding down. Great Grandpa Jim decided to sell those thirty-two hundred acres nestled up against the Double Mountain. He sat all his kids around the table in the main house and gave them each their share from the sell of the ranch, ten thousand dollars apiece, in cash. He said, "And when I die, ye'll get more. When Mother dies, ye'll get a little more."

Mother had said we were moving again.

"Where to?" I asked.

"Don't know yet. Yer Great Grandpa is selling the ranch."

"Why?"

"Needs the money, I reckon."

"What's Ike gonna do then?"

"He'll get money from the selling of the ranch, jes' like the rest 'a Jim's kids."

"What's he gonna do with the money, where's he gonna go?"

"He don't know yet."

"Will we get any money?"

"No." And that was that.

On one hand, every day I stayed on that ranch was a day I was thankful for. But the other hand said something different. It said that every day I sat at the ranch was just one day closer to not being there, not being close to Ike. I knew they were looking for someone to buy the place, and since most folks didn't have the money for a big ranch, I figured we had a little more time.

'Cause hardship was coming. I could smell it. I could feel it in my bones.

CHAPTER 42

Fresh Air and Dusted Britches

1940

LAST WEEKEND MR. Green asked Delma and me if we wanted to spend a night with him and his wife. I think maybe he'd heard a few things about what was going on at my house, about how Dad was treating me. Either way, it sure was good to get away for a night.

Mrs. Green made us corn on the cob with fried chicken, and I ate every bit of mine. Then we played checkers, and we even taught Delma how to play. It was like leaving a desert that had no water for a vacation in a place with fresh air and cold iced tea. It was a full belly.

The next morning, before we were about to leave, Mrs. Green hugged Delma and then turned to me and said, "Now Cono, you keep sittin' on the shiny side 'a that star."

It sounded like a real nice thing to say, but I'm still trying to figure out what in tarnation she was talking about.

The day before, I had apologized to Mackerel for being mean to him. I told him I understood that he couldn't stop crying just because he cut himself. We haven't been together since that picnic, but I reckon that's OK by me. He's not Gene. At least there's no hard feelings between us. We're all settled up.

On Monday, school shows up as usual, but this time I get flagged by my buddies.

"Cono," whispers J. T., with Hubert and Jack standing close behind, listening. "We're thinkin' about playing hooky tomorr'a, walk on up Double Mountain. Wanna come?"

"Nah, Dad would beat me to death if I got caught. But if ye wanna go, ye can go on ahead through our place."

It's the truth, me telling them about getting a beating by my dad if I got caught. But after how good Mr. Green has been to me, I'm not about to break his trust. He doesn't have many rules, but missing school is something he doesn't tolerate unless it has to do with family.

"Tomorrow'll be a good day if you wanna do it," I tell them. "Ya'll can go ahead on through our place."

Sure enough, the next morning I show up to school. Mackerel and Hoover are there, but J. T.'s, Jack's, and Hubert's desks are empty.

"Anybody know where those boys are?" asks Mr. Green.

"Yes sir," I say, thinking I owe him some honesty. "They're climbing up Double Mountain."

"Why aren't you with them, Cono?"

"'Cause my dad would whup me good if he found out." More honesty.

"Well, let's just take a look." Mr. Green pulls the field glasses out of a desk drawer and looks towards Double Mountain.

After a few seconds, he's says, "I'll be doggone."

"What is it, Mr. Green?" we all seem to say at the same time.

"Sure enough, there they are," he says, pointing out the window.

We all get a chance to take a peek through the field glasses, all laughing our asses off about how their asses were gonna be busted come tomorrow.

Hoover looks through the glasses and says for what seems like an hour, "Looks . . . like . . . they've . . . stopped . . . to . . . have . . . themselves . . . a—"

"A what?" we ask, trying to hurry him up.

"A . . . smoke!" We all bust our guts open again knowing they're done for.

The next day Mr. Green says nary a word about those boys and neither do the rest of us. But I know what's coming; it's time to separate the sheep from the goats.

School's about over when Mr. Green says, "J. T., Jack, Hubert, you fellas need to stay after school for a bit. I need to have a word with you." The rest of us start snickering, and Mr. Green tells us to go on out and wait for the bus.

When they finally come out, I thought I'd die laughing. They walk towards us with wet in their eyes and rubbing their butts.

"Well," I say to them, still laughing, "what'd ye tell him?"

"That it was your idee," they said.

"Well I guess yer right about that. I didn't go up, you did, and now yer britches are dusted butt good." And after saying, "butt good," I die laughing all over again.

"Cono, you're a fine friend," says J. T.

My fine friends and I had planned to run around together this weekend after our chores. If I decide to go I think I'm gonna have to keep one eye in the front and one in the back just in case they're still holding a little grudge. But it was all worth it. It surely was. A good laugh is hard to come by.

CHAPTER 43

Living in Dirt

1941

CHRISTMAS IS DONE and gone. There wasn't much to it anyhow: a new shirt and a pair of tie shoes that fit.

Ike comes in and says, "Well, it's done. We sold the ranch."

"When do we gotta move?" I ask real quiet-like since I don't really want to know the answer to my own question.

"Soon, I reckon. But here's what I hadn't told ye yet. Ye'll never guess in a million years who's buying it."

Mom and me just stare, waiting.

"Mr. Sammy Baugh."

"Who's he?" I ask.

"He's a big football player is who."

I don't care how big he is. I don't care if he plays football unless it's for the Yellowhammers.

"He grew up in these parts, ya know."

Well, I reckon that makes things a little better in my book. Still, I don't want to leave.

"Ike," says Mother, "do ye know what yer doin' yet?"

Ike grins like he's been keeping a long-held secret. "I'm movin' to Temple, Texas, boys and girls! Gonna own myself a café."

"Well I'll be damned," says Mother. "What about yer ranchin'?"

"Time to give it a little rest, Elnora. 'Sides, it's a cute little place. Not far from the bus station, so I should git plenty 'a business. And Camp Hood is close by and the soldiers gotta have a place to eat, when they're not on base."

"That's good then," she says.

But I reckon she's thinking the same thing I am. What about us? How are we gonna make it if we have to depend on Dad to take care of us? I find myself wishing that Aunt Nolie still lived in Rotan, that maybe we could stay with her. But she and Uncle Red have moved back to Ranger. Besides, if we did move back into town I'd have to go back to the primary school and see Mr. Pall and Mrs. Berry again. That wouldn't do a'tall.

☆ ☆ ☆

It doesn't take Dad long to find us a place to stay, I'll give him that. But it's the worst place we've ever lived. I'll give him that too.

The Kennedys next door to our ranch—or rather, the Baughs' ranch—say we can live in their dugout. It's just like it sounds. The dugout is dug out of the side of a hill. The front is enclosed by wood. It's big enough for a cookstove and two mattresses for the four of us to sleep on. That's about it.

There's more wood to chop. Mother's quiet, more quiet than usual. What was it Ike told me? Oh yeah. "Ya can't help where you live." I think about Great Grandpa Dennis, how he and Granny had to live in a dugout. But it was when they first got married, first started out. Seems like we're always just starting out.

I know that everybody here at the Wright School knows where we're living now. I wish they didn't. I felt proud to live at the ranch, telling those boys to "go ahead on through our property" to play hooky. Now I don't feel like saying a damn thing.

We're in the middle of arithmetic when we hear something outside. We all look out and see the best cowboy in the world coming down the road singing "Take Me Back to Tulsa, I Don't Wanna Marry," Ike's favorite song. Him singing that song didn't surprise me as much as what he was doing. Ike was riding on old P. A. and leading sixteen of his horses in single file, taking them all the way into Rotan by himself, the last thing he had to do before moving. I wonder how long it took him to tie up the horses from tail to neck, but knowing Ike, probably not long. I've never seen anything like it. By the looks on their dumbfounded faces looking out the school window, I can tell the other kids haven't either. Even Mr. Green. Damn if I'm not proud of my grandfather. Then Ike takes out his tobacco pouch, puts the tobacco in the rolling paper, folds it up and lights it, all with one hand, as usual. His other hand waves to us parade watchers.

Before I know it, Ike's moved on to Temple.

⊰ ★ ⊱

Dad says he needs to do some trapping and shooting. God knows we need the money. "C'mon, Cono" he says, "Let's see what we can find out there."

Not far from the dugout I shoot my first bobcat. I don't do

such a good job at first; I only graze the top of his head, stopping him but not killing him.

"Finish him, Cono, don't jes' hurt him!"

I raise Dad's rifle again and this time I shoot him right square between the eyes. I feel better now, knowing that he's dead, not wandering around stupefied trying to figure out where to go.

I watch Dad skin the bobcat. He says that when that cat's all dried out he's going to put it right beside his bed so, instead of dirt, he'll have something clean to put his feet on when he wakes up in the morning.

When Dad wakes up the next morning, he says, "I'm goin' ta Sweetwater."

"What fer?" asks Mother.

"Gonna open up a domino hall."

"Another one? I thought ye were done with that."

"A new town, Elnora. It's s'posed ta be a good spot." Usually he takes Pooch with him when he leaves. Not this time. Pooch is told to stay with us and to be a good boy.

"An' ya'll watch out for him. He likes to go off sometimes." Dad finished getting dressed, and before we know it he's stooping out the low door of the dugout, leaving the three of us feeling like rats in a cave.

It's good, him being gone, but it's hard work on the rest of us. There's no time for much schooling, except for Delma, who still gets to go every day. But there is time for me to pick bolls.

It's been two weeks since he's been gone, and since Dad hasn't sent us any money, the Kennedys have hired on Mother and me to work on their cotton field. She can get all the way up to a dollar a day. I can't seem to get past eighty cents.

"Where's Pooch?" I ask Mother and Delma. It's suppertime.

"He lit out early this mornin'," Mother says.

"He's been gone all day?"

"Guess so."

"Shit! Delma, we better go find him."

It's starting to get dark. Delma and me keep calling him, but all we hear back are the chirping night bugs and rustling in the mesquite trees.

"Ain't no two ways about it, if we don't find her by the time Dad gets back, we're all gonna be skinned rugs fer him te put his feet on in the mornin'." Come hell or high water, I know we have to find him, alive and well.

"Ye think he's OK, Cono?"

"Has te be. Jes' has te be."

The dark was settling in around us. I tell Delma we have to head back.

"I'm worried, Cono."

"Me too," I say worrying about Pooch as well as the rest of us.

We get home to hear Mother ask, "Where ya'll been?" Then we see Pooch sitting by the old rickety door of the dugout.

"Pooch!" yells Delma wrapping her skinny arms around him.

"Pooch, ye had us scared te death, boy," I say, rubbing his head.

"He's wore out," says Mother. "Brought back a dead squirrel 'n more porcupine eggs. Eat yer supper then ya'll can git those burrs off 'a him."

Even the same old beans taste good tonight.

Dad finally comes back but with empty pockets. He's lost his tail in Sweetwater. I guess I should have told him that Sweetwater was a no-account place. Whenever I think of Sweetwater, Texas,

I still get the smell of donkey dung, or the lack of it, straight up my nose. And then I see Sunshine giggling her ass right off that bar stool.

But at least, thanks to me, Dad has a bobcat rug to step on when he rolls out of bed.

⊣ ★ ⊢

The dugout's a little warmer now. My wood chopping has slowed down a bit, and I get to go back to school. I'm only back with Mr. Green for about a month when Ike comes for a visit. He and Dad have a little powwow, and it's decided that we're moving to Crane to open up the Idle Hour Domino Hall. Yeah, a new town, another good spot. Since Dad's pockets are only full of lint, I suppose Ike has lent Dad some money to get him started—again. So we're heading out—again—but this time Ike's going with us to get us settled.

The dugout

CHAPTER 44

12 Miles to Temple

IT WAS IN Crane where Ike bought the prettiest saddle I'd ever seen, a MacPherson with sheepskin lining, a lariat holder, and detailed tooling. It was curious to me at the time, him buying that saddle since he wasn't ranching anymore. I guess some things just stay in your blood, and somehow Ike knew he'd go back to it.

I started school and finally got to play a little football on Crane's junior high team. I still wasn't big. I was in the sixth grade and weighed only sixty-nine pounds. But I was fast, and that's what they were looking for.

I also took up boxing training. I never missed a practice in either football or boxing. I got matched up for my first real fight with Skeet Qunilin, a fight that never happened. Someone got wind of the fact that I was too small to fight this Skeet kid and canceled the fight. Back then I thought I was ready, and I thought I could have whupped that boy. Now I'm not so sure. Still, I can't help wondering if that fight would have happened, would my dad have shown up to watch?

It was in Crane that I got more bad news. As it turned out, little Ervin Clay Carter had drowned in Rotan's new swimming pool over that summer. Little Ervin Clay Carter, the boy with the powder on his face, the boy who had a mother that hugged and kissed him and told him she loved him on the first day of third grade, was dead. I sure felt sorry for his mother. Why the hell wasn't somebody watching over him, is what I wanted to know? I remember thinking back then that at least Gene would have someone his own age to pal around with in Heaven.

In December, we got more bad news.

It was December 7th, 1941, a Sunday. It was unusually hot for that time of year, and most of us boys slipped off our shirts to play some football in the vacant lot across the street from our house.

Dad came out to see me, slaps me across the face saying, "Get your shirt back on!" Along with my shirt, I put on my best "I don't care" face, and kept on playing. After another hour of sweating, one of the mothers came out and said, "Boys, somethin' really bad has happened."

That's when I learned about the attack on Pearl Harbor. It was a bad day, not just for me but for the whole country. Suddenly the slap didn't carry much importance. While all I had was a sting on my face and humiliation in my bones, many of our fighting boys were dead—all because they were standing up for something important. I remember thinking about Jessie Perkins and hoping he wasn't at Pearl Harbor.

The very next day all the of-age men were rushing around getting ready to join the military. Nobody around there, and I guess nobody in the rest of the country, put up with something like that.

Not their country, no way, no how. Back then I wanted to go with them, go straight to the recruiter's office to sign up. But I was only a kid.

Being no surprise to the rest of us, Dad got tired of the Idle Hour Domino Hall and had started coming home drunk almost every day. One early spring day I was outside chopping wood when I heard Mother scream from inside the house. I took my axe with me and ran into the house to see what was wrong. It didn't take me long to figure it out. She was lying across the bed with the back of her hand resting on one side of her face. Dad was standing over her. My hand gripped the handle of the axe like a fist ready to punch. I stood there, still as a fence post, and stared straight into the eyes of a maniac. A train roared in my head, not the soft and soothing type I'd learned to love in Ranger, Texas, and not like the one I'm on now, but the kind that gets derailed and takes off a head.

"Mother, are you alright?" I asked, not taking my eyes off my father for one second.

"I'm fine, Cono," she mumbled.

Dad looked over at me and said, "What 'a ya doin' with that axe?"

This time my words were loud enough for him to hear, but they came off my tongue as cool as a cucumber.

"I'll tell ye what I'm gonna do with it. I'm gonna chop your goddamn head off with it. If you ever, ever hit my mother again, I don't care where you live or what you're doing, if I have to catch you asleep at night, I will cut your head plumb off. Or, I can just kill you right now." What was interesting about that day was remembering my exact words and the power I felt from my anger. I'm sure my skill with that axe didn't hurt much either. I can't even say if Delma was around since my eyes were too fixed on my poor mom and my sorry dad.

To my surprise, Dad just turned and walked away from me, and that was the end of the conversation. I thought about the words of Joe Louis. "You can run, but you can't hide." I'm still thinking about those words.

Before the school year was over, we were back living in the dirt at the Kennedy dugout.

CHAPTER 45

Kicked Out and the Feel of a Gun

1941–42

IT'S THE SAME dugout alright; a little shelter above our heads to keep us dry, but this time, smaller, not big enough to cuss a cat.

Dad's figured out how to make a little money. The Rushings and the Gallaghers are still bootlegging, but P. V. seems to be breathing down their necks a little hotter and heavier. That's why they asked Dad to store their liquor for them in our dugout. Every time they show up, I help to unload their truck. Now we have to step over the booze to get to our mattresses on the dirt floor.

We have new uninvited guests in the dugout. Pooch has brought with him a family of fleas, and Mother's fit to be tied. Just as we fall asleep, we wake up to scratch. We do that all night long. Delma has so many bites she's starting to bleed in spots 'cause she won't stop scratching. Dad won't let Pooch sleep outside. He says they're too many coyotes or bobcats that could take him down.

Finally, Dad's gone into town to buy some kind of special soap that's supposed to make the fleas go away. I think there are too many fleas to be killed off by a bar of soap. I think we should just bomb the whole place and call it a day.

I sure do like the ranch's new owner, Mrs. Sammy Baugh. She's real good to me. I know she must miss her husband since he's gone a lot playing football. But she's not alone there. She's got plenty of ranch hands, so she doesn't have to do the ranching herself. Sometimes I see her big white Buick pull up and I'll open the gate for her. She'll say, "Cono, you wanna ride with me to the mailbox and wait for the mailman?"

"Yes ma'am!" I say. And that's what we do.

Mrs. Baugh is nice to talk to and always seems like she cares about me and wants to know about my family and all. She knows we live in the dugout, and I can't help wondering if she feels bad that we don't have the ranch anymore. I wanna tell her it's not her fault, that Great Grandpa Dennis needed to change his shoes is all. And when he did, so did the rest of us, for better or worse.

Things have changed. Somehow or another Mr. Kennedy's son, Jack, found out what we were doing. He came over and read Dad the riot act, told us to be out by the next day. We've been thrown out of dirt. I don't blame Mr. Kennedy one iota. We shouldn't have been storing bootlegged liquor on property that didn't belong to us. Our dugout wasn't free after all. Our bootleg-ging business cost us.

Mother seems to be a little more relaxed now that we're leaving the dugout. I've caught her smiling a couple of times when Dad's not looking. We've been invited to live on the Poseys' screened-in porch. No more dirt living. No more fleas that don't seem to want to leave the old mattresses on the ground.

⊲ ★ ⊳

Dad says to chop wood. He says we have to pay the Poseys back, so me chopping wood is one way to do it. It doesn't bother me to chop wood for the Poseys. They're real nice to let us stay on their porch, even though we get a little wet when there's a big rainstorm. Besides, they have a radio and we get to listen to it just like when we were at the ranch or at Aunt Nolie's. Dad's way of paying him back was to make sure Pooch wasn't still carting around a city of fleas. He even bathed him again with that flea soap.

Dad says that Mr. Posey "is richer 'n four feet up a bull's butt." But he doesn't act anything like Great Uncle Will McCleskey. He'd never pull me off a horse with a walking stick, even if he had one.

Most of the time we even get to have supper with them, and since Mr. Posey talks almost as slow as Hoover, supper conversations take a long time. At least Dad isn't doing us any harm while we're here. Mr. Posey doesn't go off half-cocked like Dad does. He doesn't hit his wife or Hoover, so I guess Dad doesn't want to be the only one who clobbers two outta three of his family members.

Hoover asked me to ride out with him on a couple of their horses. I was supposed to be chopping wood, but the idea of riding sounded like chocolate cake. We had a good time riding around their property. It made me think of riding with Ike: the sound of hooves, the click of his left cheek. I sure do miss him.

We were trotting along just fine until my horse swallowed his head and threw me off into a prickly pear cactus. I landed on my right hand and it smarted something awful.

"Cono," said Hoover, "I . . . think . . . you . . . gave . . . him . . . just . . . a little . . . too much . . . spur." And right then, my laughter took over my pain.

Since then I've been trying to hide my bad hand from Dad so he won't catch on that I'd played hooky from my wood chopping. For the last couple of days I've even been chopping wood with my left hand until my right one starts to feel better.

Now the Poseys have invited us to supper, and I'm favoring my left hand, trying to keep my right one hidden. It's hard to eat with my left fork but I manage pretty good. Maybe with a little more practice I can eat like Ike, dancing both the knife and fork around like a circus trick.

For a brief second I forget and reach for a piece of cornbread with my right, shining the cuts and the redness across the table.

"Cono," says Mrs. Posey, "what'd ye do to yerself?" Shit.

"I got bucked off a horse," I say, looking at Dad and wondering if he's gonna reach across the table and slap me.

"I know," Dad says. "I saw ya git bucked off."

Well, kiss a fat man's ass.

⊰ ★ ⊱

The Poseys' place is closer to the Wright School, so we don't have to take the bus. Usually, me, Delma, and Hoover walk together. But today, Hoover's waiting for his mother to finish the cookies she's baked for the class, so it's just Delma and me walking to school like we used to.

"Cono, I like it at the Poseys. Do you?"

"Yeah."

"I sure like their food. I got sick 'n tired of beans and lamb's-quarter."

"Me too," I say, thinking about me and Delma trying to find lamb's-quarter on the Kennedy property like we did in Rotan.

She'd always mix in some other kind of weed with the lamb's-quarter that Mother would have to pick out of the bunch.

"Those beans," she says. "You and Dad pooted all night long."

"So did you."

"Dad-gum-it, I did not!"

"Delma Jean, you poot just as big as everybody else." She tried to keep her laugh in but it came out anyway, just like one of her poots.

"Ye think we kin stay with them fer a while? I don't mind the front porch, only when it rains hard and Dad and Pooch get all tied up in knots."

"I don't know. Dad's known fer gettin' a hair up his ass."

"The hair that makes us move again?"

"That's the one," I say.

After school, when the three of us are walking home, Hoover says real quiet-like so Delma won't hear, "Cono?"

"Yeah?"

"I . . . saw . . . somethin' . . . on the way . . . to school . . . this . . . mornin' that . . . I think . . . ye . . . oughta . . . look at."

We walk off the trail a bit, and there it is, laying in a patch of prairie grass—a thumb buster, .45 cock-and-shoot five-bullet gun. It's the kind you can tie the hammer down and fan like in the western picture shows. I look around for a dead body, but I don't see one. Instead, I see Sheriff P. V. Hail up in the distance. He's sitting inside his pickup, looking our direction. Knowing him, he's probably caught us in the lenses of his field glasses.

"Whose gun is this, Hoover?" I ask.

"I dunno, Cono," he stammers.

"Delma, go ahead on. Ye can see the house from here. I wanna talk to Hoover a bit." While she girly skips back towards the Poseys', I pick up the gun and feel that it's cold and hot at the same time. I look in the chamber. It's fully loaded. I wonder who had left it there and if it was planted just for me.

I stare back up at that pickup and think about the man sitting inside of it, the man who had arrested my dad, the man who had arrested Ike and had beaten him for no reason. I know what that feels like.

I hold it in my hands for a while, turning it over and over, feeling the weight of it, feeling the power, feeling the end of a problem.

"I could use this, Hoover."

"No, Cono. That would be the end 'a ya," he drawled out, making me wait. "Ye don't wanna do that. Give it back to me, Cono."

Lots of pictures go through my head, moving almost as slow as Hoover's words. I don't tell Hoover about those pictures; I just stack them up in my head like a deck of cards.

He sticks out his hand, wiggling his fingers up and down. "Give . . . it . . . to me . . . Cono." With enough hesitation to make him wait this time, I place it on his open palm for him to take back to his dad.

That night I laid on my cot and thought about that gun, knew that I could find it if I wanted to. I also realized that Hoover was worried that I might use that gun on Sheriff P. V. Hail in order to get back at him for arresting Dad and Ike. I wouldn't. I was thinking that maybe Sheriff Hail was counting on the fact that I hated Dad as much as he did.

The next morning I wake up still thinking about that loaded gun when Mother says, "Cono, we're movin' te Temple. Ike's sent us a letter. He's found us a cheap place te stay."

No more dugout, no more front porch. But no more Hoover and Mr. Green either. Still, living in the same town as Ike? It doesn't get much better than that.

"Ike says ye kin work fer him at the café."

"Doin' what?" I ask, although it wouldn't matter if I was going to clean toilets as long as I'm with Ike.

"Prob'ly sweepin' up, maybe makin' sandwiches."

Making money from a man that pays sounds fine by me. The only problem I see is that Temple is in a wet county. Ike's told us that. No worries about getting caught by P. V. for bootlegging, but it'll be easy for Dad to fill up on liquor. Still, it's probably a good thing we're leaving. I can let that gun stay where it's at.

Dad doesn't waste any time. He's told us, "We need to hightail it outta here." He's arranged for his friend, Mr. Hutchings, to drive us in his cattle truck. If only it was a train. I could sit in my own seat, stare out the window, and watch West Texas slip away with the rhythm and hum and think about the comfort of Ma and Pa's farm. I've still never been on a train. It's only been inside me.

My last day of school is not the last day for everybody else. There's still a month to go before school's out for the summer. Mr. Green tells me he's sorry that we're leaving, but to try to stay in touch. He shakes my hand and tells me to take care of myself. Then he hands me an envelope.

"Cono, I wrote you a little good-bye letter. You don't have to read it now; read it on the road. Maybe it'll make the time pass a little faster."

"I shor 'preciate ye, Mr. Green."

"Likewise, Cono. Now get on to Temple. See what's waiting for you."

I say my good-byes to Hubert, J. T., Jack, and Mackerel. Then

I shake Hoover's hand real hard, knowing it'll probably be the last time I ever see him.

The last thing I do on moving day is put Mr. Green's letter in my silly box of specials, tuck it under my arm, and hop into the truck. Sure enough, the cattle truck's a rickety old thing with wooden slats on the sides that look like they've been gnawed on by termites and could fall off at any second.

Me, Sis, and Mother sit on an old couch placed in the back of the truck, a truck that's meant for moving cattle. Dad sits up front with Pooch and Mr. Hutchings. While most of my friends go places by car or train, here I am in the back of a goddamn cattle truck, and the worst part is we have to drive right past the Wright School on our way out.

When we get close to the school, Mr. Hutchings slows down like he thinks I need to see my friends again. I do, but not like this. When he honks his horn, I think I might just die of shame. The faces of my friends pop out the door one after the other, same as Mr. Green's. I stick my hand out between the wooden slats and wave.

It's nothing like Ike's parade: a tall, proud cowboy leading sixteen horses, single file, all by himself. Instead, it's me and my family in a cattle truck, sitting on an old torn and broken-down couch, going two hundred fifty miles to the unknown. I keep thinking on the fact we're gonna be with Ike again, be with somebody who's worth knowing.

But then I see Hoover and hear him yell, "See . . . ya . . . later . . . Cono," and it feels like nothing's ever gonna be the same ever again.

I go to the open end of the truck, trying to stand up tall and straight. I wave one last time out the back of the truck.

An hour passes and Mother and Delma have been put to sleep by the swaying and bumping of the truck. I open my box, pull out Mr. Green's letter, and start to read.

Dear Cono,

You did a fine job on your paper. In fact, I learned so much about you and your family that I'm really sorry to hear that you are leaving. Maybe you will come visit us someday?

After reading your paper I had a sense that maybe it would be a good thing for you to get away for a bit. We all need that sometime you know! You are a strong young man (and I don't just mean muscles), and I know you can do anything you set your mind to.

As your teacher and friend, I would like to suggest a few things that might help you along the way. First, no matter who you have to stand up for, whether yourself or someone else, always remember who you are, where you have come from and what makes you "Cono." "Cono" is someone to be proud of.

Second, times may be tough, but never give up, even if you get tired. Just like your boxing coach told you, "Fight when you're tired." Tired is just a temporary state; it doesn't last.

Finally, it doesn't really matter what other people do as long as you remember what is right. Think about the charisma of the people you admire and aspire to be like them, but of course, add your own "Cono-ness" to the equation and that will be good enough.

It was a pleasure knowing you, Cono, a real pleasure. Please try to keep in touch.

Your teacher and friend,

Mr. Sam Green

P.S.: Mrs. Green says for me to tell you to "Keep sitting on the shiny side of that star."

Our ride isn't the smooth jostling of a train. It's the bumping and tossing of a cattle truck that still smells like a cow's fear, wondering why it's not chewing on the grass it's supposed to be standing on.

I sit on that old couch and look out the back. Instead of seeing where I'm going, each passing mile shows me where I've been.

There goes Aunt Nolie and Uncle No-Account Red. There goes my garden seeds and my donkey. There goes that goddamn dugout. No more Tommy Burns and Mrs. Shit-for-Brains Berry.

I think about the slaps across my face and give names to the ones that stand out the most and holler at me: "Toothbrush," "Lunch," "Zexie," "Apple Pie," "Pearl Harbor." I even name one for Mother. I call it "Cono's Axe." Maybe that's the end of them. Maybe they're dead and gone, like Gene, part of West Texas.

I think about Uncle Joe beaten to a pulp by knucks and tire tools. I think about little Ervin Clay Carter up in Heaven with powder on his face and poor ole Wort Reynolds without a head. I think about Gene. Then I think about H. Govan with his smiling "Ever'thin's gonna be alright" face.

For the first time, I picture myself sitting on the shiny side of that star, where it's so bright I can see forever. Maybe my box of specials isn't so silly after all. And with that thought on my mind and my butt on the torn and beat-up couch that still holds the smell of cow dung, I fall asleep next to Delma and Mother.

Location of the former Wright School, below the Double Mountains

CHAPTER 46

8.7 Miles to Temple

WE MADE SEVERAL stops on the way there: once to pull over
and sleep the night through, and the other times for Mother and
Delma to have to get out and pee. Me, I had just preferred to pee
out the side between the slats.

When we finally got close to Temple, Dad told Mother to get
on in the front of the truck. I thought I knew why he wanted her
up there. I thought he wanted her to see where she's going instead
of where she'd been.

I peeked out the slats and saw that up ahead was an old run-
down house. I had hoped to God that it wasn't our new place, but
when we pulled up that dirt driveway, my hopes lit out and stayed
gone. Yep, it was ours, a true Dennis house. It was then I realized
that Dad had made Mother sit up front so we couldn't see the look
on her face when she saw the house or, maybe, so she couldn't see
the look on ours. The house was made of wood and had little holes

gnawed through from the inside out, like it had been feasted on by wild animals.

We got out and stood in front of the house and cocked our heads a little to the left to make the house look like it was standing up straight. We went inside and intruded on the rats who had mistaken it for their own Tourist Court. I remember thinking to myself, *Cono, welcome to Temple, Texas.*

After we settled in, I learned that the weather there was a lot better than in the western part of our state, except for maybe the thunderstorms. On the third night in that rickety old house, the wind was blowing the air and the rain around so hard that Mother and I had to use our four hands to hold up one of the walls. Come to think of it, maybe it wasn't the storm that was so bad; it was the *house* that couldn't be trusted.

There was other bad weather waiting for me in Temple all right, real bad weather. But it wasn't the kind that came from Mother Nature.

We only had to live in that shack for a month before we got to move into a real house, closer in town and with two bedrooms. We rented it from Doc Llewellyn. He had a daughter who became good friends with Delma. The Llewellyns lived across the field from us, the field I would grow to hate. Delma and I even had two mattresses and didn't have to share a bed. Dad was working for Ike at Weber's Café and, while money was slim, at least it was steady.

⊰ ★ ⊱

Later, I found out more about Temple's past. On Christmas Day, 1932, Clyde Barrow walked out of a store towards his car and stopped alongside a Model A roadster with keys in the ignition. Clyde thought the Model A looked a lot more appealing than the car he was driving. Clyde got in the car and tried to start it. The man who owned the car ran up and started yelling at Clyde to get out, but Clyde told him to back off or he'd shoot him. That man, Doyle Johnson, reached through the window and grabbed Clyde by the throat. That's when Clyde made good on his word and shot him. Bonnie and Clyde started the car and lit out of town.

⊰ ★ ⊱

We just went through Belton so it won't be long now before the train arrives in Temple. I can't help wondering if Dad's gonna make good on his word and spar with me when I get there.

A fellow with a gray fedora hat carrying an umbrella is walking up the aisle. What kind of man carries an umbrella? Doesn't he know that's what hats are for? He's probably a politician. I saw him get on earlier when we picked up passengers from Austin. Sure enough, he's walking over to me.

"Is that seat taken?" he asks, pointing to the seat next to me.

"I'm afraid it is," I say, knowing full well he'd have plenty of room to sit there now. It seems as though my memories have jumped out of the seat next to me and have crawled in my lap like ants at a Sunday picnic. And those ants are crawling back in my head and making me remember that first fall in Temple.

It had started off on a bad note or, rather, with a bad sore throat. I guess I'd lived there long enough to pick up Temple germs from the junior high school I was attending. My throat hurt something awful, and I thought I'd surely come down with scarlet fever like Delma had that time.

A kid in one of my classes told me about a doctor I should go see who was within walking distance from my house. He also gave me a Bible. "What's this?"

"It's a Bible."

"I can see that. Why're ye handin' it to me?"

"Just thought you'd like ta have it, you know, to read."

"I don't wanna take yer Bible."

"Well it's not really mine. I work at the Baptist Church, and I can get them anytime I want."

"OK, then," I said, taking the Bible he'd stolen from his church.

"I'll pray for your throat, Cono."

"OK," I hoarsed out of my throat, thinking, *Yeah, and praise the Lord too.*

I took him up on his advice, and right after school I went straight to that doctor's office. He told me to come back the next morning and to not eat anything. So that's what I did.

The next morning the doctor handed me two little yellow pills and said, "Here's your breakfast." Then he left me in a chair that leaned back. I waited there until my head started to feel fuzzy, like I was sitting at the bottom of a well looking up towards the light of the sky.

"Cono, are you ready?" I stared up through the well and saw the long-nosed face of the man talking to me, the man in the white coat who made a little loop out of some kind of wire and pulled one, then two tonsils from the back of my throat. And, if that wasn't bad enough, he decided that my adenoids weren't doing me any good, so he yanked them out too. Fuzzy or not, I felt every damn bit of it.

He laid a pack of ice on my neck for a while and told me to go home and get some rest. I did. I rested for a whole week because I got sicker than a dog. I got a bad fever and thought for sure I was gonna die. That's when I picked up that Bible. I remembered Ma saying, "Cono, thar ain't nothin' wrong with readin' the Bible." Plus,

I thought that if I was about to die, I might as well find out who was going to open up the pearly gates to let me in.

Once I got through all that "beggetting" stuff, it wasn't a bad read. I didn't understand much of it since there were so many people to keep up with. I got the gist of most of it, though. But I was still trying to figure out why it said "an eye for an eye" one minute and "turn the other cheek" the next.

During that week, Delma came in once with a pot on her head and stared at me sober as a judge. "Delma, ye need te get yerself a better lookin' hat." She laughed and left the room probably thinking she made me feel better. I guess in a way she did.

Mother would bring me canned soup, and I finally was getting to where I could drink the whole cup.

Dad came in towards the end of my bad week in bed and said, "Feeling any better yet?"

"No."

"Well, try ta get yourself better. Ya don't wanna miss anymore school. Besides, we need help making those sandwiches at Weber's."

"OK, I'll try." I don't think he cared I was sick. He just needed the extra money for the household.

But it was when Ike came to visit that things turned around. "Cono, well aren't you smart," he said, smirking and tipping his head to one side. "Yer tougher 'n a wood hauler's ass, that's all there is to it."

And just like that, his words were of the same magic as his knife and fork. So instead of dying, I went to school the next morning and, later that afternoon, to Ike's Weber's Café to become a maker and salesman of "fine sandwiches."

It was Dad's idea to start a business selling sandwiches at the

Greyhound bus station. After agreeing to pay Ike seven cents a sandwich for letting us use his ingredients, we made the sandwiches and took them to the bus station to sell them to the traveling soldiers from Camp Hood. We also paid the manager of the bus station, whose name also happened to be Temple, five percent of our gross sales for each day. We sold spiced-ham and cheese sandwiches, which included my special relish mayonnaise, for fifteen cents and soda pop for ten cents. (Mostly Dr. Pepper since they're made in Waco and easier to get.)

When things got going real good, we built a little cabinet against the back wall and got an icebox for the soda pops. We also ordered a few novelty items from San Antone and sold them too. Those little plastic Alamos became our biggest sellers.

On my very first official day of business, I made a bunch of sandwiches and put them in a basket. I rented a white cap and white vest from the laundry and then walked over to the station with the basket. When the first busload of soldiers pulled in, I got on the bus with my basket of sandwiches and walked up and down the aisles saying, "Sandwiches for sale." Right away, a soldier said, "I'll take one, son." It was my first sale and I was about to make eight cents!

I gave him the ham sandwich and said, "Fifteen cents, sir." He handed me a two-dollar bill. Holding it in my hand I stared at it for a bit and realized I had made my first mistake in business. I didn't have any change.

"I'm sorry, sir. I don't have any change, but I'll run in real quick and get some."

He looked at me for a brief second and said, "That's OK, son. You keep it."

I couldn't believe it! I'd made one dollar and ninety-two cents on my very first day! Right then and there I knew it was going be a lucrative business and it might pay off in a way I didn't even know yet. I pictured myself telling Aunt Nolie about making all that money on my first day. She would have spit out her beer in amazement and pride. And just like she must have known when the four of us lived with her, I knew that most of the money I earned would go right back towards keeping food on our table and beer in Dad's belly.

Besides selling little Alamos, we also rented a small tabletop slot machine from Jack Sprot, a traveling salesman who lived in Temple. We charged five cents for every pull, and if you got three bell pictures in a row, it paid out three dollars. The money we made from the slot machine was divided up three ways. At the end of each week, me, Jack, and Temple made fifty dollars, more money than a sideshow at the circus.

Pineapple came often to the bus station. He was an MP from Camp Hood who hung around so he could enforce the midnight curfew for the soldiers. His real name was Ferguson, but we called him "Pineapple" since that's what he learned to love when he was stationed in Hawaii. Sometimes Pineapple would see the bus drivers cheating the slot machine. He'd tell us when he saw someone trying to dig into it or walk away with it. Usually, as soon as the door hit those cheaters on the butt after we'd kicked them out, they'd call the Texas Rangers and tell them we had a gambling racket going on. The Rangers would then call our sheriff and tell him they were on their way. Then our sheriff would call Jack. By the time the Rangers showed up and asked, "Where's that slot machine?" we'd say, "What slot machine?"

We had other troubles on occasion. Once, Dad was helping Ike close up the café when a soldier walked in, looked at Ike, and said, "Give us a beer, old man."

"Sorry, son," said Ike, "we're not open, so I can't sell you no beer."

"Then I'm gonna come around that counter and get my own."

"No you're not," said Ike.

As the soldier walked around the corner, Ike was pulling a pocketknife out of his trousers. But before Ike had a chance to get that knife open, Dad pulled out his pistol and slapped the soldier upside the head with it.

"We're closed," Dad said.

We all watched as that stupid soldier walked out the door rubbing the bump on his head.

Later on, after Mary had moved to Temple to live with Ike, an army lieutenant was sitting at the café's bar and was getting more than a little Cooter Browned. He was also starting to get a little belligerent.

"Settle down, hoss," Mary told him.

But he kept mouthing off, being loud and annoying.

"Settle down, or I'll hit you with this billy club."

She pulled that weapon out from under the bar and I had no doubt that she would have used it. Before she got herself into trouble, I said, "Here, give it to me and I'll do it." I was fifteen at the time, and my body had finally decided to grow taller. Besides that, my muscles were starting to pop up and ask to be accounted for. I thumped that billy club on the palm of my hand and watched him turn around and leave.

The year before, when I was fourteen, another Cooter Browned man had walked into the Greyhound bus station and changed the course of my life. A man with fire in his eyes, a man I knew all too well.

CHAPTER 47

A Blade as Shiny as a Coon's Mirror

1942

BETWEEN SCHOOL AND sandwich making I stay real busy. I sure do like making money and living in a good house. The only thing I hate right now about this town is the school I go to, mostly because of the assistant football coach. He teaches English and tells me "Cono, you don't have any more sense than a bulldog."

I'm in spring training, though, and the coach likes the fact that I'm a ruthless football player. He's right about one thing. I'm not any good at English, and I'm even worse in my woodworking class. We were supposed to take a two-by-four and make a perfect square out of it. I had all the tools, the plane and saw, but by the time I was finished, I could have used that piece of wood as a toothpick. That was a real pisser.

The girls like me, though. Delma's friend and our neighbor, Patsy Llewellyn, is sweet on me. I can tell by the way she bats her eyes at me, nudges me when she laughs, and likes to sit real close to me on her couch, even though there's plenty of room for three people. She's cute enough, I guess. She has short blonde hair, and she's skinny—not like a post, more like a thin door to a storm cellar.

Delma says, "Cono, ask her out on a date, fer cryin' out loud."

She's a year older than Delma and a year younger than me. I decided to give Delma's suggestion a try.

Patsy and me walk to the drugstore, and I buy her a root beer. She starts talking like she's been storing up words her entire life and finally gets to try them out on me. She talks about boys she can't stand in some of her classes, some who I know and some I don't.

"Why do ye talk to them, then, if ye don't like 'em?" I ask.

"Cono, I don't wanna be rude!" she says and twists the curls on her forehead. She said "rude" with three syllables instead of one so that it sounded like "rue-a-duh." It was the strangest thing I ever heard, right up there with Mrs. Berry's "you-uh."

When I walk her home, I tell her good-bye, but she says, "Cono, let's sit on the step for a while."

So we do.

"Cono, why don't ya sit a little closer to me, huh?" So I do. Then she adds a little tee-hee-hee after I've moved close enough to almost touch her. She smells good, I'll give her that.

"Cono, do ya like my new dress?"

I don't think I'd even looked at it. So I look at it now. It's blue. "Sure I do," I say. Then she starts talking and tee-hee-heeing and talking and tee-hee-heeing until all I'm seeing is Sunshine sitting on the stool at the Lucky Star Bar.

"Well," I say, "time for me to head home."

"Already, Cono?"

"Yeah, gotta get home." I stand up and she sticks out a hand for me to help her up. When I do, she says, "Cono, I sure had fun tonight."

"Me too," I say.

"Maybe we can do this again sometime."

"Sure," I say. Then before I know it, she leans towards me and gives me a peck on my cheek.

As I'm walking home, I'm thinking that if she'd only left that "tee-hee-heeing" at home, instead of bringing it with her on our date, I'd have felt a lot better about the whole evening. Still, after that peck on my cheek, I'm remembering my cousin's spewing contest in Ranger. I bet I could win right now.

☆ ☆ ☆

Dad has started cooking at Weber's. He wears a white apron and a chef's hat and makes things like fried chicken and barbecue. He also makes a good open-steak sandwich, which is thirty-five cents, the most expensive thing on the menu.

He likes the job, but I think it's funny how his dad is also his boss. I'd hate it if Dad was my boss. The bad thing about his new job is that he hurts from so much standing. He can't wait to get home and pour beer down his gullet.

We're still in spring training, and even though I have to listen to that sorry-ass assistant coach, who's about as callous as a corn-cob used to wipe your ass, I like it well enough. We had a pre-game with a nearby school, and one of their running backs was being eyeballed by all the high schools: Ed Castello.

Last week I got my name in the *Temple Telegram*. Castello was running across the field towards the goal post when I caught up to him. I knocked him out and was listed as one of Woodson Fields' "fastest people."

At our next game, I'm going offense. I'll be the opening quarterback, and damn, I can't wait.

Business is good tonight at the Greyhound bus station, and Pineapple is filling us up with stories of renegade soldiers who play jokes on each other. Damn, he makes me laugh with that dry sense of humor of his, kinda like Ike's. I look at the clock. Ten, almost quitting time.

I start to say my good-byes when the door opens and Dad stumbles in from the dark, drunk as a skunk. He's got blood on his lip and a cut over his right eye, the blood still running down his cheek. I walk over to him, sit him down, and bring him a wet cloth. I dab the cloth at his cut, but he swats me away.

"What happened to ye?" I ask.

"Playing pool at the pool hall."

"Yeah?"

"Man was cheatin' me," he says, slurring his words.

"Yeah?"

"I called him a prick, jus' what he is."

"And?"

Dad yells, "He hit me with a goddamn cue stick! Couldn't get to him. Cue stick too long."

"Wait here, I'll get us a taxi."

"Don't want no goddamn taxi. Get me a goddamn beer!"

I ignore him and go to the phone to call for a taxi instead.

When I come back he says, "Where's my goddamn beer?" He didn't forget.

I open one from behind the counter and pour half of it out,

hoping he won't notice. He drinks it down in one gulp and stares at it, confused like something's missing.

"Need . . . to go . . . home," he says.

I walk beside Dad towards the door, staying close enough to him in case he starts to fall. As soon as I get him into the taxi, he lays his head against the window and mumbles, "Beaten by a goddamn taxi driver!"

"Huh?"

"I said I was beaten by a goddamn bricklayer!" I rest my head on the back of my seat and think to myself, *Well don't that beat all!*

The driver pulls up to our house, and after I pay him, I help Dad out of the taxi and into the quiet house. Dad is slumped over on me now; half of his weight is on my right side, my right arm under his. I walk him to his side of the bed hoping Mother won't wake up and see how drunk he is, see the blood I didn't get the chance to wipe off his face. He lies down and is out cold. He's good for the night.

I go into my room and see Delma asleep on her bed. I lie down on mine and stare up at the ceiling. There's a dim light coming through my window. A half-moon is paying me a visit, casting shadows of a kid named Cono who never could beat Hicks Boy. Well, I guess Dad has met his own Hicks Boy.

I can't believe I'm not jumping up and down, celebrating. I feel kinda sorry for him, my dad beaten by a cue stick. The same man who, to my knowledge, never lost a fight except for in the boxing ring with Shorty Houghton when I was three years old.

I also feel pretty good that I was there for him, did something for him that maybe he'll remember. But it doesn't really matter if he remembers. I will. For the first time, I felt useful to him.

I hear Mother scream. I snap back into the present, out of my daydream. Maybe she's woken up, has seen blood on her sheets reflected in moonlight, seen the blood on Dad's face. I start to get up but the quiet has taken over. I think I might just go back to sleep but the silence only lasts for a moment.

I hear a voice I know is Dad's but it's different somehow, guttural like a wolf's growl. I hear Mother say, "Stop it, Wayne!"

My feet touch the floor before the rest of me knows what it's doing. I open my door. Mother is backing towards me, away from the bloodied-face man holding a butcher knife. The blade glistens in the moonlight, shiny like a raccoon's mirror. He's stumbling towards her. My mind freezes. It's a scene from a scary picture show. *No, Cono,* I tell myself, *this is real. Real life, real time.*

Dad's stopped walking. He's swaying back and forth like an old porch swing. No, more like the swing of a hanged-man's noose. His eyes are glazed, like a film of anger is lying on top that he can't wipe away. He glances over to the couch where Pooch is sleeping.

I whisper, "Mother, keep backing up towards me." She stares at my father but listens to my words. Dad stops at the kitchen table, puts his empty palm on the table for balance, the butcher knife in the other hand swaying by his side.

"C'mon, Mother, keep coming to me," I say softly, feeling a surge of calm and determination at the same time.

Mother has backed all the way up to me. I pull her behind my door, into the bedroom where Delma is still sleeping. Mother is shaking. My hands are doing the same now. I see our .22 sitting on the open shelf just a few feet away. It's so close I can almost feel it. It's like the .45 that Hoover found, the one I felt in my hands, the cold steel of it. Now, I want to feel the warm safety of it.

A fear invades my body like a sickness. I'm drowning, but not in water. I'm drowning in the fear of what to do next, what I need to do to protect my family from a madman. I step a little closer to the pistol. Is this how it's going to end up?

Dad is staring at me, cold and empty eyes, determined eyes. They are the eyes of a man who holds fury as easy as he holds a new puppy. The eyes of my own father, who planted a seed and helped to create me. He made it possible for me to be in this impossible situation. I hate him.

"Cono, Cono," whispers Mother. I don't have time to think about hatred now. I have to think about survival for myself, my mother, and my little sister. I know I can't talk to him. Anything I say might set him off.

I step closer to the gun, but only a half step, because now Dad has taken a step towards me. It's too late for the gun. I back up inside the room and close the door.

"Wake up Delma," I tell her.

"What're we gonna do?"

"Wake up Delma!"

While she goes to Delma's bed, I take a chair and put it under the doorknob, hoping that will hold him off for a bit. I stand on my bed and start punching out the screen of my window, the same window that had given me easy moonlight just moments before.

"Where are you?" slurs Dad.

"Don't say anything," I whisper to Mother and Delma.

The screen is being stubborn, but it's dented now, open on one side.

"OK, Hicks Boy, you're time is up," I say to myself.

I hear the banging of knuckles on the door, not the kind

knuckles of a man like Cleave Barnes, who tried to help us find Delma when Dad had taken her. No, more like the banging of knuckles that want revenge, want to feel power.

I watch the doorknob turn back and forth, like the ticking hands of a clock when I don't want time to pass.

I finally get the screen knocked out. "Climb out, Mother!" I help hoist her out the window.

"What's going on, Cono?" asks a sleepy Delma, my sister who hasn't seen the glisten of the butcher knife.

"I said, get out!" I help her from the inside and Mother helps her from outside. The door is rattling now, Dad's knuckles still pounding it. I stare at it one last time, think for a second about the man behind it, and then hurl myself out the window.

The three of us pant our way across the deserted field, the same field I walked across from Patsy's a few nights ago.

We reach the Llewellyns' and bang on the door. We stand on the porch looking back across the field. There are just a few trees swaying in Temple's springtime winds. No one has followed us.

It's late and the Llewellyns are still asleep. We keep banging on their door. Doc finally opens the door. He looks confused seeing the three of us standing there. "Dad's gone crazy, Doc. Can we come in?"

"Of course." He lets us in and asks what happened. We give him the shortened version, still including the butcher knife.

Mrs. Llewellyn comes into the kitchen and starts to make coffee. Patsy walks out in her bathrobe.

"Doc, if you give me your shotgun, I can put a stop to this."

"I can't do that, Cono."

"But if he comes here, he's liable to kill us all."

"If he comes here, I'll give you that gun."

We wait. We listen. Nothing.

Patsy comes over and says, "Sorry about your troubles, Cono."

I know she means it when she says it. But it's no use. I'm tired of talking. Even more, I'm tired of listening.

I stay up most of the night with one eye open. I can still smell the spiced-ham sandwiches, now mixed with the smell of my fury.

I hear Speedy Dale's words, "Ye oughta be better to that boy, Wayne, or someday he'll git ya."

I hear H. Govan say, "Everythin's gonna be alright."

Then, before I finally fall asleep on Doc Llewellyn's couch, I hear Ike say, "Ya can't hep who yer parents are."

Still, I know, I feel it in my bones. It's time to leave.

Cono, Age 14

CHAPTER 48

2 Miles to Temple

I CLENCH MY jaw and my fists at the same time. We're almost there.

Dad didn't come up to Doc's place until the next morning. I heard him say, "Mother, what have I done?"

She told him the story, but I wasn't listening. I already knew what he'd done, and I wasn't likely to forget it. I didn't want to walk next to that son of a bitch, so I just walked home behind them thinking about how I'd been forced to turn the other cheek.

I knew I was gonna leave, but I didn't want to say anything to Mother or Delma since I didn't want to hurt them. I was tired of being up against the ropes and backed into the corner all at the same time. I felt like Zexie, like I was gnawing at myself just so I could get free from a trap. I was the last in a row of dominos destined to fall.

I knew that if I left I'd have a much better chance of standing right smack dab in the center of the ring, where I'd be in the advantage for a change. I wanted to head out and never turn back. I wanted to take care of my own self. I'd been doing that for a long time anyway.

I made myself a plan. I went to the Santa Fe Railroad station and asked how much it would cost for a one-way ticket to Ranger. Then I walked over to Ike's Weber's Café, where I'd made about fifteen thousand dollars making all those sandwiches. Everything I had earned I'd given to my family. I only wanted just enough money to cover the ticket. The girl that worked behind the counter gave me the money, and then I left.

I got on the train, my first train ride, and went straight into Ranger. I remember again seeing Ma and Pa and feeling that flicker of light on my pillow. When I found out that Fire Chief Murphy would let football players stay in the firehouse, I signed up for practice. He said I could stay there and he'd pay me ten dollars a month to help keep up the place, sweeping and stuff. Ten dollars was all I needed. Since summertime was closing in, I trained with the other football players. I could run a ten-second flat, and I was the fastest man on the team.

I stayed around Ranger for a while and did all right. But even though I was looking forward to the football season, there was something I was aching for even more, the company of good horses and real cowboys.

After a few weeks in Ranger, I sent a letter to my Uncle Thurmond, who was the foreman at the Martin ranch outside of Hamlin. I asked him if I could work for him. I got a letter back that said, "Dear Cono, I'm shorthanded, and I can use you, and I'll pay you thirty dollars a month plus room and board."

I left the next day.

I got on the next train to travel the hundred and forty miles to Rotan. From there, remembering the mailman's route, I knew the back way to the Martin ranch. If I could just get to Rotan I could hitch a ride with him. And that's exactly what I did.

The mailman dropped me off at a crossroad, me holding my one little suitcase that contained everything I owned. I walked for a while before I got to the Clear Fork of the Brazos River. I waded through the river a bit and then put my boots back on and walked a little more. The main house was seven or eight miles away, but the foreman's house, the number two house, was just ahead. As luck would have it, I got there just in time for supper.

After supper, I saddled up for the evening routine with Uncle Thurmond, Coots Rutherford, Whiskey Bill, Dope, and Chicken Dougherty, the ranch cook. I couldn't believe it, but they put me on Ike's colt, the one he'd broken a long time ago at the Dennis ranch. Yep, I was riding on old P. A., Ike's favorite horse, the very one he rode when he led those sixteen horses into Rotan.

It made me think about P. A. standing for "Pissant" unless the women were around, and then he'd say P. A. stood for "Prince Albert." That's Ike all right, wanting to be the gentleman. He always told me that if you treat women like cattle, you'd be in good shape. He'd said, "When ya take cattle on a drive, ya go nice and slow, real gentle-like. That's what women like when ya take them on a date, nice and slow." The real reason for driving cattle slow is because you want them to eat all they can since the more they eat, and the more they gain, the more money they're worth. The Martin ranch was like the Dennis ranch in that they only raised Herefords since they're known to have a good temperament.

As soon as I started riding old P. A., I heard Coots Rutherford say, "He rides jes' like Ike." Considering I think that Ike is the best cowboy who's ever lived, I grinned from the inside out.

We rode 'til a little after dark, when we noticed the wind picking up pace and the clouds rolling in.

"Reckon we better head on in," said Uncle Thurmond. And that's what we did.

Lying on a cowhand bunk I worried about Delma and Mother. At least they both knew where I was after Ma had called them up, but it didn't make me feel any better. I kept thinking that Dad would do something else, come after Mother and Delma again and that I wouldn't be around to protect them. I'd only protected myself, and, I suppose, I'd protected my Dad by not being near him.

It didn't rain much during the night, but the next day it rained like a cow peeing on a flat rock. We were about to cross the Brazos when Uncle Thurmond reminded me that his horse, Blackjack, was a river horse. That meant that if he felt a bog underneath him while crossing a river, he'd roll over to keep from getting stuck and drowned. Luckily, the water wasn't so high that our horses had to swim while we held on to their tails. But it was high enough that we had to give the Brazos the attention it deserved.

"OK, Uncle Thurmond," I hollered. "I'm goin' on acrost."

I charged my horse forward and made it across without any problem. Then came Uncle Thurmond on top of Blackjack, and sure enough, just when Blackjack hit that bog, he started to roll. Uncle Thurmond jumped off as soon as he could in order to keep from getting drug under and pinned down. I loosened my rope in case I needed it and watched as Uncle Thurmond made it across the Brazos, half swimming and half running.

"Whew," he said as I started laughing. And when he started drying off his glasses with his soaking wet shirt, I laughed even harder.

A few days later I rode on McKeever, another good mare. Coots and I were out with the cattle and saw a cow that needed to be treated for screwworms in her eyes. Herefords are bad about getting screwworms. As Coots sat atop Blackjack trying to rope the eye-boogered cow, my horse stepped into a badger hole. I landed flat on my back, McKeever's big body lying across me. Then Blackjack, who also happened to be heavy on the rope, got hit on the nose when the rope broke, and he threw Coots flat on his back. There we were, two cowboys lying on their backs being looked down upon by a cow with worms in her eyes.

Coots told Uncle Thurmond later, "Damn, Cono was lying so still with that horse on top 'a him I thought he was dead."

Nope, I thought, *if I was dead there'd be worms in my eyes too, six feet under the Texas soil.*

Sometimes I think there's nothing better than a rock for a pillow and the sound of a horse nickering to put you to sleep at night. One thing's for damn sure, it's a helluva lot better than having to kick your way out of a madhouse.

Maybe ol' Blackjack and I had something in common; if we think we're in trouble of getting bogged down we just roll over and get out, come hell or high water.

Maybe that's why I went back to Temple. Uncle Thurmond said to me, "Cono, don't you think you should go back to school?"

"Nah, not yet," I said.

But a few days later Dad showed up and said, "Son, if ye come back to Temple, you can live with Ike, and I won't bother you none."

Dad had come all the way up there just to ask me to come home, like everything was gonna be fresh and new, a new Temple, Texas.

I thought about it, stared at him for a while, and tried to figure out whether he was just speaking out of the side of his mouth, like that time right after he got out of the hospital and said, "Cono, if I get better and get outta here, I'm gonna be nicer to you."

This time he didn't bother to say he'd be nicer to me. He'd just said he'd leave me alone. Maybe that was honest enough.

I went home, knowing that I was a river horse. I'd get out of the bog if I needed to and no pissant was gonna stop me.

⊣ ★ ⊢

Back in Temple I stayed with Ike in his apartment, owned by a gal friend of his. One night I got home about two a.m. (and I'm not saying where I'd been), and Ike wasn't home. About four in the morning I heard Ike stumble up those apartment stairs.

"Ike, what're ye doin' up so late?"

"I was out dancin'," he laughed.

He might 'a loved Mary, but he also loved being a lady's man, probably since he was born on St. Valentine's Day. There had been another time, at Weber's Café, when he'd nodded over to a good-looking lady with a healthy bank account and said, "Cono, if I cut her meat a couple of times, we'd have ourselves a good place to stay."

I couldn't help but laugh, but part of me wondered what he was waiting for.

"Ike?" I said. "Remember Miss Bandy in Rotan?"

"Shor I do."

"If ye would 'a stayed and married her, then you'd have yer own ranch now."

"I reckon yer right about that," he laughed.

"And then, when you died, I'd have yer ranch."

He looked up at the ceiling as if he was picturing it, and then I added, trying my best Ike imitation by tilting my head sideways and letting out a little smile from the corner of my mouth, "Well aren't you smart." We both laughed.

He went over to the cabinet and pulled down a tall glass. After opening the refrigerator, he took out four raw eggs, broke them into the glass, and started stirring.

"What're ye doin' now?" I asked.

"Jes' puttin' a little lead in my pencil's all." And with that, he threw his head back and swallowed down the entire contents like it was a shot of whiskey.

I went back to school for a bit, but nothing felt right. I got my driver's license, something I knew I'd need if I ever got lucky enough to own a car.

Since the cowboy in Ike just couldn't simmer down, he took on a job as foreman of a small ranch in Walburg, a German settlement thirty-eight miles from Temple. He finally got to use that new saddle he bought in Crane.

Ike being gone meant that the sandwich business was over, and it also meant that I was back living at home. I got various jobs painting houses and saved two hundred dollars.

Dad told me one morning, "C'mon, Cono. Let's go to Rosebud. There's a car I wanna look at. And bring yer checkbook." We hitched a ride from a man going the same direction and rode the twenty-four miles to Rosebud.

Dad stared at the 1928 Chevy and asked, "How much ya want for that car?"

"One-fifty," said the owner.

"Cono," he said, still looking at the car, "write him a check."

Not only had I lost one hundred and fifty dollars of my own hard-earned money, I kept thinking about the light reflected in the butcher knife. Dad had been pretty much true to his word and didn't bother me none, but still, I'd had a taste of being on my own and I liked it.

In Temple, I felt like Dad was always standing over my shoulder, crowding me, making me want to keep more than an arm's length away from him. I don't know how to explain it, exactly, other than to say that this "new" Temple was like wearing out a new pair of shoes you learned to tie by yourself but still felt full of sticker burrs.

So, just like Mr. H. said about leaving the barbershop, Ike did the same thing. He left Temple because he was "all done with that." And then I knew that I, too, didn't have to settle for stale bread any longer.

I packed up my things, went back to the Martin ranch, broke a few horses with Uncle Thurmond, and soon felt another itch in my craw to do something different. I went to Pampa to dig a pipeline.

These days Dad is working at a construction company. He never had much schooling, having left school in eighth grade to try to get out from under his mean ol' mother, Lizzie. But he's smart as a whip when it comes to math. He can figure out dimensions and fractions in his head and is good at adding and subtracting the money he doesn't have. I'm glad he doesn't have to depend on me anymore for money. Now the money I make is mine.

Uncle Thurmond (standing up) on the Martin ranch

CHAPTER 49

Temple, Texas

I FINALLY STEP off the train, and I'm met only by the dark. I walk the fifteen minutes to the house, all the while grateful for the time to stretch my legs. I'm eager to see Mother, Sis, and Pooch, but my hands sweat when I think about seeing Dad again. It's not because he can beat me anymore; I know he can't. It's because I've promised myself to show him a thing or two from a man's perspective, this man's perspective. I want him to know he's done us wrong over the years, and I want him to be accountable for it. It's time to separate the sheep from the goats.

The house looks the same. I stare at the window, the one I'd escaped from. I see the light shining in the kitchen window. I smooth out the wrinkles in my uniform as best I can. I take a deep breath and walk into the house.

"Cono!" yells Delma.

I give her a big hug and pick her up at the same time. I wrap my arms around Mother, and like always, she pats my back a few times. I lean down to get licks from an older Pooch. Dad gets stiffly up of the couch, limps over to me sticking out his big paw for me to shake, and says, "Son."

"Sorry I'm late. The train took longer 'cause of the strike an' all."

"Well, I'm starved. Let's eat," Dad says.

While Mother takes the kept-warm food out of the oven, I stare down at Dad's hands. He's twirling his index finger around his thumb like he always has.

"Roast beef, green beans, and mashed potatoes, jes' like ye like."

"Can't beat that with an ugly stick," I tell her.

As soon as we start plowing into our supper, Delma asks, "Cono, what's it like there?"

"It's good, real good. I'm a physical training instructor in charge of ten thousand men."

"What's that mean?"

"I teach men how to be strong, build their muscles, and increase their stamina."

"Like ye did yerself?" Mother asks.

"I guess so."

"Ye look so strong, Cono!" says Delma.

"Sorta," I say, looking at Dad. "I teach a little boxing too."

Dad doesn't say anything. He gets up and gets himself another beer from the icebox.

"What do ye do fer fun?" asks Delma.

"Go to the movies sometimes, swim. Make a little money on the side. This sure is good, Mother," I say, taking another bite of tough roast beef.

"Thank ye."

"What do ye mean, 'make a little money on the side'?" asks Dad.

"I run a little gamblin' house on the side."

"How's that?" asks Dad. So I tell him.

A lot of our men play craps, so I decided to run a little gambling casino in my barracks on the weekends. Anyone who wants to be a part of my gambling night has to ante up by putting a quarter in the black box. In other words, if you want to place a bet you have to pay the house. The black box is mine. The house is me.

I watch all the gamblers pretty closely, and usually I'm good at figuring out which ones are gonna cheat and which ones aren't. After they've had a few beers and a long night, I usually hear some of them say, "Damn, where'd all my money go?" And then I answer to myself, "It's in my little black box that I'm gonna take back to my barracks and hold like an extra pillow."

Dad says, "Ye gotta cut that out. Ain't right. Trouble's all you're gonna get."

I think I'm about to choke on my food. Dad telling *me* to stop gambling? Talk about calling the kettle black. Suddenly I'm not hungry anymore. I push my plate away, staring at the food still left there.

"Done already, Cono?" asks Mother.

"Yeah, full as a tick. Any more and I'd pop green beans all over Delma," I say, winking at her.

Truth is, any more words from his mouth and I'll pop a blood vessel in my neck.

"I think I'll take Pooch for a little walk, work off this supper."

"Not too far," says Dad. "He's gettin' on in years, not as active as he used to be. We both have arthritis, ya know."

"I know," I say, feeling like I'm two years old again and Delma's just been born.

"I'll come with ye, Cono," say Delma.

We walk out of the house and Delma says, "Let's walk across the field to the Llewellyns'. Ye can see Patsy. She's dyin' te see you."

"Nah, not tonight, Sis. I'm not up for any giggling."

I don't tell her, but I don't want to walk across that field ever again. We start walking the other direction, towards town.

"So, how's Dad been treatin' ye?"

"We don't talk much, but he's OK to me."

"Good. And with Mother?"

"Fine. He still yells at her, but he doesn't hurt her." At least there's that.

We get back to the house to find Mother still awake and Dad in bed. I start to unpack and see my boxing gloves, the ones Colonel Posey lent me, lying at the bottom of my duffle bag.

"Mother, where are the gloves I gave Dad?" I ask, eager for him to try them out in our sparring session.

"He sold 'em."

My head turns one side to the other until I think I could spin it around on my neck like an owl if I wanted to.

"He what?"

"He sold 'em."

"Well I'll be damned. Why?"

Mother shrugs her shoulders.

"We were supposed to spar."

"What's that?" she asks. The water is running over the dishes she's washing in the sink.

"Nothin', nothin' a'tall."

I don't want to wait until the end of my trip to see Ike. I need to go tomorrow, put a little lead in my pencil, the one that doesn't seem to be able to write.

"I'm gonna go see Ike tomorrow," I tell her.

"I know Ike'll be glad te see ye."

"Yeah, I'll be glad to see him too."

Mother has set out a pillow and blanket on the couch for me. My room, the one I'd shared with Delma, has only one bed now, a double, just for Delma. Fine by me, I don't want to sleep in that room anyway. I'd rather be out here on the couch with one eye open.

☆

Early in the morning Mother is making bacon and eggs for breakfast.

"Where's Dad?" I ask.

"He walked to town. He left the car fer ye."

"Pooch go with him?" I ask, noticing I didn't get a morning lick.

"Yeah, usually does when he walks te town."

"He doesn't mind me takin' the car?"

"Reckon not. That's why he left it."

I eat my breakfast and take off in Dad's car. It's good to drive for a while and clear my head a bit. I think about Dad teaching me how to fish, how to trap, how to chop wood, how to stand up for myself, how to cover myself when I'm being beaten, and how to hate him. This isn't such a bad car for a hundred and fifty dollars—*my* hundred-fifty, that is. It's worth it if it takes me to see Ike again.

I arrive at Ike's house and see sweet Mary looking out the kitchen window. She walks out with her arms spread wide.

"Cono!" She gives me a warm bear hug, and I give her one back.

"Sure is good te see ya. Boy, ya look fit as a fiddle."

"Sure good to see you too, Mary. Where's that old man?"

"Out feeding the cows, jes' a little over yonder," she says, pointing in the direction of the barn. "I know he's chompin' at the bit ta see ya."

"Better go find him then. Don't want him to bite through anythin'!"

"Alrighty then, see ya'll when ye get back. I'll have some dinner waitin' fer ya."

I take off walking towards the barn, speeding up my pace. About fifty feet away is the best sight in the world. Ike is standing there surrounded by Herefords, all looking at him like he's their lord and savior, which I imagine he is. Sometimes I look at Ike the same way. Today is one of those times.

He feels my presence before he sees me. "Cono, 's'at you?" he says while turning around. "Well I'll be damned. You've shot up like a weed and out like Tarzan."

"Came to see what no good yer up to." We shake hands, and he pats my back.

"Ya look real good, Cono."

"Same as you, Ike."

"Now don't go sayin' that. Yer still young and spry." Then he says with a wink, "Well, I'm still kinda spry."

"I'm sure Mary's pleased 'bout that!" We both laugh.

"Say, I gotta meet a friend 'a mine at a bar nearby. He wants to talk about purchasing some cattle and needs some of my know-how. Ya ride with me?"

"Sure."

We get into Ike's car and do a little sightseeing on the way. I see a cute little house on the left with a front porch and picket fence.

"Who lives there?"

"Oh, that place belongs to a German Bohemian man. Nice fella."

Further up on the right is another house. It looks kinda like an old Wayne Dennis house, falling down on one side. Car parts litter the front yard.

"Who lives there?"

"Oh, some damn white man."

"Still like that Cherokee part 'a ye, huh, Ike?"

"Damn straight."

We get to the bar and meet Andres, Ike's friend. "This here's my grandson, Cono," Ike says.

"Pleasure," I say, shaking his hand.

The three of us sit down at a table for four and a short little old lady in a pink uniform comes over to take our order.

"Bring us three Pearl beers," says Ike.

"No beer fer me," I say.

"Still not a drinker, Cono?"

"Still not."

"Sody pop then?"

I turn to the waitress and say, "Ye got Nehi Grape?"

She nods and says, "Be right back."

For eleven o'clock in the morning the place is busy. The early lunch crowd has come in. Andres starts to talk while Ike listens. And I'll be damned, Ike's twirling his index finger around his thumb. They say an apple doesn't fall far from the tree. This is one habit Dad's pulled down from his father, but as far as I can see— and unfortunately—the only one.

Ike starts to talk but Andres keeps saying, "What are you saying? I can't hear."

Finally, after gulping down his beer, Andres says, "Hell, let's go someplace quiet where we can talk." I pull out my wallet to pay, but Ike says, "Put that away, Cono. You need ta save yer money." I do as I'm told, grateful for the man beside me who appreciates my hard work.

Ike and me gulp down our drinks and head down the street to a little dive of a bar, a place that doesn't sell food.

"This is better," says Andres. We all sit down at a table and order another round from the bartender, the only person working there.

In the middle of cow talk, a man with a black mustache that matches the color of his eyes opens the door, pulls out a pistol, and shoots a bullet right past Ike's ears and into the mirror behind the bar. The bartender pulls out his shotgun, aims it at the shooter, and says, "José, you drop that gun right now. This ain't no way to settle a bar tab." The man backs down and yells something I don't understand, and then he leaves.

As cool as a cucumber, Ike clicks the left side of his cheek, turns to Andres, and says, "Ye got another quiet place ye wanna go?"

Damn, it all happened so fast I didn't even have time to get scared. So I laughed. Good ol' Ike. He sure does look at the world in a whole different light. I just wish I could see things the way he does. He takes care of business without any fuss.

I remember the last time I lived with him before he moved to Walburg. There was a Peeping Tom outside of Ike's window on South 9th street. Ike pulled out his pistol, opened the window, and yelled, "Hold it right there, or I'll shoot ya where yer gallasses cross."

It turned out to be the sheriff, who was looking for the Peeping Tom.

"It's just me, Mr. Dennis."

"Well, go on ahead then," said Ike. I guess he felt he was still in the wide-open part of Texas, where you took troubles into your own hands and settled the problem with a ride on a good horse.

Back at Ike's place Mary has set our dinner on the kitchen table. I watch Ike twirl his fork and knife around, his magic way of eating that I've never understood and have always missed when I'm not around him.

I don't tell Ike about the sparring session I was supposed to have. I don't tell him about Dad selling the gloves I gave him. I tell him that it was sure good to see him and Mary and that I look forward to my next visit. I get into Dad's car and watch Ike walk back over towards the barn. I watch him mount up on his mare. I watch his lips move as he talks to his horse and pat his neck. I watch the best cowboy in the world roll up a cigarette in one hand, tip his hat at me, and ride off to the pasture.

On the drive back to Temple, I try to think about what's next. I try to imagine asking my dad why he sold my gloves. I know Ike would just let it go, not say a word. Instead, he'd just think to himself, "what is, just is." I think again about the words he said to me just after that apple pie night at the ranch: "Ye can't help who yer parents are."

The sun is just starting to set when I get back. Temple, Texas, seems quiet, like it's settling in for the night. I pull up to the house and see Delma running in a panic towards me. "Cono, Cono," she sobs, "something terrible has happened!"

Ike and Cono

CHAPTER 50

Train Back to San Antone

WHEN DELMA CAME storming out, I was thinking that Dad had gone and done it again, he'd unleashed his fury. But that wasn't what happened. Mother and Delma were home, but Dad had taken Pooch to the vet to have him put down. She told me that Pooch was out walking with Dad when a mean Afghan hound tore into him. As always, Pooch tried to defend himself, but this time the other dog got the best of him.

"He was in real bad shape, Cono," Delma sobbed into my shoulder. I wondered who was in worse shape, Pooch or the man who loved him beyond means.

"Where's the vet's office?" I asked. She told me where it was, and I took off on foot, just like Dad had when he carried Pooch the six blocks to the vet's office. I saw Dad before I made it there. He was walking home slowly, his head down.

"I'm sure sorry, Dad," I said with tears in my own eyes. I loved Pooch too.

Dad started sobbing. I'd never, ever seen him cry.

"I tried to shoot him, put him out of his misery. But I couldn't. Jus' couldn't." And he cried all the way home and into his room.

The three of us left him alone to grieve in his own way. We grieved too, for the only dog we'd ever owned, the dog that defended us, the dog Dad had defended by spraying that car with bullets when it tried to run him over.

I think we all grieved for Dad too. We were used to seeing him fragile with illness, used to seeing the mad inside and outside of him. Seeing him sad was a whole nuther thing.

After making supper, Mother took a plate to him in their bedroom. When she came out, she was holding something familiar, something I hadn't seen in a long time.

"Yer Dad found this today," she said, holding it towards me to take. In her hands was my cigar box, my box of specials.

While Mother went back to doing dishes, I sat down on the couch, opened the lid, and took out each item one at a time. The top part of a toothbrush, the one I'd bitten in two that left my face stinging; a devil's claw, like the ones I used to stack up and compare; a stick I'd called Tiger that protected me and grew me a little sister; the pocketknife given to me by Ike when Delma was born that I'd tainted with a bully's blood in first grade; Uncle McClesky's penny that I never spent; and an old worn lace from the pair of boxing gloves I'd fought with for the first time, when I chipped my tooth.

And, dirtied from the cookstove's ashes I'd scooped out for Little Gene Davis after he had died, were two letters. The one I'd written to Gene and the one from Mr. Sam Green.

"Mother, did Dad look inside this box?"

"I reckon he did. The box was open when he left this mornin'. Why?"

"Jes' wonderin'," I said, knowing that those letters were never intended for Dad to read. Or were they?

I unfolded Mr. Green's letter first, skimmed through it, and read

As your teacher and friend, I would like to suggest a few things that might help you along the way. First, no matter who you have to stand up for, whether yourself or someone else, always remember who you are, where you have come from, and what makes you "Cono." "Cono" is someone to be proud of . . . Finally, it doesn't really matter what other people do as long as you remember what is right. Think about the charisma of the people you admire and aspire to be like them, but of course, add your own "Cono-ness" to the equation and that will be good enough.

Did Dad read this? Then I unfolded and read over the letter I had written to Gene.

Gene, I want to kill my Dad. Send him right up there to Heaven, where maybe you can teach him a few things, like how to be nice to me. But then, I guess it would be too late. Unless he was Jesus, and got alive again to come back to do something good. That'll be the day.

Dad had read those letters. I knew it when I held them in my hands, sitting on that couch. I could feel it in my bones just like I was able to feel storms brewing around me when living at home. I had wondered if he was going to say anything to me, but as it turned out, and as usual, he didn't say one word.

The next day, before my train was to leave, I helped Dad pick up our dead Pooch and together we buried him on the side of Elm Creek. It was hard for both of us. The breeze was soft, and I kept hearing "Down in the Valley" playing its tune in my head. "Down in the valley, valley so low, hang your head over, hear the wind blow."

When we got back to the house, I packed up and got ready to leave. I kept my borrowed gloves hidden at the bottom of my duffle bag, and as far as I knew, Dad hadn't seen them.

Dad was trying to be easy and calm. He was trying to put Pooch behind him and think about other things; maybe he was even thinking about those letters.

He said, "So, Cono, ya teach all those boys how to take care of themselves, how to fight?"

"That's right," I said.

"So, if I were to come at ya and do this, what would ya do?" He got up from the couch, came towards me, and started to throw a slow punch at my chin. Before he knew it, I had spun him around and had him in a choke hold. It was as easy as eating a piece of apple pie is supposed to be.

"I'd do something like that," I said.

I let go.

He grinned. Not a big toothy grin, but a Dad grin. Turning to Mother he said, "Elnora, that boy can go!"

It was my turn to grin. My Dad had just paid me my first compliment. I think for the first time he was proud of me, not jealous, but proud. "That boy can go!" was his way of saying that I was alright, I could take care of myself, and he knew it. He sat back down on the couch and lit a cigarette.

I said good-bye and hugged Delma, who whispered two things to me. "Do you have a girlfriend yet?" to which I gave her a smirk worthy of Ike, and, "Cono, you're the best brother ever. You were right to leave when you did. I would 'a hated to have seen ye in jail at fourteen years old."

I nodded, hugged her again, and tried to maintain control. I hugged Mother after she'd said, "Take care 'a yerself, Cono."

Dad managed to get up, despite his pain, and shook my hand and said, "Guess we'll see ya next time, then."

"Yeah, next time." I watched him limp back to the couch to seek comfort in a Pearl beer and the lit cigarette that was smoldering in an ashtray on the coffee table.

Before turning to leave I looked at Dad and said, "I jes' have te tell ye what happened to my boxing gloves."

He looked up at me, his forefinger making circles around his thumb, and listened to my story about Vargo. I told him the whole story about getting in free to the movies, swimming, and skating. I told him about how I'd loaded up my own stolen gloves on a bus to Philadelphia. When I finished, he laughed. He didn't just grin, he laughed and said the same words I had said when I learned that Dad had sold the gloves I gave him: "Well I'll be damned."

When I walked out the door, he was still smiling.

☆ ★ ☆

The chug in this train seems steadier somehow. Heading away from Temple, the air seems lighter, easier to breathe.

Dad didn't want to spar with me after all. Was it that he'd had enough of hitting me, or was he afraid he'd have to live with the memory that I could beat the tar out of him and he wouldn't stand a chance? Did he have any regrets?

Some of my friends say that I never would have hit him. Others say that if I'd started hitting him, I never would have quit. That might be right. I'll never know. Colonel Posey had told me that the way I'd pictured things might not be the way they'd turn out. He sure was right. The idea of sparring with Dad was nothing but a snipe hunt.

Maybe he learned his meanness by watching and listening to his mother, the one who was supposed to hug him and say goodnight to him when he went to sleep, hover over him when he was sick or scared, but did none of that. Instead, he learned that hitting hard was the best way to make himself feel strong. Now he's a man whose body defies him, mocks him, and has stripped him of any strength and power he once thought he had.

I like to think my next leave will be different. No more harsh words. Some kind ones would be all right, but Dad doesn't use many words, not since the Great Depression when they cost money. Not with me anyway.

I saw him break down and cry like a baby, like I'd seen Mother do when she was beaten, and Aunt Nolie do when her Joe got killed; like Delma did when Dad beat me senseless over a piece of apple pie. Still, there's gotta be a kindness in there somewhere. But when I was born, he didn't know where to start. He hit below the belt, and he knows it.

I might not have sparred with him, but I stopped him cold, and I don't just mean by showing off my defense skills and putting him in a headlock. As sure as a sharp axe can cut through and splinter a log and slice a thin piece of paper, a sharpened pencil can do the same thing. Words are powerful; they can be weapons as sharp as an axe. "Gene, I want to kill my Dad" are words that I bet reverberated and echoed in his ears just as loud as a shot from a sawed off shotgun or as jolting as a steer must feel when blue lightning bounces off his head. And just as sharp as a hard slap across my face. I don't think I meant for him to find those letters, but he did.

Sometimes I wonder if Gene had anything to do with it. I wonder if, when you get to Heaven, you can move the people on earth in certain ways, make them do things, like they were marbles that you could flick in any direction you wanted to. Gene knew what I'd done to Tommy Burns, jabbing him with that pocket-knife in first grade. Maybe he didn't want me to do that again.

I see Gene grinning sometimes, even still after all these years. He says to me, "We don't give up, do we, Cono?"

That time in Temple, when Dad came at us with a butcher knife? I realize now that when he was staring at us, it wasn't us he was seeing. It was his Hicks Boy he saw that night, the one at the pool hall who had beaten him with that cue stick and left him feeling small, like a cockroach you have to squash so you can get on with your supper.

I don't think he hates me. He's just not what you call "standard issue." Besides, I didn't make my dad; he made me.

I know where I've been, and for the most part, where I'm going. I can be around Dad and see him through a man's eyes. I'm no longer a towheaded kid hiding his dad's booze, protecting his family, escaping. Could it be that I don't need that one man to respect me? I'm on a train back to San Antonio, where ten thousand might be enough. Ain't that something?

I'm eighteen years old, and I'm safe.

⊰ ★ ⊱

Something else has settled into the seat next to me. I'm not real sure what it is until it nudges me and asks, "So, Cono, what are you looking at?"

It's the future, the future who's sitting next to me. I shrug my shoulders and think, *Yer more likely to know that than me.*

But I have a feeling it's something better than what's behind me.

I close my eyes, and before I know it, I'm out like Lottie's eye.

Cono on leave with Pooch

CHAPTER 51

San Antone, Texas, Lackland Army Air Force Base

THE FIRST THING I did when I got back was retire my little black box. Maybe Dad was right, that trouble was all I would get from it. I don't want any more trouble. It doesn't mean I'm going to stop gambling a time or two. In fact, that's where I'm headed in a few minutes, to the Rec Hall for a soda pop and a game of craps.

I lather up my face for a shave and stare at my reflection in the mirror. Looking into my own eyes, I see the eyes of others. I've become real good at reading eyes: Dad's eyes when they were full of fury and I had to take cover; Dad's soft mushy eyes when he looked at Pooch; and the calm, cool eyes of Ike. And I see the eyes of H. Govan, eyes I could look into and see past the color of his skin and into his goodness resting inside.

My eyes are looking towards the future. Even though I regret the things we have missed out on, Dad and me, I know we can never make up for the time we lost. Maybe someday we'll be friends. I guess I'll just have to see how it plays out.

I've met a lotta good men in this man's army; some who've been a whole lot worse off than me and some who've had it a whole lot better. Those fellas in Pampa who got to the paratroopers office before lunchtime? Most of those boys died on D-Day in June of 1944.

I have another buddy here in the army, a Zuni Indian named Eddie Beyuka. When he was still a private, he was shipped out to the Philippines and was taken prisoner along with seventy-five thousand other soldiers. As a POW, he somehow survived the Bataan Death March, maybe because he prayed to his "Great Being." He's still carrying on, not giving up.

The Great Depression was hard on many folks. Some people have told me it takes time for a blind man to find the right pair of eyeglasses. Not Ike, though. He kept smiling all the way through the Depression. And he makes me realize that there are at least two ways to think on things: the way they were and the way you can still make them.

In the Rec Hall, I'm winning game after game. I think I should quit while I'm ahead, but I keep on going. I'm gonna win bigger than this, like I'm about to ride Polo like a wild Indian.

Hutch finds me in the back room. "C'mon, Dennis, there's someone I want you to meet."

"Tell him to come back."

"I would but it's not a he. It's a her. Katie's friend from Kelly Field. Her friend works payroll there."

"OK, be right there."

I spend another fifteen minutes in that back room, winning three more rounds before it occurs to me that I'm supposed to be doing something else. I leave the craps table and go out to the front where the regular action is, food and music. I scan the room and see Hutch waving his hands back and forth. I walk over towards Hutch, nodding at Katie for only a second.

There's a woman sitting next to her, a woman I've never met but for some reason I feel I've known all my life. She's the most beautiful woman I've ever laid eyes on. Her medium-length brown hair is curled in the right places, framing her greenish-blue eyes. Her shy but confident smile welcomes me to the table.

"Ray, this is Amelia Eckhardt, but we call her 'Mallie.'"

And at this moment, I can see the chiseling in the stone, where my life is heading, and who I'm going to share it with.

How often at night, where the heavens are bright
With the light of the glittering stars
Have I stood there amazed and asked as I gazed
If their glory exceeds that of ours.

Looking at her I knew. There was no more wood to chop and no axe to grind. I had won again. I stare back into her eyes and lose myself there, in a place called "Nothing Else Matters." Nothing else.

Now there's gonna be someone else in Cono, Texas. I feel it in my West Texas bones. Her name is Mallie, and she's gonna be sitting right there next to me on the shiny side of that star.

Home. Home on the range.

Amelia Eckhardt Dennis and Connel Ray Dennis

EPILOGUE

EDDIE BEYUKA LIVED on an Indian reservation and became well known for his mosaic inlay kachinas and dancers that double as standing figures.

Great Uncle Will McClesky lost his fortune and finished his life ironing clothes for thirty dollars a week.

The train station in Ranger, Texas, is now the "Roaring Ranger Museum" and contains pictures and artifacts from the McClesky oil boom.

Aunt Nolie (Nola Griffice) died at the age of seventy-one and is buried in Ranger, Texas, next to her first husband, Joe Pugh. Ma and Pa (Jim and Luffy Brewer) are also buried in Ranger.

Ike Dennis retired back to Rotan, Texas. Although he never "officially" married Mary, she stayed with him until he died of a heart attack at the age of seventy-six. Mary "Dennis" is buried next to him in Rotan, Texas.

As Cono grew older, he and Mamaw Lizzie developed a close relationship and stayed in touch over the years. Bill Preston was an important part of her family.

Cono remained close to his Aunt Eva and Aunt Marguerite.

Towards the end of Wayne's life, he walked with a cane and was so stooped that lifting his head was an effort. He died at the age of fifty-two from apparent heart failure.

After Wayne's death, Elnora moved to Springlake, Texas, to be close to Delma and her family. Elnora died at the age of seventy-five and is buried beside Wayne in Temple, Texas.

Delma is eighty years old and lives in Springlake, Texas, close to her two children, grandchildren, and great-grandchildren.

H. Govan became an assistant trainer for the Rotan Yellowhammers, rarely missing a game even after his retirement. Rotan's football stadium is named after him.

Cono Ray Dennis married Amelia Eckhardt in 1948. An only child, Amelia (Mallie) taught him a new meaning for the word "family." Cono received his first-ever Easter basket from her parents the first year they were married. Cono and Amelia moved to Austin, Texas, where they raised their two daughters. As time passed, three grandsons and one granddaughter were born to Amelia and Cono. "Grandpa" continued to pass along to them old rifles, old spurs, but especially his stories.

Cono resented his father for the majority of his life; not so much for the abuse but for the years wasted. After Amelia died in 2008, and a few months before his own death, Cono stared at a picture of his father hanging in the middle bedroom of his house and uttered these words for the first time: "Dad, I forgive you."

Cono followed the Rotan Yellowhammers until the end, always looking in the Saturday paper for their game scores. In fall of 2010, after his death, the daughters of Cono and Amelia purchased a new scoreboard for the Rotan Yellowhammers, replacing the weathered scoreboard of thirty years. The night of the dedication ceremony, many of the characters from this story came alive through the conversations with the people of Rotan. Carolyn and her family spent the night at the former Dennis ranch, now the Baugh ranch. Carolyn had met Judy Baugh, daughter-in-law of Sam Baugh, seventeen years before when her children attended the Child Development Center in Austin, Texas, where Carolyn was the director. The community of Rotan welcomed Cono's family with open arms, and for that they are immensely greatful.

The signage at the top of the scoreboard reads, "In honor of Cono R. Dennis." Now he can sit on the shiny side of his star, look down on home-game nights, and know the score.

Ain't that something?

Scoreboard erected in September 2010, Rotan, Texas

Today, Yellowhammer Stadium named after H. Govan, Rotan, Texas

Cono at age 80, Rotan, Texas